The Deathly Dolls

HELEN GOLTZ

THE DEATHLY DOLLS – The Lady Mortician's Visions, book 4.

PUBLISHED BY: Atlas Productions. First published 2024.

Copyright © Helen Goltz

Cover design by Karri Klawiter, Art by Karri.

PLEASE NOTE: This book is written in British-Australian English.

Chapter 1

Tuesday 4 November 1890. Brisbane, Australia. Clear skies, 30 degrees daytime.

The *Doll and Teddy Hospital* on Elizabeth Street was open for business. Having only been open thirty minutes, it boasted three customers inside and one looking through the window at the display like a child outside a sweet store. The young lady studying the window's contents—Miss Phoebe Astin—was doll-like herself. Her long blonde hair was tied loosely with a pink ribbon that matched her pink and cream dress, and she was dainty in appearance.

Phoebe was amazed at the range of dolls and bears on display; some were very old, some were in mint condition, and others needed adoption. She took the opportunity to enter the store as a couple departed, thanking them as they held the door for her. Inside, the quaint little shop smelled of sandalwood and roses, the latter featured in a glass vase on the counter.

While she waited for the comely lady behind the counter to wrap a customer's repaired doll, Phoebe opened a small bundle she had been carrying, revealing a delicate doll with a porcelain face in some disrepair.

'Mrs Crandle at your service, my dear,' the lady behind the counter said as she approached. She was small and round in stature with a bun of grey hair and a kindly face. 'Oh my, what do we have here?'

'Good morning, Mrs Crandle; I am Phoebe Astin. A pleasure to meet you. This is my grandmother's childhood doll, and I hoped to have it restored for her birthday.'

'How thoughtful of you, dear. Goodness, what a delicate doll!'

'Yes. You see, my grandmother only found it recently in a chest of her mother's belongings that arrived from England. She was overcome with happiness to see it again but distressed by the state of it.'

Mrs Crandle paused, leant behind and moved a curtain aside a little. 'Mr Crandle, are you free? There is a doll you must see.'

A portly gentleman of similar size and shape to Mrs Crandle appeared. Both wore white aprons as if it really were a

hospital, and they were the orderlies caring for the ill dolls and teddies.

'Good morning, Miss,' Mr Crandle said.

Phoebe returned his salutation and eagerly awaited his thoughts on the doll before him. The face was pretty, with large blue eyes, long fair hair and a cream lace dress that had yellowed with age and featured moth-eaten holes.

'Oh, she is lovely, isn't she, dear?' he asked Mrs Crandle. 'Well over eighty years or older and in quite good condition.'

'Yes, my grandmother is sixty-five; it was her mother's before her. Sadly, the doll's face has cracked, and the chest has caved in.'

'Nothing we can't repair in our hospital, I assure you,' Mr Crandle said and keenly accepted the doll. 'We will take great care of her.'

'Thank you, Sir,' Phoebe said with a smile, enjoying their dedication to their patients. Mrs Crandle took Phoebe's details and, thanking her, Phoebe opened the door of the small store to depart and nearly tripped on a bundle in the doorway. She stooped to pick up a large parcel wrapped in brown paper and string.

'Mrs Crandle, I believe this is for you,' Phoebe said, carrying it to the counter.

'Goodness, how odd that it was not delivered into the shop. I did not even see it delivered.'

'Nor I.'

'Let's see what we have,' Mrs Crandle said, inviting Phoebe to stay. 'There is no address or letter.'

She cut the string and peeled back a layer of brown paper to find a small card inside that was not enclosed in an envelope. Within moments, Mrs Crandle had pocketed it and, seeing Phoebe's surprised look, the shop owner added, 'Just a note saying it is a gift, a donation... that happens quite often.'

'Truly? I could not part with my childhood bears and dolls. That does sound uncharitable,' Phoebe said with an apologetic look.

'Neither could I,' Mrs Crandle said in confidence, and laughing, she added, 'I suspect you guessed that. But people often find dolls or teddies, send them to us, or gift them when their owners are deceased. We are always pleased to see them go to new homes.'

Mrs Crandle removed a second layer of paper, and her smile faulted momentarily before catching Phoebe's eye and altering her expression again.

'What a lovely doll,' she said. 'Look at that pretty dress.'

'Indeed,' Phoebe agreed as both ladies admired the beautiful doll before them. It was easily two feet in size and wearing a yellow dress with cornflowers hand-stitched around the hem. On its feet were little white socks and slippers. The doll had long brown hair, large brown eyes, and a cherubic look with her rosy cheeks. By contrast, her neck had been squeezed tight to such thinness with a bright red ribbon that the internal filling had bulged and torn around the neck, making it appear like her head was almost cut off, the cloth dangling around the doll's neck.

'What a great shame, the poor little girl,' Mrs Crandle said. 'Nothing we can't fix with clever stitching and a little re-stuffing.'

'Rather nasty though,' Phoebe said.

'Yes, I suspect naughty boys; perhaps the doll owner's brothers may have gotten hold of it.'

'Ah yes, I have some of those,' Phoebe said, narrowing her eyes and making Mrs Crandle laugh. 'I shall leave you with your new patient and my thanks, Mrs Crandle.'

'You are most welcome, my dear. We shall see you in a week then.'

Phoebe departed in haste, late for her work as a mortician at *The Economic Undertaker*. Fortunately, she knew the boss very well, as he was one of those pesky brothers, but not the one who stole her dolls and dressed them up as pirates.

Chapter 2

THE FUNERAL PARTY WAS fortunate that the deceased's plot was well placed beneath a large fig tree that provided shade for the mourners, the priest, and the funeral directors, all attired in black on a day when the temperature was exceedingly warm.

'I am thinking of a new career,' Ambrose Astin whispered to his brother, Julius, as they stood back, allowing Father Morris to conduct the blessing over the grave.

Julius rarely faulted when it came to decorum at a funeral. Tall and strikingly handsome with his dark hair and firm jaw, he was the epitome of dignified, but just for a moment, his eyes widened.

Ambrose continued. 'Just for the warm months, I'll return to service in winter.'

Julius's eyes narrowed at his brother's ill-timed jest, and he ignored him as he had learned to do from years of practice.

'Your turn,' Julius muttered, nodding to the lady on his right, who appeared to be overcome from heat.

'But she is young; therefore, I am sure she is swooning for your attention.'

Julius nudged him, and suppressing a smile, Ambrose hurried towards the young lady and saw her into a nearby chair, provided for the elderly and grieving. The look she gave him confirmed his suspicions.

He returned to his brother advising, 'She has made a speedy recovery.'

Julius made a humph sound as Father Morris said the final words – their cue to lower the body into the ground.

'May the love of God and the peace of the Lord Jesus Christ bless and console us and gently wipe every tear from our eyes ...' Father Morris made the sign of the cross, and the gathering said 'Amen' with him in unison.

With that, the mourning party broke up, and as a small group stopped to console each other, a young boy and girl, no more than eight years old and dressed in black, joined Julius and Ambrose at the gravesite. They both looked into the hole where their aunty's coffin now rested.

'What if she is still alive in that box?' the girl asked, looking at Julius and then Ambrose, with more curiosity in her voice than emotion.

'She's not, Millie. I poked her at the viewing, and I pinched her really hard, but she didn't move at all, and you know she would have slapped me,' her brother said.

Millie nodded. 'She would, Marty, really hard too.'

'Do not be concerned, I assure you, she is very dead,' Ambrose said. 'She has been in our waiting room for several days and has not moved at all or eaten a thing.'

'Dead as a doornail then?' Marty asked, folding his arms, and Julius suppressed a smile. 'That's what my father said.'

'Yes, I think we can all agree on that,' Julius said, giving them his best reassuring look.

'Or stiff as a board,' Ambrose added. Marty repeated it after him as if committing it to memory. 'Dead as the Dodo,' Ambrose continued.

'For the love of God, please do stop,' Julius said quietly and with a pained expression. 'That may be repeated, and we have our business reputation to consider.' He glanced at the parents and back to Ambrose.

'Quite right,' Ambrose agreed, 'but yes, in answer to your question, young lady, your aunt is definitely dead.'

'I guess she was old. Forty!' Millie said, and Marty nodded.

'Can we throw the dirt on top of her?' Marty asked.

'You'll get your clothes dirty,' Millie told him.

'Don't care.'

'She made good cakes. I'll miss those. Has anyone ever come alive again when you've been burying them, Mister?' Millie asked Julius.

'Not once. I imagine it would give everyone a big fright,' he said, and Ambrose chuckled.

'Have you seen a ghost, Mister?' Marty asked Ambrose. 'I bet you've seen lots.'

'Marty, Milly, we are leaving,' a voice called from behind the twins, and they made no haste to depart.

'Best go then; you don't want to be left here tonight when it is dark and spooky,' Ambrose said, making a ghostly noise. They both scampered off as he grinned, and Julius threw his hands up in despair.

'Do not carry on so; it won't hurt them. Children love ghost stories,' Ambrose said, defending himself as the two gravediggers shovelled the dirt in, and the men stood aside. 'So, have you ever seen a ghost, brother?'

'Ambrose, Ambrose, Ambrose,' Julius said with a sigh. 'One day, when it is too hot and you are too annoying, you will find yourself six feet under!'

Ambrose laughed, enjoying getting a rise from his brother. 'Someday soon then?'

'I suspect so,' Julius agreed.

'Mum, that man said Aunty was as dead as the dodo. What does that mean?' young Marty's voice could be heard, and Julius shot Ambrose a look that helped drop the temperature a degree or two.

'Ah, sorry about that,' Ambrose muttered and hurried into the empty hearse to return to *The Economic Undertaker* office.

Across town, Detective Harland Stone arrived at the Botanic Gardens and alighted from the hansom cab, along with his detective partner and protégé, Gilbert Payne. He would have preferred to stay in the hansom and enjoy the breeze while moving than to face a death scene in a tent on a warm day.

A collection of spring activities had opened to the public in the Botanic Gardens and would remain open until after Christmas. A miniature village display was one of them, but today, as the scene of a crime, it was closed, disappointing young and old alike. Walking under the shade of the trees along the riverside path, even from a distance, the two men could see the fenced display around the large tent where a small crowd had gathered, and several constables were keeping them well at bay.

'Brace yourself, Gilbert. It is never easy to see a deceased young lady,' Harland said, adjusting his hat and quickly wiping the sweat from his brow before re-pocketing his handkerchief. He was a tall man, athletic and strong. His face bore the traits of his sporting endeavours—a slight tilt to his nose, a scar or two above his eyebrow—but his voice had the polish of a good education. His partner was neat and respectable, a young man who had not been sporty but appreciated the finer things in life – art and poetry, balanced by a scientific mind.

'Thank you, Sir. I find it helps to be prepared. I am reading an article by the eminent psychologist William James, who believes that anticipating an emotion can bring feelings or sensations into being.

'Most interesting,' Harland agreed, storing the fact away. He was never quite sure which of Gilbert's facts might be useful at some point in time. 'So, by that conclusion, if we anticipate seeing something dramatic, we can begin to feel the dread but then harness it before facing the scene?'

'Well, Mr James believes the body reaction comes first and then the emotion, so I will finish the article and let you know if that is a conclusion he draws. It's rather complex,' Gilbert said, frowning.

They arrived and were granted admittance by Constable Wright, manning the entry gate. Closer to his fortieth year than his thirtieth, the constable was a solid man of cheery disposition who had no ambitions to rise any higher than a foot slogger and did his job with good grace.

'Not an exhibition anyone would want to see, Detectives,' he said in a low voice. 'The owner of the display arrived early this morning to check all was in order before unlocking the gates and found the young lady dead.'

'Did the owner recognise her?' Harland asked.

'No, Sir, and if you don't mind me saying, he seemed more upset that the dead body had flattened the miniature shopping precinct than about the loss of life.'

'I welcome your observations, Constable Wright,' Harland assured him. 'Has the young lady been identified by anyone else?'

'No, Sir. There is nothing on her person that tells us her name or address. I stopped the staff members from seeing the body, but the manager did not claim to know her, nor could he suggest why she was inside the exhibition. He assured me no one was on site when he locked up last night.'

'Excellent work, thank you, Constable. If you can assist with getting statements, we'll make our way to the deceased.'

'Right you are, Detective.'

The two men entered the tent and wandered through the exhibition on the set paths that allowed viewers to enjoy the miniature displays of their city.

'It is very well done,' Gilbert said.

'Indeed,' Harland agreed and added in jest, 'We'll have to find our miniature police station later.'

They made their way towards where another constable stood guard, and he moved aside, grimacing as he looked over his shoulder and indicated where the body lay. A young lady was sprawled over the miniature street display, like Alice in *Alice in Wonderland,* after drinking from the bottle that made her too large for the room.

Her chestnut hair was spread around her like a halo; she wore a yellow dress with little blue cornflowers handsewn around the hemline, white stockings and little white slippers, and around her neck was a red ribbon tied tightly, perhaps enough to strangle the life from her.

'It's not as gruesome as I expected,' Gilbert said, relieved, 'oh, but still a tragic sight.'

'Did I miss anything?' a loud Scottish voice asked as the coroner, Dr Tavish McGregor, walked gingerly towards them. 'Ugh, I hate miniatures; I feel like a bull in a china shop.' Before the men could address him, he stopped short, ran a hand through his red hair and added, 'Well, look at that.'

'Good morning, Doctor,' Gilbert greeted him.

'Good morning, Tavish, a most odd one indeed,' Harland agreed as they stood over the young woman's body and studied her.

'A stage actress perhaps, vaudeville?' Tavish asked.

'It is like theatre make-up,' Gilbert agreed, 'and the exaggerated rouge on her cheeks is most doll-like. It was not that long ago that women were poisoned by their white lead makeup.'

'Very true and an interesting observation, young Gilbert,' Tavish said. 'Your boss tells me you store some interesting facts.'

Gilbert flushed like a schoolboy, unsure if it was an insult or a compliment.

'None that would be of value to your line of work, Dr McGregor, I am sure,' Gilbert said modestly and turned to address Harland. 'But, Sir, is it not interesting that out of all the displays she might have fallen upon, she has demolished a city strip in Elizabeth Street?'

'I wondered about that too, Gilbert, and if it were significant,' Harland agreed, looking around. 'She doesn't appear to have been dragged here, and nothing else is askew that would have indicated a struggle. It is as if she dropped from the sky,' and all three men looked up at the top of the tent to see nothing of consequence.

'Right then,' Tavish said, 'let me look at the little lady.'

The detectives leaned closer as the coroner moved the body to observe its manner of death. Tavish made a few sounds—huffs and puffs—before stating, 'Well, she may have been strangled, but I can't rule out other methods of death just yet.'

'No?' Harland asked, surprised. 'The ribbon appears tight, and there is some bruising around her neck.'

'Yes, but I believe her cause of death might be...' he paused. 'I won't speculate; it's a hunch only. I may have more insights if you want to drop by later today. Bring the lovely young journalist with you if you like,' he joked.

'Ah, Miss Lilly Lewis?' Gilbert said with a smile. 'I am sure she will find us as soon as there is a whiff of a good story.'

'No doubt,' Harland agreed, but he warned the coroner, 'I think you have competition if you seek Miss Lewis's hand.'

'No! Is that possible?' Tavish said in jest.

'Hard to imagine,' Harland agreed with a grin. 'A certain private detective.'

Tavish scoffed. 'That handsome, rich, charming bore, what can she want with him?'

'No accounting for taste, Sir,' Gilbert said, getting into the spirit of the conversation.

'Precisely so, young Gilbert, thank you. Well, I am done. Can the lads take her?' Tavish asked with a look toward the young men waiting near the door to remove the body to the morgue for examination.

'Yes,' Harland said and waved them over. The detectives thanked and farewelled the coroner but remained to study the area and conduct interviews.

'Perhaps there is a pantomime in town, Sir; it is the holiday season. Maybe this lady is a performer, and someone can identify her,' Gilbert said.

'It is worth a try,' Harland agreed. 'A human doll in a miniature setting. Most odd indeed.'

Bennet Martin, an occasional private investigator and passionate painter, did not like seeing clients before 11am. That was his painting time, but as the gentleman in question was unavailable later, his clerk, Daniel Dutton, booked him in.

'I should fire you for cutting my morning painting session short,' Bennet muttered as he entered his office, adjusting his tie and straightening his jacket.

'Except you need me, and no one else would put up with you,' Daniel said in jest, but there was an element of truth to it. Not because Bennet Martin was a difficult man, far from it, but he was disorganised, and the office and the business worked because of Daniel Dutton.

'Fortunately, you have made yourself indispensable,' Bennet agreed. 'Is there any paint in my hair?' He ran a hand through his blonde hair, which often featured strands of blue or red depending on the subject on his easel and how frustrated he was while painting.

Daniel studied his head. 'No. It must have been a good morning's effort.'

'Hmph.'

'I'll bring tea and cake into the meeting room when your client arrives, Mr Martin,' Mrs Clarke said as she entered the room.

'Thank you, Mrs Clarke. Don't feed him too well; I want the meeting to be over quickly.'

'Thank you, Aunt,' Daniel parodied him. 'I'll have whatever cake he does not consume.'

'Hollow legs you have, Daniel,' she said with a shake of her head and left to return to her preparation.

'He is here,' Daniel announced, and they watched a well-dressed middle-aged gentleman alight from a private hansom. 'If you play your cards right, this will be a good income source, and it might become a regular pay cheque.'

'Insurance fraud,' Bennet faked a yawn.

'It's not quite that dull. He wants us to investigate some large insurance policies taken out for children whom he believes do not exist but have since died.'

Bennet's expression did not change, and Daniel laughed. 'Buck up; it might just be the client that frees you to paint more while toiling less.'

Mr Earnest Webster entered, was introduced to Bennet, shown to the meeting room, and plied with tea and cake.

'So, you see, while it is a common practice to insure your child—we currently have 70,000 policies in existence—we believe there is fraud afoot!' Mr Webster concluded after explaining his visit.

'But do they not insure for around the cost of a funeral, say seven or eight pounds?' Bennet asked, confused.

'Many do, and the purchase is prompted by honourable motives such as self-respect in wishing to meet their bills and to ensure their children are given a proper burial, especially in households where there might be five or more children and illness is rife. Plus, there can be medicinal expenses and mourning costs like clothing and drapes.'

'Ah yes,' Bennet said, immediately thinking of his closest friend, Julius, and the mourning dress wear store recently opened.

Mr Webster continued. 'But of late, we have a large number of clients who are insuring their children for up to one hundred pounds.'

'Good Lord,' Bennet said. 'That is suspicious to begin with, surely?'

'Not necessarily. Some may never cash in their policies if they are fortunate. There is no law to stop them insuring to that amount.'

'Perhaps there should be,' Bennet said.

'Yes, we think alike, Mr Martin.' He slipped a list containing ten names across the table to Bennet. 'We believe the following clients took out their life insurance for improper purposes. The children are deceased, but we do not believe they ever existed.'

'But that means a doctor, or a coroner was in the parents' pocket to provide a death certificate.'

'Or it was a particularly good fake and needs to be revisited,' Mr Webster said. 'Can we ask that of you, Mr Martin?'

Bennet agreed. Mr Webster accepted the terms presented by Daniel, and they showed the new client to the door where his ride awaited.

'That is challenging; looking for ten deaths that never happened.' Daniel summed it up.

'As they said during the black death, bring out your dead,' Bennet gave him a wry look.

'Sadly, there is no immediate reason to visit *The Economic Undertaker*... no physical body to seek, no body at all if Mr Webster is correct,' Daniel said and pouted at his boss.

'I am no longer pursuing Miss Astin and don't intend to elaborate further. Miss Astin and I shall remain loyal friends.'

'Ah, I am sorry to hear that,' Daniel said, capable of sincerity when needed.

Bennet nodded his thanks. 'Do not despair. Another lady has caught my attention, a most intriguing lady.'

'I expected nothing less,' Daniel said, and before Bennet realised what was happening, Daniel was running up the stairs to Bennet's studio, calling behind him, 'I shall see her for myself in oil paint, shall I?'

Bennet laughed and took to the stairs in hot pursuit.

Chapter 3

WILL AND CLAUDE PLACED the body on the table indicated by Phoebe and removed their stretcher.

'There you go, Miss, we'll leave you to your work then,' the younger man, Claude, said.

Both had recently been promoted in the business, with Will stepping up to assist Ambrose in Julius's absence twice a week, Claude managing the stable yard, and overseeing the newcomer, Charlie.

'Thank you, Claude. I think you should call me Phoebe. You have been working here for several years, and surely we are friends.'

He coloured slightly. 'I hope so too, Miss, but it wouldn't be right. But I'm at your service.'

Phoebe nodded and smiled. 'How is Charlie settling in?'

'He's determined to prove his value to Julius,' Will said and chuckled. 'Can't do enough to be helpful and show he was worth employing. He's a good lad.'

'He's bright too,' Claude added. 'He knows what needs to be done without us asking.'

'I'm pleased. Julius could see the good in him,' Phoebe said. She did not seek company, but she was at home amongst the tight-knit family of employees at *The Economic Undertaker*.

They spoke for a little longer, Phoebe asking after Will's wife and newborn, but all the time, she could see the lady seated and waiting for her in the corner. Once the men had left and were heard walking across the floorboards above, she turned to the lady in question and offered a small bow and smile.

'Good afternoon, Miss Phoebe Astin at your service.'

'Miss Astin, forgive the intrusion. I do hope you are well.' The lady spoke with a voice that spoke of professionalism. 'I am Miss Charlotte Faithful, or Nurse Faithful if you would be so kind to address me as such.'

'Of course, Nurse Faithful. I am sorry you find yourself in my company.'

Charlotte Faithful smiled. 'I am not sorry, Miss Astin. I had a good life and a quick death. Who could ask for more?'

'A positive view of life indeed,' Phoebe said, smiling at her. 'You have a very pretty name, like a heroine from a romance novel.'

Charlotte Faithful laughed. 'Yes, it is rather romantic, and I believe my patients found it reassuring. But unlike the romance novels, I never married. I have been called Nurse Faithful all my working life; I dedicated myself to the profession,' she told Phoebe. 'Oh, I had my share of proposals, but I had a calling.'

'I understand, Nurse Faithful. I, too, love what I do. It is a great honour to be here for families when their loved ones have departed this world and to ease the burden by presenting them at their best.'

'Well, I am in good hands then,' Nurse Faithful said with a smile. 'May I join you?'

'Of course.'

Nurse Faithful rose from the chair, approaching her body where Phoebe stood. She was a tall woman, thin, with a fair complexion and reddish-grey hair that would be wiry and unruly if not tied back.

Phoebe uncovered Nurse Faithful's face. 'I believe you are not having a viewing, so there is no work for me to do before your departure unless you would like me to do so for your peace of mind?'

'No, I am not so vain as to wish to be preened for my coffin, but thank you. I must, however, beg your indulgence.'

'Of course. How might I assist you? Is there a message you would like to give to a loved one? Mind you, that can be tricky, but we can work it out. Or perhaps something you would like collected and passed on?'

'That's very thoughtful of you, Miss Astin, but nothing of that nature.' She took a deep breath. 'I would like to do something I should have done years ago. I would like to confess to a crime... several, actually. Could you assist me?'

Miss Violet Forrester, the store manageress, found her thoughts interrupted by her junior seamstress.

'Mr Astin and Mr Astin are coming past with the hearse,' young Miss Mary Pollard piped up as she saw the horses pulling the vehicle past the windows of *The Economic Undertaker*, soon to pass the premises of *In Mourning – Attire for the Family* where she worked by the front window.

'Thank you, Mary,' Violet said, hiding her amusement.

Mary was the youngest member of the dressmaking team and was timid by nature, but Violet was pleased she was becoming more confident with her and the head seamstress, Mrs Nellie Shaw.

The concept of the mourning wear store was the brainchild of Julius Astin to meet the needs of the bereaved of the city. Those who knew of an illness might prepare their mourning clothes, but many found death unexpectantly on their doorstep and hurried to dye their clothing black while mourning wear was made for them. On meeting Miss Violet Forrester, Julius knew he had found his manageress, and the venture was launched. Her innovative idea of having a selection of pre-made clothes that could be hurriedly altered to fit if needed was a risk that had paid off. Despite outlaying the cost of the fabric and manufacture before purchase, the ladies had found their clothing much in demand for those caught unprepared and mournful. It was a most successful business, and the manageress was also the flame of the business owner's heart.

Young Mary had the best view of the street and the comings and goings; she missed nothing. To the ladies, she looked the picture of sweetness, with her light brown hair tied back, the occasional natural wave escaping, and her large doe-like brown eyes that were easily startled by the entry of the Astin gentlemen to the business. Violet had interviewed several seamstresses for the junior role, but Mary's skills surpassed them, and she had settled in nicely.

'Here they are now,' Mary announced as the vehicle came into view, travelling at a respectable speed given it was designed to carry the dead.

Violet looked up, and even though she knew Julius could not see through the windows of the dress store with the sun's reflection upon them, she had an excellent view of him in command of the horses and watched until he had passed. Violet turned to see Mrs Nellie Shaw offering her a teasing smile.

'I believe Mr Astin wears that shirt you made him more than any other shirt in his collection,' Nellie said.

'Oh, he does, Miss, he must love it,' Mary agreed. 'So romantic.'

'Very,' Nellie agreed with a laugh on seeing Violet's pained expression. 'Best you make him another couple soon, or he will wear it out.'

Violet smiled and shook her head at the pair of them. 'If you do not think it too forward, I should do so. I still have some of the leftover fabric in Grandma's sewing basket. It is a very good quality.'

'It could not be too forward a gift, surely, Miss,' Mary offered. 'You have been on several dates now, and it is a thoughtful gesture, as my mother would say.' Mary then flushed. 'Not that I know anything about romance; my father scares away any beaus that may call.'

Nellie gave her a sympathetic look. 'You are only a young slip of a thing, Mary. Maybe next year, he may be more willing to part with his little girl and allow you to step out more. It is hard for parents to imagine their children moving on.' Mrs Shaw looked to Violet. 'But I agree with Mary; it would be a thoughtful gift. Did you enjoy your outing together on Saturday evening?'

Both ladies looked at Violet with great interest.

'I wanted to ask too but thought it might be improper,' Mary added keenly.

Violet smiled at them both. 'I see no harm in telling you about our evening as we stitch. It was a lovely night, and he is very charming company.'

'I would die,' Mary sighed and then, remembering her promise to Mrs Shaw, quickly added, 'That is, I would faint away.'

'That is better. We hear enough about dying around here. Your day will come to swoon and faint, Mary, my dear. So where did Mr Astin take you, Violet, if we may ask?'

'You must tell us what you wore too,' Mary added. 'And is Mr Astin fully healed, or was he still in pain from the knife wound?' She saw the look of amusement both ladies gave her and added, 'I shall be quiet so you can speak.'

Violet laughed. 'That is quite all right, Mary. Let's see, well, I was very pleased to be collected at my home by Mr Astin in his best suit. He waited with my brother, Tom, who enquired what time he might expect me home.'

Both ladies laughed at the thought of 15-year-old Tom, who was employed by Julius Astin and his cousin Lucian as an apprentice carpenter, laying down the law about his sister.

Violet continued. 'If Julius was in pain, he did not show it; he thought only of my comfort.'

Mary sighed again to their amusement as Violet continued. 'I wore my new lavender and lace dress... I am still in light mourning for my grandmother, but Julius says it is a colour he loves on me. He arrived with a large bouquet of cream roses, and the scent was truly beautiful.'

'How romantic,' Mary said. 'I am sure he is the perfect gentleman.'

'We then went to the Queensport Aquarium on the moonlit excursion to dance and hear the band.'

'Oh, I have longed to go there, but Mr Shaw is not of a fancy to wander around the aquarium of a daytime or to dance of an evening. He is not as steady on his feet as he once was and not one for crowds.'

'Then he would have been most uncomfortable, Nellie. There were a lot of people there,' Violet said, giving her a sympathetic look. 'We took the steamer – it was part of the moonlit excursion package.'

'And did you dance?' Mary asked.

'Many waltzes.'

Mary sighed again. 'Oh, I long to dance the night away with a handsome man and to think of you both on the steamer crossing the water to get there. Was there a bright moon?'

Violet laughed. 'Mary, you are a hopeless romantic.'

'I am very much so,' she agreed.

'You will be pleased to know it was a very romantic night, and I shall say no more on that subject,' Violet said coyly, 'except to say the electric lights installed there were a marvel.'

The ladies began peppering Violet with questions, and she laughed at a memory.

'Tell us, please,' Mary begged.

'It is silly,' Violet assured them. 'We were looking around the aquarium before the dance, and this fish seemed to follow us. Truly, it never left us the entire way along the glass. Julius said Tom sent it to chaperone me.'

The ladies laughed at the idea.

'Tom has been coming by a lot lately to walk you home,' Nellie said. 'Such a good young man, quite mature.'

Violet noticed Mary flushing; the young seamstress was very much taken with Tom Forrester, one year her junior but much more mature of nature. Not that they had said more than hello and goodbye to each other.

'He has had to grow up before his time and is the man of the house now,' Violet said. 'He is like Pa, though. Very much a family person and keen to have his own family one day.'

Mary continued to look industrious, not making eye contact with Violet or Nellie.

'You are lucky,' Nellie said. 'My father was never around. He found the company of his friends and the pub much more interesting than his family.'

'My father does a little of both,' Mary added.

'That is a good thing, I'm sure,' Violet said. 'A man must have his amusements, as must the ladies. But I am sure my brother will make a wonderful husband and father.'

The door to the business opened, and a mature pair of women entered. The conversation stopped, and Mrs Nellie Shaw, offering condolences, rose to her feet to assist them, leaving Violet and Mary to return to their sewing dutifully. Violet was pleased to see the hint of a smile tracing Mary's lips as she no doubt dreamt of a romantic liaison of her own.

Chapter 4

Phoebe smiled. 'Goodness, I was just about to suggest we take a seat, but of course, you no longer tire on your feet,' she said to Nurse Faithful, who laughed in return.

'No, but do sit down if you wish, and I shall join you. May I tell you my confession if time permits you?'

'Please do. I am at your disposal,' Phoebe said, and the two ladies moved to the seats underneath the window, sitting together as Nurse Charlotte Faithful might have with a friend when living.

The thin, wearied-looking woman placed her hands in her lap and, after a moment taken to gather her thoughts, said to Phoebe, 'I am sure that many you meet on the way to the next life are full of justifications at this late hour of our lives, and I am no different. I can honestly say, Miss Astin, that I thought my actions were correct, and I thought I had received a sign from God to do them.'

'I will not sit in judgment, Nurse Faithful, fear not.'

The woman nodded and began. 'Thank you. I have been nursing for many years and have seen great joys and tragedies. Despite my faith, I have come to realise there is no sense or logic to the laws of life – those who deserved to die lived, those wanting children so desperately and who would be wonderful parents cannot conceive... God works in mysterious ways.'

'I have felt the same disillusionment myself,' Phoebe said. 'I see many young people taken too soon, and my parents were taken when I was a child.'

'I am sorry for that,' Nurse Faithful said with the warmth in her voice cultivated from many years of nursing. 'For me, it was as if it were meant to be, the way it all came together. Forgive me; I shall start at the beginning.'

'Please,' Phoebe encouraged her.

'I enjoyed delivering babies more than general nursing and thus worked largely in that area. But despite the joy of bringing a new life into the world, sometimes it caused abject misery.'

Phoebe nodded. 'I understand. If one has to battle to put food on the table and a roof overhead.'

'Precisely so, Miss Astin and Mrs Liddle was one such case. I delivered all five of her babies in her humble home, and the woman was on the edge of despair. Oh, Miss Astin, if you could have seen her misery. Mr Liddle wanted his husbandly rights in the bedroom with no thought to her condition or the number of children under his roof. He drank away a good deal of his income while the family went hungry. Poor Mrs Liddle did her best, but she was this tiny, thin and exhausted woman with five bairns under seven years of age beneath her feet. The final time I visited, she was expecting twins and quite distraught about how they might all live.'

'The poor woman, I can only imagine,' Phoebe said sympathetically, her hand going to her heart. Her upbringing had been on a budget as her grandparents unexpectedly inherited three children to raise, but they were comfortable. No luxuries, but all the necessities could be met. 'It must be so distressing to struggle to feed your children, and I can't imagine the despair.'

'Oh, it was pitiful and so sad. Mrs Liddle was a woman too proud to ask for charity, and she had no family to fall back on. She was a lovely little lady and always remembered to ask after me each time I visited.' Nurse Faithful paused, took a deep breath, if possible for a spirit, and continued. 'Another of my regular clients was Mr and Mrs Dellow. A young couple that so desperately wanted a child and Mrs Dellow had lost three in childbirth. She feared her husband would leave her, and I feared she might harm herself.'

Phoebe shook her head. 'It is, as you said, sometimes an unjust world.'

'So true, and that is how it began... what we did. A small group of friends and I—all involved in the business of babies—had trained together and enjoyed working together. Do you have similar friends?'

'I am very fortunate to have a group of lady friends; we call ourselves *The Vexed Vixens*.'

Nurse Faithful laughed. 'Very good, Miss Astin. We called ourselves the *Storks*. There were five of us – two midwives, myself a nurse, and two wet nurses.'

'It is a fitting name.'

'Yes, in more ways than you might realise. Are you aware of Greek Mythology?' Nurse Faithful asked.

'Only a little. My mother chose my brothers and my name from ancient Greek folklore. So let me see,' Phoebe mused, 'The stork delivering babies was connected to the goddess Hera, was it not?'

Nurse Faithful looked surprised. 'Indeed, Miss Astin, you are well read.'

Phoebe blushed. 'I know very little more on the subject.'

'Well, in Greek mythology, Hera, the goddess of childbirth, discovered Gerana was having an affair with Hera's husband, Zeus. She turned Gerana into a crane, and as Gerana could not bear to part with her baby, she wrapped the baby in a blanket and flew off with it in her beak. Thus, the stork was believed to steal babies.'

'Oh. I see,' Phoebe said, making the connection. 'But you said these were desperate situations.'

'They were, and I assure you we only interfered when times were desperate. I was the eldest, at 36, when we began the *Storks*; the youngest was one of the midwives, aged 20. We all had clients like Mrs Liddle, who should not have more children, and clients like Mrs Dellow, who were desperate for a family, and so, we ensured women got what they needed.' She held up her hand. 'I know we were playing God, but we believed God had put us in a role where we could do some good in the world... well, that was my justification, and I know the other ladies felt the same.'

'But what if Mrs Liddle wanted the twins despite being unable to feed them?'

'No, my dear girl, she did not. She was beyond exhausted, and we both knew it would drive her to an early grave. Each day was survival. Of course, the inherent love for her children was there, but feeding and clothing them, making the rent, and avoiding her husband's drunken displays were her daily burden. Then something happened that made me think it was a sign to do what I had been considering.'

Phoebe leaned forward, wide-eyed with interest.

'Mr Liddle was killed in a workplace accident.'

'Oh, my goodness. What would become of Mrs Liddle and the five children now?'

'My thoughts exactly, Miss Astin,' Nurse Faithful nodded. 'Mrs Liddle was given a small amount from the company to pay for the funeral, and she told me it would pay the rent for several months, but then, she did not know how they would survive. She had no relatives who would take in five children and herself, and no amount of sewing or cleaning on her behalf would provide the funds needed. At the same time, Mrs Dellow was just about to give birth and was beside herself with anxiety, and rightly so, I'm sorry to say.'

'So, you swapped the babies?'

'Yes, that was the first time. But there were more incidents. Many more, I'm afraid, and perhaps it is time to reveal all.'

Alex Cowan could never be accused of being a patient man. The editor of *The Courier* dismissed two of his senior staff members from his office and bellowed for his two youngest—Lilly Lewis and Fergus Griffiths—to attend him. The young pair hurried in. They had achieved great success with their reports in the last six months and not only earned a name for themselves and a following but proven they were ready to be moved from the *Births, Deaths and Marriages*

column, affectionately known as the *Hatches, Matches and Dispatches* column, and the *Shipping News*, respectively.

Lilly entered first. She looked demure in a pale lime dress, minimal jewellery, and her chestnut hair restrained in a neat knot at the back of her neck. Even dressing modestly and in a manner deemed professional, her beauty shone through – blue eyes that sparkled with intelligence, a figure proportioned in all the right places, and confidence that came from being the only girl in a family of five boys and very much loved and indulged.

Three years her senior at twenty-five years of age, Fergus Griffith followed her into the editor's office, undertaking his habit of running a hand through his hair that was too long in the front for the editor's liking but very much in favour with his young wife, now the mother of his first child.

'Ah, it's the young trailblazers,' Mr Cowan announced as they entered. 'I've got a job for you both: a spate of thefts from several antique stores.'

'Oh, Mr Cowan, that sounds very meaty, but we have a breaking story that you will not want to miss the opportunity to share with our readers. Imagine if our competitor got their hands on it.' Lilly looked to Fergus, who looked confused. Then, he seemed to catch on to her plan and nodded furiously.

'Tell me about it then, Fergus,' Mr Cowan said, putting him on the spot, recognising the ruse underway and affectionately impressed with Miss Lewis. He sat back, pipe in mouth, and gave them an indulgent smile.

'Uh, it's a mystery that the readers will find intriguing, Mr Cowan,' Fergus said. 'We are about to bail up Detective Stone and beg his indulgence for an exclusive story again in return for fairly representing the police force and calling for public help when required.'

'I see.' Mr Cowan nodded. 'Who is the victim, the star of this mystery?'

Lilly stepped in. 'Sir, let us pitch you the whole story as you have allowed us to do before. We are sure that will give you a better insight into what we can deliver to the readers.'

He hid his smile. 'All right then, Lewis, Griffiths. When might I get this brief?'

'First thing in the morning if that is convenient, Mr Cowan?'

'Off with you both. I expect you at nine o'clock sharp.' He dismissed them and called for another pair of his journalists, and the young couple rushed out. Alex Cowan blew out a puff of smoke and grinned. She had guts, more than most of his men, and Lilly Lewis was worth a day's wait to see what she came up with next.

'Oh, my Lord,' Fergus exclaimed when they were far enough away from the editor's office. 'A mystery, I can't believe I said that. I have been in your company too long.' He chuckled.

Lilly grinned. 'Well played, Fergus. Spare us from having to report on a theft,' she said with a roll of her eyes. As they returned to their desks, she asked, 'Did you have anything in mind?'

'No, I was just jumping on board your wagon, and Mr Cowan knew it. He indulges us.'

'Yes, so we must not let him down. Best we find ourselves a mystery then.'

'I shall go to the morgue,' Fergus said.

'Excellent. I shall find Detective Stone. Between us, I am sure we can find a good mystery afoot!'

'Let's meet back here mid-afternoon, if not sooner?' Fergus suggested.

'Agreed,' Lilly said, and they gathered their belongings and hurried out the door lest Mr Cowan could not find a victim, that is to say, another team of reporters to write his crime story and called them back on sight.

Out the front of *The Courier* building, the young pair entered a hansom cab, one of the many waiting near the entrance, knowing they would likely get regular fares.

'If I have no luck with the detective, I shall head to *The Economic Undertaker* and see if Phoebe has anything of interest. There might be a client who is claiming foul play over the death of their relative,' Lilly said without giving away that Phoebe would have the story first-hand from the dead themselves.

The cab stopped at the morgue shortly after, and Fergus leapt from it with a wave. 'Good luck, then.'

The driver nudged the horses forward, and Lilly was on her way again, arriving shortly after at Roma Street Police Station. Lilly thanked the driver, paid the fee and brushed the horse with affection as she passed. She ran up the stairs of the building in a most unladylike rush.

'He left some time ago, Miss Lewis. I can't say where the detective has gone, but he did say he expected to be back well before noon,' the desk sergeant said.

'Thank you. I shall hunt him down,' Lilly said, making the older police officer laugh. Departing the building, she entered another cab that was one of several on hand and gave the driver the address of *The Economic Undertaker*. The clock was on, and Lilly needed a good story to present to Mr Cowan, or she would have to succumb to the editor's story whims. The thought made her more determined to find a crime underway.

41

Chapter 5

PHOEBE WAS UNSURE IF she should help Nurse Faithful. Was it really worth disrupting so many lives with the truth?

'I am puzzled how you could have swapped the babies, Nurse Faithful. They were born at home, were they not?' she asked the spirit sitting nearby.

'Yes, but we had worked out a way; remember, there were five of us in the *Storks*, and we worked from my house where I lived alone. If we had a child born early, one of the wet nurses stayed at my house with the child, and then the *Storks* substituted the baby for the little deceased child. If the timing did not work, no one was assisted, but in many cases, we could change lives.'

'It terrifies me. What if you were caught?'

'To be truthful, it was too outrageous. Who would suspect such a thing of five respectable women? One of the wet nurse's husbands made dolls and toy soldiers; it was a delightful hobby and fortunate for us as those dolls were often used as an excuse should anyone see us with a baby around my home. We would say it was a doll we gifted mothers for comfort or consolation – a doll for the girls, a toy soldier for the boys.'

'Goodness, it appears you had thought of everything.'

'We believed we saved lives, Miss Astin.'

'What happened to the lady expecting twins, Mrs Liddle and poor Mrs Dellow, who could not deliver a live child?'

'Well, Mrs Liddle gave birth first, a little earlier than expected, with the shock of the loss of her husband. That worked well for us as Mrs Dellow was due any minute with her twins. We told Mrs Liddle that her twin babies were not responding, that we must rush them to the doctor, and that if we waited for him to call, it would be too late. She was weak from the birthing and agreed.' Nurse Faithful looked at her hands in her lap and back up at Phoebe. 'The next day, I called on Mrs Liddle to tell her the children were in hospital and in the best care the doctor could give, but we feared the worst. I said she could not risk visiting them and told her I had a priest give them the last rites.'

'How did she react to this news?' Phoebe asked.

'With a sad acceptance,' Nurse Faithful answered truthfully. 'Then, I slipped her a piece of paper; I had purchased insurance for her as a gift. I explained I did not know the children would be in trouble, and I hoped it was not a painful present in retrospect.'

'She had just buried her husband; surely she would have been grateful?'

'Oh, she was, and it did not set me back much; I had so few expenses of my own. Then I was called to Mrs Dellow's home; she was in labour. One of the *Storks* and the wet nurse brought Mrs Liddle's twins—a boy and a girl—to Mrs Dellow's neighbourhood and waited nearby in a carriage. Poor Mrs Dellow's little ones did not stand a chance, but she did not know that. When she went into labour and delivered, Mrs Dellow was distraught as there were no cries from the babies. I told her to wait while I checked the babies and cleared their mouths and noses. She did not know enough to argue. I took away the deceased, and...' Nurse Faithful waved her hand as if the rest was self-explanatory.

'And then you performed the swapping of the babies?'

'Oh, Miss Astin, if you could have seen the happy scene before me – Mr and Mrs Dellow in love and so very happy, cradling these children as if their life together had begun.'

'What would you have done if Mrs Dellow had given birth to healthy children or one had survived?'

Nurse Faithful shook her head. 'I knew she was in trouble; I had heard no heartbeat, but there was little point in telling her of her loss when she was so close to delivering.'

'But surely the doctor must have warned her about the heartbeat,' Phoebe said, confused.

'She was not seen by a doctor. Trust me, Miss Astin, the doctor rarely saw the ladies unless the birth was particularly complicated and there was fear that the mother might die. The midwives managed the birthing process.'

'I understand,' Phoebe said, seeing how it might all come together.

'I then had to tell Mrs Liddle of her loss; she did not ask to see the children but wanted to give them a Christian burial. Mrs Liddle was able to pay for their funeral from the insurance I had purchased. I had taken it out for one hundred pounds, a fortune, and enough to keep her and her five existing children for years. She even repaid me for the purchase. So, as you can see, we *Storks* changed so many lives for the better.'

'It does seem that way, Nurse Faithful. You provided a future for both families. But what became of the twins?'

'That little boy and girl were loved and had everything they needed and more; I saw them often over the years. We continued to help families as we saw the need, and we always gifted the dolls, soldiers, and insurance policies.' She dropped her voice as if worried someone might hear and said, 'We charged the families that could well afford our services more, and that covered the cost of the insurance policies for the families that could not.'

'So, how many might you have helped altogether?' Phoebe asked, curious.

'About four a year, so close to twenty families over five years. But then, a couple of our group retired, and the wet nurses could not go on forever. We didn't want to replace them; it was too risky.'

'Oh, goodness, that would be complicated.'

'Indeed. But please know this was not baby farming. We were not selling children.'

'I think you did your work with much goodwill, Nurse Faithful. Why reveal the truth now if everything worked out so well? Is it not best to let it lie?'

'I'm afraid it may all come out now. You see, when the *Storks'* ceased our work, we agreed to keep each other's secret and went our separate ways. Of the five, only myself and Esther have passed to the other side. Sadly, Esther was one of the wet nurses and died young, a year after we stopped our *Storks'* work.' She sighed at the thought. 'I will not reveal the names of the other three ladies; it is for them to clear their conscience, but I want to repent, and I believe something sinister is stirring.'

Phoebe felt a foreboding chill.

Nurse Faithful continued. 'Someone knows something. I have been tormented with notes and strange gifts for the last few months. Dolls. I fear for the safety of the remaining *Storks*. You see, I believe it led to my ill health and death.'

'Forgive me, I don't know how you died.'

'Officially, I believe my death is listed as heart failure. But I died of fright, Miss Astin, I am sure of it.'

Julius washed the cemetery dust off his face and hands before joining his family for a cup of tea and Mrs Dobbs's fruit loaf. His ritual was different from that of Ambrose, who did not feel the need to clean up after a funeral and had to be reminded by his grandfather, *The Economic Undertaker*'s frontman, Randolph, to at least brush down his jacket.

For Julius—and he would not confess this to anyone—the ritual was as much about cleanliness as it was about letting go of the sorrow of a life passed. Too much accumulated grief was not good for anyone; it settled and was absorbed through the skin. And so Julius did his duty by providing a respectable funeral and easing the burden on the family. He could not carry their grief as well. With a wash of his hands and face, he cleansed himself.

Julius's mind drifted to Violet in the store next door. He was sure he could feel her presence as if his heart synced with hers when he was back in the building; she took up a large part of his daily thoughts and had him quite off balance. He wondered if Ambrose noticed and guessed not, as his brother would tease him mercilessly if he were aware.

Saturday's visit to the aquarium had been a great success. Seeing Violet laugh when he warned, 'Do not look now but I fear we are being followed,' and pointed out the fish behind the glass aquarium wall, holding her as they waltzed, and taking every opportunity to offer his hand or arm to ensure her comfort and safety made for a rewarding night. He could wait no longer, and Julius determined he would speak with Violet's brother, Tom, today and seek permission to ask for her hand; Tom was the man of the family now, and he knew Violet would appreciate the gesture.

'The tea is poured, Julius,' Randolph called to hurry him along.

'On my way.' Julius gathered himself and departed to join his family in the meeting room for morning tea.

Nurse Charlotte Faithful suddenly vanished as someone thundered down the stairs to Phoebe's workroom.

'Ah, I heard you talking to someone. Are they still here?' Ambrose asked.

Phoebe turned. 'No. So, did it all go well?' she asked of her second eldest brother and the most gregarious of the three siblings.

'Despite the heat, yes. The usual number of ladies throwing themselves at our feet,' he said with a wink, 'and of course, we buried the dead. Come up while there are no customers; Mrs Dobbs has morning tea ready.'

'I shall be there promptly. Thank you, brother.'

Ambrose departed just as quickly, and Phoebe turned to resume the conversation. Moments later, Nurse Faithful reappeared, and Phoebe encouraged her to share her thoughts on what might be done now.

'Please do go and take your tea while you can; rest breaks are important when you are on your feet most of the day. That is my story done, my actions right or wrong.'

Phoebe thought Nurse Faithful looked better for having spoken of her burden.

'Thank you for listening, Miss Astin.'

Phoebe rose. 'I am happy to be of service. Might we talk about a course of action later, Nurse Faithful?'

'Yes, thank you. Perhaps you might call on someone who could assist? A detective, a priest...' Nurse Faithful's voice trailed off.

Phoebe agreed, pleased for the break to think about the senior lady's story, but asked, 'You will return?'

'Definitely.'

With that, Phoebe excused herself and took to the stairs, entering the room just as her cup of tea was being poured.

'So, how many ladies fainted today?' Randolph teased with a raised eyebrow in Julius's direction.

'It was hot, so a few more than usual,' Julius said.

'Four,' Ambrose said what his brother would not, 'and I don't believe it had anything to do with the heat. The funeral was early and under a shady tree.'

Mrs Dobbs put the teapot down and said, 'The handsome Astin brothers would send most women into a swoon, especially when emotionally wrought at a funeral. If I were forty years younger...'

'Then you would not have been born,' Ambrose teased her, and she laughed.

'Get away with you, you charmer.'

'Well, it does not hurt our business,' Phoebe said, assisting Mrs Dobbs with passing the milk and sugar. 'I just hope when you both wed, we don't lose a large proportion of our custom.'

Julius shook his head at their nonsense. 'We are economical; that is the bottom line. No one cares what we look like; I am sure it is just a distraction from the stress of the funeral. What are you working on, Phoebe?' he diverted the conversation.

'No spirits wanting redemption or for you to solve their murder?'

'The timing of your question is interesting, Julius. Had you asked me that earlier this morning, I would have said there had been no requests for my help for a few weeks, but the strangest thing happened today.'

Mrs Dobbs gave a small laugh and added quickly, seeing their surprised looks, 'Oh, forgive me. Is it not strange enough to work in this industry and to speak with spirits? But of course, you are all used to it.'

The group around the table chuckled, and Phoebe squeezed Mrs Dobbs's hand as they partook of her delicious cake.

'Yes, you are right, of course. Perhaps I had best say something stranger than usual happened! I have had the pleasure of meeting the nurse that you brought in for her funeral tomorrow,' she said to her brothers.

Mrs Dobbs blessed herself, as she often did when the Astin family mentioned guests from the other side.

'Nurse Charlotte Faithful—'

'What a beautiful name,' Randolph interrupted.

'I thought so too, Grandpa,' Phoebe agreed, 'and I believe her to be a good person. But perhaps her death is not as straightforward as the police thought.'

'Uh oh, here we go,' Ambrose said and took a large bite of fruitcake, sitting back as if expecting a good tale.

The bell sounded over the door, and Randolph started to rise, Julius hailing him down.

'I am closer, Grandpa,' he said, going to attend to the customer. Phoebe waited, not wanting to tell her story twice when Julius re-entered with Detective Harland Stone and Detective Gilbert Payne.

'Just in time, gents, if you can stop for cake and tea,' Randolph invited them to sit as Julius grabbed a couple of extra chairs, Mrs Dobbs hurried to get more plates, and Phoebe rose to get cups and saucers.

'Apologies for interrupting your break, and thank you, Mr Astin; I think we can definitely make our query over a cup of tea. Who could resist Mrs Dobbs's baking?' Harland asked.

Phoebe poured as Mrs Dobbs returned and cut the extra slices, her face alive with pleasure. As a widow, the staff and guests at *The Economic Undertaker* were the fortunate recipients of her baking, and they were profuse in their praise.

'It is well worth timing your visits around morning and afternoon tea time,' Ambrose agreed.

'I am sure you could go into business with this fruitcake, Mrs Dobbs,' Gilbert said, accepting a slice as he sat beside Phoebe, forcing Harland to sit beside Julius and Ambrose.

Phoebe was relieved; sitting so close to Detective Stone would make her nervous, and her brothers would no doubt notice. She held Detective Gilbert Payne in high regard and was pleased when he sat beside her.

'It is excellent,' she agreed, 'everyone comments so.'

'Now steady on, Detective Payne,' Randolph scolded him in jest. 'Do not come in here suggesting business ventures for our employees.'

Gilbert grinned. 'Forgive me, Mr Astin.' He turned to Mrs Dobbs. 'It is cut-throat out there, Mrs Dobbs. You are much safer in here,' he said in an effort to regain favour, and amused her no end.

'Your timing is perfect. Phoebe has a new visitor crying foul,' Julius said, 'but it's best you address your reason for visiting first as clients might arrive any moment.' To Mrs Dobbs's disappointment, he declined a slice of cake.

'Ah, that is bad news,' Harland said, and as all eyes turned to him, he explained, 'If they are crying foul, it means our police force has not asked the right questions.'

'Unless the villain was a genius,' Ambrose said.

'Are they ever?' Phoebe asked. 'Can evil and genius co-exist?'

'That is an interesting debate,' Harland said, and the pair exchanged a smile.

'Well, if we can have geniuses in our detective ranks, why not amongst the villains?' Ambrose asked. 'Don't you agree, brother?'

'I am sorry I wasn't listening.' Julius admitted and hurriedly finished his tea; his impatience was obvious as Harland cleared his throat and introduced the reason for his visit.

'We have a young lady we have not been able to identify, and we understand you have drawn a likeness before for Detective Harry Dart on one of his cases, Miss Astin.'

'I have. How is lovely Detective Dart? Has he not retired then?' Phoebe asked.

'This year, I believe, and he is well. I shall tell him you asked after him,' Harland continued. 'We hoped we might impose on you to do a sketch for us.' He looked to Randolph. 'The face is intact with nothing to be alarmed about.'

'Thank you, Detective, but I have not yet seen anything that alarms Phoebe despite our best efforts to shield her,' Randolph said.

'I would be happy to do so, Detective. Shall I come to you, or will you bring her by? The poor woman,' Phoebe sighed.

'I suggest we bring the body to you, Miss Astin, so you can work on the drawing when convenient,' Harland said, and Phoebe thanked him.

Again, she felt the look he gave her lingered a little longer than it should have, and she hurriedly returned her attention to her teacup.

Julius rose, his chair loudly scraping the floor. 'Please excuse me, I have to go.' He was out of the room within moments and heard his grandfather rise behind him, catching up near the exit, his hand grasping Julius's arm.

'Lad, what is going on with you?'

Julius turned. 'Nothing, I am fine. Do not concern yourself, Grandpa.'

'Are you still in pain?'

'No. I am quite healed.'

'You are not eating.'

Julius restrained from sighing, but his impatience at the intrusion reflected on his face. 'I assure you I am fine.' He softened, seeing his grandfather's look of concern. 'I... I need to speak with Tom.'

'Tom?' Randolph stopped, surprised, and then realisation dawned on him; he smiled, released Julius and gave his grandson a wave towards the door.

'Well of course, lad, don't let me stop you.'

Julius mumbled his thanks, grabbed his hat from the nearby stand and departed. Like all things in his life, Julius had decided now was the time and his feelings demanded action. He would speak with Tom, get a ring, and propose to Miss Violet Forrester this week. If all went well, she would be Mrs Julius Astin as soon as possible and, along with her brother, be under his protection.

Chapter 6

Detective Harland Stone had wasted no time in paying a call on Miss Astin. In fact, he had to hide his pleasure when he learnt of her experience in sketching for the police force and the account that existed between the two businesses for that purpose. But if Harland had hoped to have a moment alone with Phoebe, he was sadly left wanting. As Julius departed in a hurry, he heard Mr Astin senior greeting a young lady and, moments later, Randolph showed in journalist Miss Lilly Lewis. The gentlemen rose until she took a seat.

'Well, I have found you both,' Lilly said, pleased at seeing Harland and Gilbert. 'Hello Mrs Dobbs, Phoebe, Mr Astin,' she said, addressing Ambrose before returning her attention to the detectives. 'I was just at the police station.'

'Good morning, Miss Lewis. Did they say we were coming here?' Harland asked, surprised.

'No. I gave up on you and came to see Phoebe.'

Harland had to admire the two ladies who looked as pretty as a picture, as his mother would say. Phoebe, with her fair hair tied loosely back with a cream lace ribbon and wearing a pale pink dress, and Miss Lewis in mint green with her shiny chestnut hair. The pair hugged affectionately, and as a client arrived, the detectives and Miss Lewis accepted the invitation to continue the discussion in Phoebe's room. Mrs Dobbs returned to the kitchen, and Randolph greeted the new customer, assuming his most dignified expression in their time of grief.

The small party followed Phoebe downstairs, accompanied by Ambrose as if chaperoning. Harland wondered if her family insisted on it after he exhausted her last case. It pained him still that he had thought so little of her needs. It was poor form, especially in the eyes of her family, should Harland wish them to consider him a suitable suitor. On arriving at Phoebe's workroom, he noted the body in the corner covered by a shroud. The ladies sat at Phoebe's small work table while the gents gathered random chairs to join them.

'Are you here on a case?' Lilly asked with hope in her voice.

'Yes,' Harland answered and said nothing more.

The small party exchanged smiles as Lilly grimaced.

'Very well, as long as you adhere to our usual arrangement, I see no harm in you having the story,' Harland conceded.

'I will, of course,' she said, her hand going to her heart as if taking a pledge. 'Thank goodness. I have today only to find my next investigative piece. Do tell, please. And Phoebe, you are involved. Did it come from you?'

'No, the detectives have approached me this morning,' Phoebe said, 'but there is another matter I hope to speak to them about for one of my clients if their time permits.'

'Oh, how exciting! Two potential stories,' Lilly said, looking thrilled at the prospect.

'It may help to have Miss Lewis report on the unidentifiable young lady in question,' Gilbert said to his superior.

'My thoughts exactly,' Harland said. 'We may get someone coming forward to identify her.'

'Oh, this story is getting better,' Lilly said, fascinated and giving a small guilty smile when Ambrose burst out laughing, and she realised how mercenary that might sound.

Harland gave her an amused look and nodded for Gilbert to tell of the body they found.

'The stage make-up sounds odd,' Lilly agreed after Gilbert concluded.

Harland said, 'We shall release the young lady's body to you, Miss Astin, as soon as we return.'

'That would work very well for me, thank you, Detective Stone. Claude and Will can collect her if you advise on a time?'

'Excellent. Let's say mid-afternoon then, and I will ensure she is ready. Do tell us about your visitor?' He asked, hat in hand.

'If you have time,' Phoebe said.

'Oh good, let's have your mystery too, Phoebe,' Lilly said, eyes alight with excitement. 'My day cannot get any better.'

Phoebe gave a huff of laughter. 'It is a complicated case, and it might take longer to solve than identifying the detectives' victim.'

'Perfect, I shall have two cases on the go and not have to hunt another for a brief period,' Lilly said, exhaling with relief.

'Is your visitor here, Miss Astin?' Gilbert asked, looking around with much interest. He pulled out his notebook and pencil, ready to write up notes.

'Yes, she is, seated below the window,' Phoebe said with a nod and smile toward the empty seat before addressing the detectives. 'I would make introductions, but suffice to say Nurse Charlotte Faithful is present and has requested assistance as a result of her deathbed or, rather, a post-life confession.' She turned to the lady sitting in the corner. 'May I present Detective Harland Stone, Detective Gilbert Payne, Miss Lilly Lewis, and my brother, Ambrose, whom you saw earlier.'

'Gentlemen, Miss Lewis,' Nurse Faithful said as if they could hear her.

'It began with a good deed,' Phoebe said and told them briefly and concisely Nurse Faithful's story as it was recounted to her. 'And so, you can imagine Nurse Faithful's distress thinking her work might have been in vain and caused more harm than good. She also fears for the safety of the remaining three ladies of the *Storks*.'

'The best-laid schemes o' Mice an' Men,' Harland mused as he looked to the covered body in the corner that he understood to be the physical presence of the lady in question.

'Robert Burns's poetry, Sir!' Gilbert said, surprised. 'But very apt. The foresight to know what might happen would be as valuable as hindsight. For Nurse Faithful, the intention to better the lives of two families in the present would seem the best plan in her noble profession.'

Phoebe nodded. 'Nurse Faithful thanks you for your empathy and understanding,' she said, repeating the words of the lady in the corner.

'I respect that Nurse Faithful does not want to reveal her friends' names, but that does make it difficult for us to protect them or investigate if they have been threatened,' Harland said.

'If you tell us, we won't tell your colleagues that your ghost told us so,' Ambrose suggested, and everyone present did their best to hide their smiles.

Nurse Faithful laughed. 'He is a cheeky one, that.'

'He is cheeky,' Phoebe agreed and smiled at her handsome brother.

'Could Nurse Faithful tell us about one of the frightening episodes she encountered so we understand the degree of threat?' Gilbert asked, and Harland appeared pleased with the question.

Phoebe listened as Nurse Faithful began the story with a shaky voice, the experience still causing her distress, even in death; Phoebe recounted it to the detectives as best she could.

Three weeks prior, in Nurse Charlotte Faithful's words...

'I checked the doors were locked, and the windows clasped as I prepared for bed. In all the years I lived alone, I was never fearful until now, but something had changed. There was a sinister presence watching me. The notes and gifts were all unwanted, and all contained a hint of malice – a coward's act but enough to strike fear into any lady's heart.

Before I extinguished my candle, I looked out into the dark but saw only my reflection in the window softly lit by the candle's glow. There appeared to be no cause for alarm. Closing the curtain, I confess I abandoned my usual prayers and offered a small plea for a safe night ahead.

After midnight, I woke with a start; there was a noise. I froze; my breath hitched while listening. I assure you I am not a woman given to hysterics, but fear threatened to overtake me on this occasion. Everything seemed sinister; even the silhouette of the tree outside my window, with its branches stretching like fingers, caused my heart to pound faster.

The message on a card I had received earlier served as a premonition – *I know what you did.* My mind had gone there a thousand times since receiving it: *I know what you did, I know what you did.*

Who is sending them?

Who is aggrieved by the actions meant in kindness?

How does anyone know of the work done now several decades past?

I began to breathe steadily again, wondering if I had imagined the noise or if it was just the wind or a night animal. But then, no! The sound was faint, but there it was again. Was it music?

Rising, I donned my nightgown, taking comfort from its warmth, not that it would serve as a protector. My feet found my slippers in the dark, and sliding them on, I quietly moved to the bedroom door. Glancing down the small hallway of the cottage revealed little – there was nothing amiss, nor could I see the glow of any lights, shadows, or shapes to strike fear into my heart. Nevertheless, terror gripped me. You must know the feeling of intuitive fear. My heart beat so fast it caused a sharp pain in my chest.

Someone was nearby. Someone was watching; I sensed them like prey does, waiting for the hunter to strike. There was no going back now. I could not return to bed, nor stay frozen in fear in the hallway of my home. So, I shakily continued on my path and moved slowly down the hallway towards the backdoor. Now, the sound increased in volume. It was melodic, sweet even, and I recognised the tune – the sound of a child's music box playing and the song... it was called *Home Sweet Home.*

I gasped. How could something so innocent sound so foreboding in the dark of night? My mind grasped at the meaning of the chosen music. Did I place this person as a newborn in a home that they did not like? I also knew someone had to wind the mechanism; were they still present? Flattening myself against the wall, I moved as close as I dared to the back door and realised the sound came from outside, not inside. Nothing would make me open that door, but there was no turning back now, so I edged my way quietly to the nearby window and moved the curtain slightly aside. Then I saw it. On the back path, in the centre, sat a small music box lit by the glow of a lamp beside it. It was close enough that I could see it was quite beautiful, with enamelled dainty butterflies inside the lid and flower decorations. I could see the crank winder. A doll was beside it, propped upright and leaning on the box. I later discovered it was not just any doll, but the very same one we gifted years and years ago... they were all alike, our signature gift.

It looked like such an innocent scene, but I was terrified beyond all measure. I could look no longer. I gathered myself before again opening the curtain slightly, and for a brief moment, I saw a shadow. I was not alone.

Phoebe concluded Nurse Faithful's tale. 'The music box and lantern were gone in the first morning light as if they had never been there, but the doll was left behind.'

'Oh, that is sinister,' Lilly said and shuddered.

'How did Nurse Faithful die?' Ambrose asked.

'Nurse Faithful claims she was frightened to death,' Phoebe said, 'but I believe her death was recorded as heart failure.'

'Does Nurse Faithful have a record of the families she assisted?' Harland asked.

Phoebe looked to the corner, waited for the answer and nodded. 'Yes, Detective, but they were in her personal possessions left to her brother, and he may have discarded them. If required, she can recall the names of most.'

'Then, time permitting, we shall delve deeper into it. Do not be alarmed,' Harland added, anticipating Nurse Faithful's fears. 'We will be subtle and not reveal anything that might break up a family. We will see if there are any cracks to be seen. If Nurse Faithful could give us half a dozen names now, that would be a starting point.'

'I shall run with the dead, unidentified lady story first if that is suitable, Detectives? I best get to the morgue and see her for myself,' Lilly said, cutting in. 'Thank you, Phoebe.'

'We shall accompany you there,' Detective Harland said. 'I need to speak with the coroner and release the young lady's body to Miss Astin.'

'Oh good, then I shall get some quotes for my story en route,' Lilly said. 'It is turning out to be a marvellous day.'

'Except for the dead,' Ambrose said in jest, glancing at the body in the corner.

Phoebe smiled as Lilly groaned.

'Do not worry, dear Lilly, our jobs are far from conventional and we must make the best of every situation,' Phoebe assured her friend.

'A fine sentiment,' Harland said, and Phoebe smiled at him again. She might not have torn her gaze away had Lilly not begun a hearty defence of her position.

'I cannot feel guilty for my dedication,' Lilly said. 'The Reverend Dr Talmage wrote the most magnificent piece on the role of the newspaper in society, and my editor pinned it to the noticeboard and made us all read it.'

'And who might he be?' Ambrose asked, but Lilly did not get a chance to answer as Harland, with a raised eyebrow in her direction, said, 'Let me guess, he said you were the crusaders of truth!'

Lilly bore his teasing. 'Dr Talmage said a good newspaper is a mirror of life itself, and that the evil must be reported as well as the good so we know what to guard against or reform.'

'That is eminently sensible,' Gilbert agreed, in between taking down the half dozen names Phoebe quietly relayed.

Lilly added, 'And he said that the newspaper that only wrote of the bright side of life misrepresented it.'

'I agree with that. On that note, we shall go and do our best to see justice done,' Harland said with a small bow to Miss Astin, and placing his hat on his head, he farewelled Ambrose and took off up the stairs with long strides; Gilbert and Lilly hurrying behind in his wake and Phoebe staring after him.

Chapter 7

JULIUS HAD GIVEN GREAT thought to what he would say
to Tom Forrester—Violet's younger brother—but knew
there would be no resistance to their union. Not because
Julius was a co-owner of the carpentry business and, thus,
an employer of Tom and his sister at *In Mourning – Attire
for the Family*, but because Tom had actively encouraged
their union. Nevertheless, he felt uneasy arriving at the
carpentry factory – an unusual sensation.

On seeing his arrival, the co-business owner and Julius's
cousin, Lucian, approached.

'Hello cousin, is everything all right? We were not
meeting today, were we?' he asked, brushing sawdust from
his clothing.

'No, forgive the intrusion, Cousin.'

Lucian laughed. 'It is your business as well, hardly an intrusion.'

'But you are managing it. I was hoping you would have no objections if I spoke with Tom for no more than ten minutes.'

'Tom? Is his sister—'

'She is perfectly fine,' Julius assured him.

'Well... oh. Now? Goodness.' Lucian smiled. 'You were always a man of action once a decision was made.'

Julius rolled his eyes. 'Perhaps. So may I?'

'Of course. I am thrilled for you, Julius,' Lucian said sincerely, pumping his cousin's shoulder and earning a small smile.

'It is not done yet.'

'But it will be.' Lucian turned, calling loudly above the noise of the factory, 'Tom, down tools, lad, front and centre.'

Lucian turned back to look at Julius. They were the same height; only Lucian was from the fairer side of the family. He smiled.

'Don't let me hold you up,' Julius said drily, and Lucian laughed and, with another slap on Julius's shoulder, returned to his work as Tom approached, anxiety written on his face.

'Julius, is Violet unwell?'

'Fear not, Tom, she is in good health. Could I speak to you about her?'

'Of Violet? Sure. Oh, you are going to propose!' he exclaimed and extended his hand. 'That is brilliant.'

Julius chuckled and shook his offered hand.

'Well, I was going to ask if you had any objections as you are the man of the family,' Julius said, studying Tom, who had grown a great deal in the last year not only in height but in maturity. The planes of his face had lost their youthfulness, and he looked very much like a young adult. Julius could see Violet in him – the blue eyes, the shape of their noses and the full brown hair with a curl that both shared.

'I want no one else for her. You are the best thing to happen to my sister, to our family,' Tom said in sincerity, 'and thank you for asking me.'

'So, I have your blessing?'

'A thousand times over.'

This time, Julius offered his hand, and the men shook. 'You will both move in with me after the wedding. Yes?'

Tom frowned. 'I am sure you want your privacy. I can probably get a smaller home again on our street and afford it on my salary.'

'No. We are family, and you will be officially my brother-in-law. I can't imagine you and Violet separated until you find your own bride. Fear not; the house is big enough, and you will come and go as you please.'

Tom grinned. 'Then it is all set. I shall say nothing until you ask, but don't leave it too long. Violet always knows when I am keeping something from her.'

Julius laughed. 'That does not bode well for me then. I shall ask her to accompany me on a date in the next day or so and hopefully secure her agreement then.'

Tom grinned again. 'This is a good day.'

Julius doffed his hat and, with a grin to mirror that of his future brother-in-law, departed to return to the office of *The Economic Undertaker*.

The red-haired, bearded Scottish coroner, who would describe himself as ruggedly handsome, exclaimed joyfully, 'Be still my beating heart. It is the lovely journalist, Miss Lilly Lewis!'

'It is also the lovely detectives Stone and Payne,' Harland added humorously.

'So it is.' Tavish grinned. 'What a glorious day! But wait, I bet you've come to see about a body and not to visit me.' He made a face in jest.

'Oh, but we are delighted for the excuse,' Lilly teased.

The door swung open, and all eyes turned to find Bennet Martin entering.

'Another guest, hello Bennet,' Tavish exclaimed. 'Ah, to be so popular.'

'A full house,' Bennet said in his proper English accent as if he had just arrived at the theatre. 'Doctor, detectives, Miss Lewis,' he gave a small bow, and Tavish could not help but notice how resplendent Bennet Martin looked, like a man who came from money, while he wore a dull grey suit in keeping with his office role. No wonder Miss Lilly Lewis was drawn to the suave Englishman. He watched for a special exchange between them and detected a change in Miss Lewis's demeanour. The look on Bennet's face upon entry at seeing Miss Lewis in attendance left no question of his feelings.

'What are the odds that our business is one and the same?' Lilly asked with a smile, and Bennet shook his head.

'Not this time, sadly. An insurance company has hired me—I know, how frightfully dull—to look into claims of large insurance policies taken out for children who don't exist but have since died. Any chance you know of such cases, Harland and Detective Payne?'

'An interesting coincidence as we, too, have been speaking of insurance this very day, but no, I don't know of any false claims yet,' Harland said.

'Nor I,' Gilbert said, 'but it is worrying. I find it odd that insurance policies for children can be taken out for such large sums.'

'As do I, 100 pounds,' Bennet agreed. 'I shall loiter if I may until you are free, Tavish?'

'Please do. That is a clever scheme,' Tavish said, impressed, and hurriedly added, 'but very bad form, of course, if the child does not exist.'

'I could never be a criminal,' Lilly said. 'I could not come up with some of these inventive crimes. What a challenge to think like these offenders, detectives, in order to catch them!'

'Exactly so, Miss Lewis. Luckily, we have crafty minds,' Harland said in jest and earned a laugh.

'To business,' Lilly said impatiently.

'On a deadline, my dear?' Tavish asked.

'Yes, always, Doctor McGregor, and my editor is not to be kept waiting. I believe you have an unidentified lady on hand that I might report on.'

'And we are keen to hear your autopsy findings on the same lady, Tavish, thank you,' Harland said.

'Plus, we are curious about Miss Charlotte Faithful, whose body was recently released for burial,' Gilbert said.

'Gracious, one moment please, lady and gents,' Tavish said, and moving to his desk, he rifled through some files, collecting two before moving to a large cabinet where he pulled out a trolley with a body on it, covered by a cloth.

'Resting under the sheet is our unknown deceased lady. Do you wish to see her, Miss Lewis?'

'Yes, please, if I may?' Lilly said in a low voice and uncharacteristically reserved as she prepared herself to see the deceased. Moments later, after observing the face, she proclaimed, 'Goodness gracious, what is that odd face powder? Was she an actress in a pantomime or wearing a costume when you found her?'

'It is peculiar,' Harland agreed. 'Gilbert thought she might be a pantomime performer too. She was dressed in a dress that seemed most childlike, as if she were a doll.'

'Except my queries late yesterday revealed nothing currently being performed that might require her costume or make-up, and no one was missing a lady cast member,' Gilbert added.

'She was found at the Botanic Gardens miniature village display, lying in the middle of the city... crushing Elizabeth Street to be exact,' Harland told Lilly, who scribbled down the information. 'She had no identification on her, and no one has reported a lady of her description missing.'

'That bruising around her neck... does that mean she was strangled?' Lilly asked and looked at Tavish.

'I am ready to give the detectives my finding; shall I proceed?' he asked Harland, glancing at Lilly.

'Yes, Miss Lewis can be privy to it,' Harland said.

'Right then. The red ribbon found around her neck was very tight but not tight enough to take her last breath. And no, as Detective Payne pointed out earlier, she was not poisoned from the make-up.'

Gilbert nodded. 'I understand current powders and bases do not contain the toxicity of past decades.'

'Correct, Detective Payne,' Tavish said. 'You are well-read, as usual.' Gilbert flushed with pleasure. 'No, the young lady died of tuberculosis.'

A hush fell over the room as they considered the coroner's findings.

'So, you are saying she died of natural causes?' Harland asked, confused.

'Yes. Why she was dumped at the miniature show and why no one has claimed her is a mystery, but her cause of death is not.'

'Oh my, how very peculiar,' Lilly said in a low voice as she studied the young lady.

'If she was ill with tuberculosis, why would anyone dress her and apply powder to her face in such a fashion?' Gilbert pondered.

'And desert her, leaving her amongst strangers,' Lilly added.

'A touch of melancholy from our ruthless journalist... surely not,' Tavish teased her.

'Empathy is a writer's friend,' Bennet said in her defence, and won himself an endearing smile from Lilly.

'Thank you, Mr Martin. The readers do like to be moved to shed a tear or two.' She turned to Harland. 'May I share everything we have spoken of today, Detective?'

'Yes, I see no harm in that, and the sooner we find out who she is, the better,' Harland said. 'Thank you, Tavish. If you have no objections, I will transport her body to *The Economic Undertaker*'s office this afternoon. Miss Astin is going to sketch the lady's likeness.'

'She may go anytime,' Tavish agreed. 'I shall dress her as she was found, as her garments featured some nice stitching of cornflowers and may prompt recognition if Miss Astin features it.'

'Thank you; that is a sound idea. Miss Lewis, will you include details of her clothing when you write this story? Let's see if we can get someone to claim her,' Harland continued.

'With pleasure. Although that will not give me a mystery to solve for very long. What of this other crime then?' Lilly asked, and Tavish laughed.

'Ah, the journalist's relentless hunt for a story. Let me see then,' he said and opened the file on Nurse Charlotte Faithful. 'This might be a dull one; Miss Faithful died of heart failure. What makes you think her death was of a suspicious nature?'

A momentary silence filled the room as the inhabitants could not reveal mortuary artist Miss Phoebe Astin as the source of their query; everyone present, with the exception of

Dr Tavish McGregor, knew of her penchant for speaking with spirits.

Harland cleared his throat. 'A source acquainted with Nurse Faithful believed her to be frightened and threatened before her death.'

'And if she had a weak heart, her death may have been premature,' Gilbert added.

'That may well be the case,' Tavish agreed, 'but I have no means of confirming the cause of her heart failure. She was not a large woman, so her heart was not strained, but a weak heart may expire at any time.' On seeing their expressions, Tavish gave them an apologetic look. 'I'm sorry, gents, you have your work cut out for you.'

As he watched the detectives and reporter depart, he was also sorry that Miss Lewis did not care a fig for him, but he turned to give her potential new beau his undivided attention.

Chapter 8

Miss Kate Kirby cut the string and opened the brown paper around the package to view her photographs returned from her regular picture framer. Carefully lifting each one out, she placed them side by side and moved along the half-dozen images to study the final product. Tall, fair, with auburn hair that was a little skew-whiff from working under the fabric hood of the camera, she bit her lower lip with concentration.

'Just lovely,' she exhaled with relief, satisfied with the work commissioned by *The Economic Undertaker*. The first image was taken outside their store, featuring all the staff, including the men from the stable and Mrs Dobbs from the kitchen. The next shot was of management only – Randolph, Julius, Ambrose and Phoebe Astin. She studied one of those

Astin men a little longer than the rest of the family, and an involuntary smile lit her face.

'So handsome, Mr Ambrose Astin,' she whispered and looked at the next couple of images of the ladies in the mourning wear dressmaking store – Violet, Mary and Nellie, admiring how lovely they looked, especially Violet.

Kate was pleased with the quality of the images. The lighting had been perfect in the late afternoon, and the positioning of everyone in the photographs had worked to best advantage. She had asked to display an image in her studio, hoping to inspire other businesses to seek her services, and these would work very nicely. In packaging the photographs that would go to the client, Kate was quietly thrilled for the opportunity to visit *The Economic Undertaker*. She hoped Ambrose Astin would be in attendance.

Better still, she would send a note requesting an appointment to deliver them for inspection. That way, if Ambrose was genuinely interested in her, he could make himself available, along with the other Astin gentlemen – Julius and Randolph. She set to work penning a brief note to Mr Astin senior in order to make today's post.

Julius Astin was on his way back to his business but digressed. He made his way to the home where he was raised after his parents' death, to where his grandparents made ends meet, even if times were tight much of the time. Dismounting, he saw the door open and knew his grandmother was home. Moments later, she appeared on the verandah, panic written on her face.

'What is wrong, Julius? Is it Randolph?'

He held his hands up. 'All is well, everyone is well. I am sorry to frighten you, Grandma.'

She exhaled with relief and embraced him as he approached the top step. He was surprised by how petite she was; had he gotten taller, his grandmother smaller, or perhaps both? But some things never change – the way she wore her white hair neatly presented in a tight bun and her attire, as always, was immaculate.

'Well, in that case, it is lovely to see you, my eldest grandchild. Have you got time for a cup of tea, or are you collecting something?'

He realised how little he visited his ancestral home when his grandmother did not think he might have called to see her.

'I have time for a cup of tea; I have come to see you. Shall we?' Julius asked, and indicating the house's interior, followed her inside. The pair made small talk until seated with a cup of tea before them. Then, Julius broached the subject of his visit.

'Grandma, I wish to share something with you before I tell the rest of the family. I spoke with Tom Forrester today, asking permission to wed his sister.'

Maria clapped her hands together and gave a small cry. 'What joyous news, Julius. Our first wedding in the family; it has been decades. Oh, how your father and mother would wish to share this.' She reached for a handkerchief buried in the bosom of her dress and dabbed her eyes and gripped his hand with her other free hand. 'How I love such joyful news.'

He laughed. 'Well, she has not said yes yet, Grandma, but Tom believes she will.'

'Of course the lovely Miss Forrester will say yes. You are made for each other, and she is taken with you. Anyone who saw you together could tell that. Oh, Julius, a wedding to look forward to. Well, I could not be happier.'

'I had best ask her sooner rather than later,' he said in jest. 'I shall call on her today and ask her to accompany me on an outing tomorrow evening, depending on her availability. She has the *Vexed Vixens* gathering tonight.'

'Ah yes,' Maria laughed, 'those clever young ladies are so good for each other. And to think, soon you will be married to one of them.'

'I have never felt this way before, and if you had told me this time last year that an engagement was on the cards for me, I would have thought you were very mistaken, Grandma.'

'Love is a funny thing,' she agreed. 'I was gone for your grandfather the moment I laid eyes on him. It was his brother, Reggie, who introduced us.'

'Is that so?' Julius said, recalling the story. He believed his deceased uncle held a flame for Maria Astin, and it was the reason Reggie had not moved on to the next world.

'One moment, dear, please,' Maria said and rose, returning with a small jewellery box. 'As you are the firstborn, would you like to present your mother's engagement ring to Miss Forrester?' She opened the small timber box. 'It is a modest ring but one given with great love.'

Julius looked at the small, dainty ring and smiled at the thought of his father, with his meagre funds, presenting this to his mother.

'It is lovely. Thank you, Grandma, but I am in a fortunate position to secure Violet a larger diamond and would like to treat her.'

'Of course, as you should.'

'Maybe Phoebe, as the only girl in the family, should have Mum's jewellery.'

'A lovely thought and fitting,' his grandmother said, closing the jewellery box. 'So, you must let me know when I can spread the good news.'

'As soon as she says yes, and I hope she does. Her uncle tried to convince Violet we should not be together.'

'His intentions were honourable in trying to look after her best interests, but thank goodness he went home,' Maria said with a sigh. 'Does your grandfather know of your pending proposal?'

'He knew I was going to see Tom, and no doubt concluded as much. I shall tell him on my return.'

'And you've come out of your way to tell me. Thank you, dear boy.'

'No, thank you, Grandma.' He said, and their eyes locked for just a moment before Julius rose. 'I had best get back in case Ambrose has buried the wrong body.'

Maria laughed and was still dabbing her eyes when he departed. Julius was glad he had made the slight detour to see the woman who had given so much of herself and made him the man he was today. His next detour on his return to the office was to a jewellery store, and he chose that of two men—the Brooke brothers—similar to his age who had trusted *The Economic Undertaker* to bury their father a year back; Julius was a loyal businessman and would place his business with them in return. It was conveniently nearby on Tribune Street.

Arriving at the small but attractive store with its windows full of glass trinkets, Julius entered to the sound of a bell announcing his arrival. Joseph, the eldest of the Brooke brothers, appeared from a back room. He was dark of features, not dissimilar to Julius but shorter and slenderer; his brother, whom Julius could see through the open curtain working on a clock, was very similar and a few years younger.

'Mr Astin! This is a surprise.' The gentlemen shook hands.

'It is good to see you under happier circumstances,' Julius said. 'I am after a diamond engagement ring and hoped you could assist.'

'Of course, that would be my pleasure and how good of you to remember us.' Hearing the discussion, the other Brooke brother appeared, and handshakes were exchanged again before he returned to his work.

'Would you like a ring designed or to see our stock on hand?' Joseph Brooke asked.

'Your stock on hand, please. I intend to propose in the next day, and should I be accepted, I will bring in Miss Forrester for an adjustment if needed.'

'Excellent, and congratulations, an exciting time for you both,' Joseph said with a smile. 'Do you have something in mind?'

'A single diamond in a gold band.'

Joseph looked surprised. 'You have given this some thought.'

'No, I was told by my sister, who is a friend of Miss Forrester and raised the topic of their desired engagement rings, thus providing all the details should I need it,' Julius said drily, making Joseph laugh.

'Ah, the ladies are always more organised than we mere mortal men. One moment, please.' Joseph pulled out several jewellery trays from under the counter, each presenting a single diamond in various settings.

Julius cast a quick eye over the trays and looked at the jeweller. 'I appreciate your discretion, but would you have a larger diamond, perhaps?'

'Of course, I did not want to be presumptuous.' Joseph returned the trays to the shelf and, selecting a key from a chain tucked in his suit pocket, unlocked a cabinet, removed a tray, and presented it.

Julius's eyes lit with interest. 'Ah, yes, one of these will be perfect.' He selected a large solitaire diamond at a price that well exceeded the amount the Brooke brothers paid for their father's funeral. Joseph Brooke boxed it for him before taking the offered payment and writing a receipt.

'It has been a pleasure doing business with you once more,' Joseph said. 'My congratulations again, and we shall see you should you need a complimentary adjustment.'

'Thank you, Mr Brooke. Good day to you both,' Julius said and pocketed the ring, keen to see it worn on the hand of Miss Violet Forrester.

Chapter 9

THE BODY OF THE unidentified lady arrived at *The Economic Undertaker*. It was delivered to Phoebe's room under the supervision of the company owner—Julius—who had returned at the same time and wanted to ensure the relationship with the police service and the detectives remained in good stead.

'Please put her here, Will and Charlie; thank you kindly,' Phoebe said, directing them and thanking them again on their departure. Phoebe did not have time to loiter. The *Vexed Vixens*—four of her closest girlfriends—were meeting tonight at Emily's townhouse for dinner and solving the world's problems, as was their wont. They were also invited to inspect Emily's completed dance floor, where the *Miss Emily Yalden School of Deportment* pupils would undertake dance instruction. On the evenings the *Vexed Vixens* were to meet, Phoebe always left early to arrive on time, and her boss had no objection.

'I will make the illustration my priority tomorrow, Julius,' she said. '*The Vexed Vixens* await.'

'Of course.'

'I promise to give you my full attention then too, Nurse Faithful,' Phoebe said to the senior lady who had suddenly appeared; Julius ignored Charlotte Faithful, still refusing to act on his visions.

Phoebe moved to the body on the table and drew the sheath back to the chin to see the young, unidentified lady who had just been delivered.

'Oh my, I know her!' Nurse Faithful exclaimed and disappeared just as quickly.

'Goodness. Our unidentified lady appears to have been identified.' Phoebe waited a beat, but the senior woman did not reappear. 'I fear that might have been traumatic for Nurse Faithful.'

'You best go,' Julius said, avoiding the discussion.

'Yes, you are right. But did you want to speak to me about something?' Phoebe asked. She and Julius were the closest of family members and alike in nature, often seeking each other's quiet company.

He hesitated. 'I wanted to tell you in the strictest confidence—'

'You are going to propose,' she gasped.

Julius nodded. 'Tomorrow. I have bought the ring you suggested.'

'Oh, Julius, I am so happy.' She knew better than to gush too much; Julius would only withdraw. 'Do you have it on you? May I see it?'

He reached into his jacket pocket and pulled out a small gift box, opening it for Phoebe's inspection.

She gasped, her hands going to her face. 'It is perfect, absolutely perfect.'

Julius smiled with relief and returned it to his pocket. 'Not a word, promise?'

'Not a word,' she said, smiling up at him. 'Thank you for telling me.'

'Grandma knows.'

'Oh, well done, Julius.'

He laughed. 'I think she's earned that.' He moved away from her, reached for her shawl and held it out; Phoebe stepped into it, thanking him. 'You best go see the vexed ladies then.'

'You have created a challenge for me, brother; I will spend the night trying to appear very normal around Violet.'

'You will manage it,' he said with a smile. 'You are the epitome of discretion. Having said that, I am sure it is always tiresome vexing about Ambrose, but is there anything vexing that I have done? You are welcome to share it with me before airing it to the ladies,' Julius teased.

Phoebe grinned. 'No, and that would defeat the purpose as I am complaining about you, not to you,' she reminded him as they headed up the stairs and down the corridor to the back exit, where Claude waited to take her home with the horse and trap at Julius's request.

'I can only imagine what you say... overworked, stuck in a basement, and with a grumpy boss.' He narrowed his eyes, and she kissed him on the cheek in farewell as he opened the door for her.

'I assure you, Violet and I hardly ever say anything about you that isn't good. But there's always a first time,' she warned, waggling a finger and exiting with a glance to the business next door to see if Miss Violet Forrester had yet arrived at the back door.

As Claude waited to assist her into the cart, Violet exited the rear of the dressmaking store. Phoebe welcomed her and mentioned that her brother was watching. Violet turned to see Julius still at the door and waved her hand, her smile radiating her affection. The young ladies of similar age departed together, chatting happily as if they were sisters; they would soon be.

Within an hour, the small party was welcomed by Emily at her townhouse in Bowen Hills, bequeathed to Emily by an aunt who had no children of her own and found Emily to be a clever, practical soul similar to herself.

Phoebe was certain that if she had her own home, she would decorate in a similar fashion to Emily – shades of cream and pale blue, minimalist classic pieces of furniture.

'I so love it here,' Phoebe sighed, 'I can't imagine what it is like to fashion a home in your own style.'

'It has been fun, and I have done it on a small budget. Aunty was generous leaving her townhouse to me, but the renovations had to come out of my pocket.' Emily directed the ladies where to put their shawls and personal items.

'Now, let us see this room you have prepared for dancing lessons,' Kate said enthusiastically. 'We could be the first to christen it. Shall we dance?'

'You will be daintier than my herd of elephant students,' Emily said in jest and added, 'but in fairness, I only have one or two elephants at the moment; the rest are wildebeests.'

The ladies laughed at the image Emily painted.

'That is why they are your students,' Violet said. 'Their mothers most likely hold great hopes of you returning them reformed from wild to whimsical.'

Emily huffed at the thought. 'That challenge buoys me; thank you, Violet. Now, here is the room. I had the carpenters combine two of my smaller rooms into one large room and lay a timber floor for dancing. Viola!' She stood aside to show the room to the best advantage. There was ample room for students to partner up and spin around the floor and a lovely piano near the window to provide the dance music.

'Ooh, it is lovely,' Phoebe said, and the other ladies agreed.

'These doors open onto a formal dining room, so should I wish to entertain,' Emily paused, 'and I thought a small dinner dance might be something we would enjoy...'

'Oh yes!' Kate clapped her hands together. 'What a clever idea, Emily.'

'A dinner dance for friends,' Emily continued, now convinced it was a good plan. 'I can seat twelve comfortably around my aunt's... that is, my dining table, and we could perhaps enjoy some dancing after dinner and test the new floor.'

'Who would you invite?' Lilly asked as they followed Emily into a more informal dining room that she had set for dinner for six, where platters of delicious food were displayed.

'Please take a seat,' Emily said, also doing so. 'I thought we might ask the same group we had at your grandmother's charity ball, Phoebe. It was a happy party of good-natured souls, but with a few amendments.' She uncovered the dishes and passed them around.

'Lord, yes please amend,' Lilly agreed. 'I don't wish to dine with my brothers more than necessary, so please omit them.'

'And my sisters need not attend as they were only making up the number of ladies on the table we booked,' Kate agreed. 'So that leaves us with a selection of handsome gentlemen,' she said with a cheeky grin. 'But how will you invite the gentlemen without looking too forward?'

'I have given that some thought,' Emily said. 'What if we issue the invitation from the *Vexed Vixens,* not from me? With the five of us, we can invite one more lady and six gentlemen. Perhaps we could all invite a guest, and none will be the wiser on who specifically invited them.'

'That is very clever,' Lilly agreed.

'In that case, may I invite Detective Gilbert Payne?' Phoebe said generously for her friend Emily. 'I find him great company, and I'm sure he would enjoy a few turns around your dance floor.'

Emily looked delighted. 'Then he is on the list, thank you, Phoebe. I would like to invite Detective Harland Stone. I am sure the two detectives can bear each other's company for the night despite spending the day together.'

Phoebe looked delighted.

'I think the two Astin brothers must be invited to attend if Phoebe has no objections to her siblings being here,' Emily said.

'Oh, please don't object,' Kate reached out to touch Phoebe's arm. 'Violet and I would be most upset.'

'Of course I am happy for them to attend. I see little of them since Julius moved out, and Ambrose keeps his own hours.'

'I would like to suggest we invite Mr Bennet Martin,' Lilly said and earned a surprised look from all at the table. 'We have become better acquainted, and he has a little more depth than I first thought.'

'He is a very nice man,' Phoebe agreed generously before nudging Lilly, adding, 'and handsome.'

'And rich, no doubt,' Kate added.

'Perhaps he is all that,' Lilly agreed.

'If another lady guest does not come to mind, might I suggest my cousin, Isabelle?' Emily said. 'She is quite shy but loves to play the piano. My aunt always tries to get her out into society as she debuted five years ago. I am sure Isabelle will happily provide the dance music and get her mother off her back for one evening.'

'That sounds perfect, but she must dance too. I am happy to take my turn at the piano,' Phoebe said.

'As am I,' Violet offered.

'Well, I am not,' Kate said and added, 'I am sorry, but my playing would certainly put a damper on the evening.'

'As would mine,' Lilly agreed.

The ladies laughed at the thought.

'Well, that only leaves a seat for one gentleman, so we are almost finished with our guest list,' Emily said. 'Now, in keeping with the creed of our gathering, we cannot talk about flippant social events and men all evening. We are, after all, the *Vexed Vixens*. What has you vexed, Lilly?' Emily asked, throwing the meeting to her as they had now served themselves from the salads and platters prepared and relaxed in each other's company.

Lilly sighed dramatically. 'I have to pitch a story to my editor in the morning, or he will make me cover a story about theft from antique stores.' She grimaced at the thought. 'Unfortunately, my two story leads sadly lack depth. There is a senior nurse who tells Phoebe she was literally scared to death, and there is a deceased lady about our age, wearing odd pantomime-like make-up, who remains unidentified.'

'They both sound rather intriguing,' Violet said. 'Except, you cannot, of course, sell your story to the editor on the basis that your dear friend heard directly from the spirit that she was frightened to death.'

'Exactly so, Violet,' Lilly agreed. 'I have news too, Phoebe. The coroner, Dr McGregor, said the unidentified lady died of natural causes even though she was found squashing the miniatures at the display in the gardens.'

'Good grief, I am sure you can make a story out of that, Lilly; you are brilliant,' Emily exclaimed.

'Why thank you, Emily,' Lilly grinned.

'Should we ask Dr Tavish McGregor to the dinner?' Kate suggested, always easily distracted in social matters. 'That would be all seats at the table taken, and he is fun company, even at the scene of a crime when he probably should not be entertaining.'

'We could indeed,' Emily agreed.

'If only he had a more dramatic finding for me,' Lilly said crankily, as if it were the doctor's fault. 'Which story do you think I should own, Phoebe?'

Phoebe finished her mouthful before responding and quickly dabbed her lips with a serviette. 'If your editor is satisfied with a hint of your story and lets you sell him a mystery, I may be able to help.'

'Really! Do tell, please.'

The girls chuckled at Lilly's enthusiasm, and Phoebe said, 'Before I left work this afternoon, the unidentified lady's body arrived for me to illustrate. Nurse Charlotte Faithful also appeared—'

'What a beautiful name!' Kate exclaimed.

'It is, isn't it?' Phoebe agreed with a smile at seeing Lilly's impatience. 'Nurse Faithful was quite shocked to have recognised the lady I am to sketch, and then, Nurse Faithful left abruptly.'

'Ooh, so their deaths might be connected,' Lilly said, clapping her hands together in glee. 'Even if it turns out they are not, I am sure I can sell that as two bodies, two mystery deaths, somehow their paths have crossed... I will think about how I can present that given one is unidentified and the other in spirit form. But thank you, Phoebe, thank you.' She turned to Emily. 'I am no longer vexed; thus, I shall stand down.'

'Well, you may stay nevertheless,' Emily teased Lilly and, moving on, invited Violet to share her vexations as Phoebe pondered just how a senior lady who was scared to death and a young woman deserted on her death bed might have anything in common.

Chapter 10

Mr Bennet Martin was throwing himself into his new investigation with more gusto than anyone in his office expected, and the reason was nothing to do with a noble desire to please the client and give them value for money. It was about finding reasons to cross paths with Miss Lilly Lewis again. He wondered what she was doing this evening. Was she surrounded by her family, all those brothers, laughing and having fun over the dinner table? Or perhaps Miss Lewis was out to dinner or at the theatre with a friend, hopefully of the female persuasion. Or might she be at work, like him, meeting a late deadline?

'Are you sure you do not want me to stay and assist?' his clerk, Daniel Dutton, asked. 'It is not like you to leave the office after me of an evening.'

'I live upstairs; I never leave,' Bennet reminded him.

'Leave work then if you must be pedantic,' Daniel said with a smile. 'I am quite taken aback at seeing you at this hour of the day. It is after six, you know.'

Bennet gave him a wry look. 'I am sorry you are taken aback, and I suggest you take yourself somewhere else,' he said, making Daniel laugh. 'I shall lock up, and yes, I remember how to do so before you give me any more cheek.'

This had his assistant chuckling, and Daniel rose, locked his desk and reached for his hat. 'I shall see you in the morning when you surface from your studio.'

'You shall, and thank you for your report; it is most comprehensive,' Bennet said, waving a file at Daniel.

'I live to please,' the young man said with a small bow and a wave of his hand as he departed, leaving Bennet alone in the quiet of his townhome, the sound of foot traffic and horses drifting in from the street being the only noise.

Opening the file that Daniel had prepared on the number of deaths in the last year of children under the age of ten and the number of insurance premiums paid to the amount of one hundred pounds, he found a list of eleven claimants and some details about every family – excellent work by his clerk. He would have to think of a reason to pay a call, something sympathetic and appropriate as the insurance company's representative. After all, some might be genuine claims.

He then spotted a letter with British stamps that Daniel had placed in his 'IN' correspondence tray. His mother was a faithful writer. Bennet slit the envelope open and leaned back to read, happy enough for the distraction.

'My darling boy, I hope life is good in the colonies, and you have not sullied your clothing or dirtied your nails while toiling all day long.'

He saw her smiling as she wrote that with her peculiar sense of humour. He read through the family news, glanced at the included cheque with appreciation, and saw the truth in the lines that followed:

'Thank you for including the news clippings and congratulations. Perhaps, Darling, if you stop solving cases and getting professional recognition, your father will give up on his dream that you will return home and join the detective service like himself. Fear not; I know your passion remains with your art, but you are clearly skilled in your investigative work as your newspaper clippings would have us believe, and I send my congratulations. I am also so happy to hear you have met a young lady. However, the inevitable news of your betrothal to an Australian lady will still shock us. I fancy a trip to Australia for a wedding, but do not tell your father I said that.

He thought about Miss Lilly Lewis, not that she had been far from his thoughts for too long. The articles she wrote—in which he was mentioned—that he clipped to send to his mother took on a different level of importance now. What would his mother think when he declared Miss Lewis is the subject of his attention and not Miss Phoebe Astin, who was his heart's desire at the time of writing his last letter home?

He felt ashamed at how quickly he had allowed Miss Lewis to replace Miss Astin in his thoughts, but he realised that Miss Astin was right in rejecting his suit. He was taken with Phoebe Astin's beauty and with a desire to protect and love her. Bennet saw himself coming home to her, accompanying Phoebe for walks and presenting gifts to her while being a brother, legally, to his close friend, Julius. But would he have settled for the quiet life she seemed to favour? As much as he hated to admit it, she was suited to Harland. Both would be content in each other's quiet company, able to fill time capably if apart.

On the other hand, he had pondered if his attraction to Miss Lewis was because she did not swoon for him, but he did not believe that was the case. She stirred him into action, challenged him, and made him feel alive. Bennet wanted to take her to all the galleries and debate which paintings they liked the best, to go to the theatre and review every performance afterwards to see if they shared the same views, and if they didn't, that would make for a fiery debate as well.

He wanted to shower her with gifts, the best dresses and jewellery, and see her wear them and attract attention as Mrs Bennet Martin. He wanted to undress her.

He smiled at the thought of the spirited beauty and, rising, grabbed his hat, determined to see what performances were on at the theatre. He would work them into their next conversation in the hope she might express an interest in attending. The insurance claims could wait until tomorrow.

It was well after midnight when upstairs, in the rooms above the *Doll and Teddy Hospital* in Elizabeth Street, Mrs Frances Crandle, former midwife, heard a noise she could not identify. It was not a late-night reveller in the street below, a possum or rodent of the night, nor the roof creaking as the night cooled the iron sheeting. Being a light sleeper, Mrs Crandle wondered if she had imagined the noise and stilled, straining to listen. Beside her, Mr Crandle slept, a slight shuffle snore escaping from him, but that was not the noise she heard. She was well familiar with her husband's nocturnal noises after decades of marriage. He slept on, which provided some comfort to Mrs Crandle that perhaps she had imagined it.

No. There it was again, a board creaking, and she knew the very one. It was near the shelf closest to the front door in the doll hospital downstairs. Someone was in the house, in the store below.

'Frank,' she whispered, nudging her husband. He stirred. 'Don't make a sound; there's someone downstairs.'

He was awake immediately, sitting, listening. They had very little cash on the premises, but there was a day's earning in the till, and their entire business was sitting on the shelves as doll stock. Not to mention the sentimental dolls they were repairing for clients that money could not replace.

Two loud creaks had Mrs Crandle's hand going to her mouth to stop her from screaming in fright. Frank Crandle held his hand up to silence her; his brow was furrowed, and he ran a thumb over his forehead as if clearing his thought. Mr Crandle quietly rose.

'Do not go downstairs, dear. Let them take what they want,' she whispered.

'What if they come up here? What if they begin a fire and we are trapped?' he whispered. 'Stay here, my love; leave this with me.'

'I won't. There is safety in numbers,' she said, rising as quietly as she could and wrapping her dressing gown around her.

Mr Crandle reached for a small statue of the Virgin Mary that was weighty enough to cause some damage and grasped it; it would have to do for a weapon if needed. Mrs Crandle glanced around for similar but fell short. What she imagined in her mind would be far more fearful than the truth. It could only be a person, but she saw a villain, a knife-wielding slasher or a crazed madman with wild eyes ready to slay them in their home in the dark of night.

And then they heard the sound of several quick footsteps and the front door closing. Mr Crandle ran to the window and cautiously pulled the curtain aside. He saw a figure running away.

'Have they left?'

'Yes, I believe so. It was a man in a dark cape; I could not see his face; he kept his head down.' Frank Crandle closed the curtain. 'Let me go down first to check no one else remains.'

Mrs Crandle shook her head. 'We shall go together and prepared.' She felt for the matches on the bedside cabin, and Mr Crandle opened the curtain again slightly to assist with finding the lamp and lighting the wick. With the lamp ready, Mrs Crandle nodded and followed Mr Crandle slowly down the stairs.

'We are getting a door upstairs to lock at night that will separate us from downstairs. For safety,' Mr Crandle was muttering as if making a note to himself, and he turned at the small landing, glancing downstairs. 'Good Lord!'

'What is it?' Mrs Crandle stepped back with fear, but her husband hurried downstairs. She gathered herself and followed.

'Oh, my!' she gasped, and the pair stood looking at the dolls on the shelves. The intruder had turned around all twenty dolls sitting on the three long shelves, their backs facing the owners except for one. A large doll in the middle of the second shelf faced them, and on its once pretty face was painted a large red smile like an evil clown laughing at them.

'Why?' Mr Crandle said, confused.

He did not see Mrs Crandle pocket the note left on the counter. She shook her head when he turned to look at her in confusion. Having no answer, she rushed to lock the door and glanced out, but the street was deserted. Nevertheless, Frances Crandle shivered and felt someone was watching her. Later, alone, she dared to look at the note and its five-word message: 'I know what you did.'

Chapter 11

Phoebe felt a little naughty for stopping on the way to work to collect the doll she had left for repair, especially since she had left early the day prior, but her grandmother's birthday was only a couple of days away, and the *Doll and Teddy Hospital* was on the way to the office. Her hours were often irregular and unpredictable—the dead did not abide by work hours—and Phoebe knew she had done enough overtime not to earn the manager's ire for running late. She smiled at the thought of Julius scolding her; she couldn't recall when he had ever done so except in trying to get her to leave or come up for air from her basement hideaway at *The Economic Undertaker.* Now, he was to be engaged, and to a lady Phoebe happily called a dear friend. She mused how lucky she was to soon have Violet as a sister, knowing the beautiful dressmaker would consent to her brother's proposal.

Phoebe entered just as Mrs Crandle turned the sign on the door to read "Open".

'I am sorry to crowd you right on opening time,' Phoebe said after greeting her, 'but you are on my route.'

'Not at all. Do come in,' Mrs Crandle said, and Phoebe thought the senior shopkeeper looked most agitated. Mrs Crandle's eyes darted to the shelves as if seeking something, so Phoebe reminded her of the doll she had dropped off for repair, lest she was looking for it.

'Oh, that's right. My husband enjoyed restoring your delicate porcelain doll,' she said, looking below the counter and carefully raising a box. 'I am sure you will be happy with the result.' Opening it, she showed Phoebe the restored and cleaned doll.

'Oh, how wonderful! That is much better than I ever imagined. Thank you both, and for repairing her so quickly,' Phoebe gushed. 'I am sure Grandma will be delighted.'

'It's our pleasure. Mr Crandle was keen to work on her; he likes a challenge,' Mrs Crandle said and seemed in a hurry today even though Phoebe was the only customer; last visit, Mrs Crandle would have talked all morning had Phoebe not had work to attend.

Phoebe settled the bill and looked in the direction where Mrs Crandle's eyes kept glancing.

'Oh, you seem to have one doll facing the wrong way.'

'So we do. I just noticed that too,' Mrs Crandle said and gave an odd-sounding laugh that was more of a sharp bark than a laugh. 'Our cleaning lady has an odd sense of humour. Sometimes, she dusts the dolls and mixes them up or puts them the wrong way. Never mind, she is well-intentioned.'

Phoebe smiled and thanked her again, noticing Mrs Crandle did not rush to turn the doll around until Phoebe was at the door. A glance back showed Mrs Crandle tentatively looking at the doll's face before turning it as if expecting it to say something.

Perhaps working in a doll and teddy hospital leads to talking to your charges, as working in a mortuary leads to talking to the spirits, which Phoebe could attest to doing. She hurried on to the office with her parcel in hand. There was a sketch to do, and Phoebe hoped Nurse Faithful would return to identify the lady without a name.

It was Julius's day behind the desk under the new arrangement whereby his grandfather spent the day assisting his grandmother, Will undertook burial duties with Ambrose, who was in charge, and Charlie assisted Claude in the stables. Everyone stepped up.

Seeing Phoebe approaching, he opened the front door of *The Economic Undertaker*.

'And what hour do you call this?' he asked, trying to be serious and hide a smile.

'I assure you, Mr Astin, I have a good excuse,' she teased and waved the small package at him as she stepped inside. 'I was collecting Grandma's restored doll for her birthday. They have done a brilliant job, and the store was on my way here, so...'

He shook his head. 'It is so hard to find good people.'

Phoebe laughed. 'It is quiet; where is everyone?'

Mrs Dobbs appeared. 'Ah, you are here, dear. Will you have a cup of tea?'

'Good morning, Mrs Dobbs. I better not, I'm already late.'

'I shall bring it down to you,' Mrs Dobbs said with a wink and returned to her kitchen.

'Ambrose and Will have a funeral to deliver this morning. Lord help me, I hope they bury the right body in the right plot.'

Phoebe grinned at her brother. 'You have more faith in Ambrose than that.'

Julius raised an eyebrow but did not respond. 'Claude and Charlie have gone to collect a body from a private home. The family would like a viewing tomorrow morning but cannot have it at their home due to illness. Can you prepare the gentleman in question?'

'I shall begin as soon as the boys bring him in. I'll start the sketching now until they arrive,' Phoebe said. 'Hopefully, Nurse Faithful will reappear and identify the lady I am drawing.'

'If it gets too much, call for me.'

'I will, but it won't. She is very respectful.' Phoebe hesitated. 'Speaking of the dearly departed, I have not seen Uncle Reggie for some time. Have you?'

Julius glanced toward the kitchen, where Mrs Dobbs might have overheard had she not been humming. He gave a curt shake of his head in the negative. He did not like to speak of his seeing the dead. 'I'm sure he is all right. After all, he is dead. What is the worst that can happen?'

Phoebe chuckled. 'You are very amusing today, Julius. Are you happy about something?'

He gave her a wry look. 'Yes. I am happy you are here. Now, might you consider starting work?'

She gave him a mock salute and a grin as she hurried down the first few stairs to her workroom, pausing moments later.

'Oh no, that burial that Ambrose and Will are attending... it is Nurse Faithful, is it not?'

'Yes. We cannot hold the body any longer without embalming. Harland will need his unidentified lady back rather quickly, too.'

'You are right. I had best make haste. I had hoped Nurse Faithful would be with me longer, but she may return despite being put to rest.' Phoebe studied her brother for just a moment. 'I love that you are happy, brother,' she said, continuing down the stairs, her footsteps fading.

Julius sighed. Was he so dour that a lightening of his mood amazed everyone? Again, his mind wandered to tonight's plans as it had done since he had asked Violet to accompany him for a dusk walk through the Botanic Gardens. He touched his jacket pocket to confirm the ring was still there and felt the small box. He had already done so several times this morning, and no doubt would continue to feel for the reassuring ring box until the walk and proposal late this afternoon when, all going to plan, he could slip the large diamond onto Violet's finger.

The door opened, and his appointed clients entered right on time. Julius noted his grandfather did not book many clients on the days he was not there, concerned he might overload Julius, who took the opportunity to get his accounts done, but time was of the essence in matters of death and the young couple dressed in black who entered did indeed look like they needed an economic undertaker. They had dyed their clothes black to save money, and the quality of the fabric and cut of the clothing left no doubt the garments had been stitched up and worn many times.

'Mr and Mrs Taggart, I am Julius Astin, at your service. My condolences on the loss of your sister, Mrs Taggart.' He said, having checked his grandfather's notes prior to their visit.

'Thank you, Mr Astin,' she said, crying anew. Her pale face had already shown the telltale signs of grief... reddened eyes, swollen nose and lips. 'It was quite unexpected,' she said, regaining control.

The men shook hands, and Julius showed them into the meeting room. Mrs Dobbs, having the list of appointments for the day, arrived moments later with tea and cake, for which Mr Taggart thanked her profusely and helped himself. Julius thought the young couple could both use a good meal.

'My parents are deceased, and my sister is my responsibility, was, I mean,' Mrs Taggart said. 'We want to give her a good funeral, and I heard you have a funeral plan we could pay off.'

'We can pay,' Mr Taggart added hurriedly, 'I'm working.'

'Of course,' Julius assured them, 'do not concern yourselves with that. We have three burial options and several payment plans, ensuring a dignified funeral for your loved one. I give you my word; your sister will be well cared for regardless of your budget.'

'Thank you, Mr Astin,' Mrs Taggart said, slumping slightly in relief, followed by an abrupt blow of her nose into her handkerchief. Mr Taggart patted her hand. Julius assumed they were not long married as they were both young and seemed very much in the early stages of love. He recognised the look they exchanged.

After considering the three exceedingly affordable packages, Mr Taggart said, 'We had best take the top package; it is only right.'

Mrs Taggart gave him the most grateful look, but Julius could not abide the thought of them extending themselves even that little further.

'The middle package is by far our most requested by families.'

'Is it?' Mrs Taggart brightened.

'It is my recommendation,' Julius said, wanting to remove any stigma in their minds that they must spend money to be respectable.

'Then if you think so, Mr Astin—'

'I do.' He could see the relief on their countenances. 'I will include a lovely pine coffin, which we produce ourselves.'

Again, Mrs Taggart's eyes widened with surprise. 'Truly?'

'Mr Astin, thank you, but no. We don't need charity, and you have a business to run,' Mr Taggart said, clutching onto his pride.

'I assure you it is not charity, Mr Taggart. Sometimes we have too much stock and can include a coffin with a package if we have to make more room for the next orders,' he said, which was not quite the truth. He could hear his grandfather saying he was a soft touch, but Julius always added a small fee to the well-to-do funeral customers who chose to be cheap, to provide a number of free coffins for those in need. No one need know. It was business, after all.

'It is just timely for both of us,' Julius concluded.

'The pine coffin is acceptable, isn't it?' Mr Taggart asked Julius, 'It's not damaged? My wife would feel terrible if that were the case.'

'It is new, and you are welcome to inspect it.'

'On no, that won't be necessary,' Mr Taggart said embarrassed, 'thank you, Mr Astin, we are grateful. I was ensuring I had thought of everything.'

'Of course. We favour local timbers for this climate, and most of our orders are for pine. Again, it is a much-in-demand choice.' Julius did not mention cedar or English oak; he had a few in stock for customers who preferred spending money on a better-quality coffin. Cousin Lucian produced most of their coffins in the local hoop pine or bunya pine, the cheapest option.

'That is a relief and more affordable than we dared imagine.' Realising she had implied they were struggling, Mrs Taggart gave her husband a pained look and said to Julius, 'Forgive me, Mr Astin, I am quite confused in my distress,' she said in a quavering voice.

'There is nothing to apologise for, Mrs Taggart.' He gave a little of himself. 'When my parents died, I was a child. My grandparents could not afford the funeral packages and went into considerable debt to bury them both. I will never forget the pressure on them to pay that back while raising three children they did not expect to inherit. I promise you this package, which you can pay back with generous terms, will ensure your sister is seen right to the next life.'

This caused Mrs Taggart to burst into fresh tears and thank him many times, while Julius suggested Mr Taggart might want to finish another piece of cake; he gave them a moment alone as he departed to get the receipt book.

Death, a strange business indeed, he mused.

Chapter 12

THE YOUNG WOMAN WITH the chestnut hair and theatre-like make-up lay on the table adorned in a yellow dress with little blue cornflowers handsewn around the hemline that looked most feminine. She had been re-dressed for the illustration, and finishing her outfit were white stockings and little white slippers. Around her neck was a red ribbon that did not match the carefully chosen outfit.

Phoebe stood gaping, the shroud dangling from her fingers. It was the first time she had completely removed the covering from the unidentified lady. Until now, Phoebe had only glanced at her face, but seeing the lady from head to toe, she was surprised by what lay before her.

'I know you,' Phoebe whispered, then shook her head slightly. 'No, I don't think I do, but why do you look so familiar?' Folding the shroud, Phoebe placed it on the shelf, grabbed her pad and a pencil, and pulled up a high chair next to the lady. She got to work with little time to spare, but her sketch was remarkably accurate; like her grandmother, Phoebe had a talent for etching.

'Who are you, Miss?' She whispered and glanced around, hoping the young woman might appear, but she did not. 'Why do I know you?'

The room was silent, with just the sound of Phoebe's pencil making quick strokes on the paper.

'Are you a friend of my friends? No, I cannot recall meeting any of Kate, Emily, Violet or Lilly's friends of late.'

Her mind went to the recent dance they attended for the hospital ball. No, the woman could not be placed there.

A stage production? Phoebe dismissed the thought immediately. It had been some time since she had been to see a show of any kind.

In a quiet voice that the departed might only hear, Phoebe said, 'If your funeral has been conducted and you find yourself free, Nurse Faithful, I would welcome your visit. You might tell me who this lady is, perhaps.'

Phoebe continued working, stopping occasionally to ensure she was alone. No one appeared.

'Uncle Reggie, then? Might you drop in to tell me all is well with you and help me with this riddle?'

But no, Phoebe found herself very much alone. 'No one is seeking my company today. Perhaps I should get a cat.'

'God spare us, they make me sneeze,' a male voice said, and Phoebe looked up with delight.

'I have missed you, Uncle Reggie, not that I ever knew you in life, but I have become accustomed to your visits.'

'Thank you, my dear,' the debonair ghost in his riding outfit, who would always be forty years of age, gave a small bow. 'Forgive me for being absent, but a friend arrived on this side, and I had duties.'

'Is that so?' Phoebe said with interest.

'Yes, and I shall not be telling you anything more, so do not try to wheedle it from me with your big blue eyes and pleading looks,' he scolded her in jest.

Phoebe laughed with delight. 'All right then, but I am pleased you are here, and I am pleased to know a friend might meet me when I go to the other side.'

'I shall attempt to do so myself,' he promised her. 'As requested, I am here to make myself useful. I heard you asking questions of the recently departed Nurse Charlotte Faithful, and I introduced myself.'

'You charmed her!'

'I did my best,' Reggie said with a small smile on his handsome face. 'She just arrived—'

'Interred today,' Phoebe agreed.

'Which made it a little difficult given a lot was going on, and she was adjusting. But to your question. All the lady would say was that she recognised the unidentified young lady.' He glanced at the body on the table in the corner. 'Apparently, Nurse Faithful knew her as a child and saw her grow over the years, and claimed the deceased has a twin brother.'

Phoebe inhaled sharply. 'She is one of the twins exchanged at birth. No wonder Nurse Faithful was shocked to see her, and wearing this odd make-up. Thank you very much, Uncle Reggie, that will help with identifying her.'

'If her brother, her twin, is still alive, why is he not seeking her?'

'Perhaps he does not know that she is missing yet,' Phoebe suggested.

'Miss Astin, may we enter?' A voice called from the top of the stairs, and Reggie gave a small bow and disappeared.

'Yes, I am down here, thank you, Claude,' she called back, and moments later, Claude and Charlie began the descent to Phoebe's rooms, gingerly carrying a covered body on a stretcher.

'This is the gentleman for the viewing tomorrow morning,' Claude said.

'He looks very dead, Miss. You'll have your work cut out for you making him look alive,' Charlie said, and Phoebe gave a small huff of laughter.

'That would be a challenge, Charlie. But luckily, I just need to make him look a little like he did in life, and I have some good powders that make the skin look warmer.'

They placed the body where directed.

'Thank you both. Might you have time now to return a body to Dr Tavish McGregor at the morgue and then drop a note to Detective Harland Stone at the nearby Roma Street Police Headquarters?'

'Of course, we are at your service, Miss Astin,' Claude said, taking his promotion and responsibility very seriously, and that Phoebe Astin was the boss's sister prioritised her needs.

'Is that the lady there, Miss Astin?' Charlie asked.

'Oh yes, sorry.' Phoebe hurried to cover her, and Claude assisted, undeterred by the sight of the dead. Charlie was more curious than hesitant but remained out of the way. Before covering her completely, Phoebe briefly touched the young lady's cheek and wished her well. Then, grabbing her pad and pencil, wrote a quick note to the detective advising that the illustration was ready at his convenience, sealed it, and handed it to Claude. Phoebe did not risk sending the drawing with them lest it should fall into the wrong hands or be damaged en route; that was the arrangement she had with Detective Harry Dart previously. Besides, she wanted to tidy her drawing a little more before it was collected.

'Thank you, Claude and Will, the lady may go.'

Phoebe watched the boys leave with the unidentified lady, remaining still and affording her the respect of seeing her off. Once out of sight, Phoebe sighed at the cycle of life that would take one as young as herself. She turned her attention to the recently arrived gentleman who needed preparation, her mind preoccupied with why the unidentified lady was so familiar. And then it occurred to her!

Reporter Lilly Lewis drew a quick breath as she finished her pitch to *The Courier* editor after being summoned first thing this morning. She wore her blue gown, which brought out the blue of her eyes; Lilly was not averse to using her charms to help get the story over the line.

'So, you see, Mr Cowan, with the special relationship we have cultivated with the detectives and access to the sketch of the unidentified lady, not to mention the mysterious connection between the two deceased ladies and the odd make-up on the younger lady's face, we believe a story and mystery is demanding to be told.'

'The readers will love it, Mr Cowan,' Fergus agreed, 'especially if they feel they are assisting by having the opportunity to identify one of the ladies.'

'If the sketch is ready, we could run it tomorrow, Mr Cowan,' Lilly finished.

Their crusty editor, who was not a morning person—nor an afternoon person, for that matter—grunted as he puffed cigar smoke in their direction. Lilly marvelled at his ability to look dishevelled and grimy before the day began; she was sure his wife had not let him leave the house in such a condition. But his cigar habit and the constant tugging at his tie and running his hand through his hair did not assist his appearance.

'I don't like it. Too ambiguous for my liking, and I think you are both clutching at straws.'

Lilly nodded, knowing when to shut up but feeling a rising dread that the story of the antique shop thefts was about to land in their lap.

'But, given your track record with your last three stories, I'm prepared to give you some leeway.' He held up his hand to stop them as Lilly opened her mouth to thank him. 'I'm giving you three days. I want a story every day, and if I'm not impressed...' he ran a finger across his throat to indicate the story would be cut and then waved them off.

'Yes, Mr Cowan,' Lilly said.

'Thank you, Mr Cowan,' Fergus said, and both departed before he changed his mind.

Returning to their desks with a sense of urgency hanging over them, Lilly and Fergus shared a small smile. One did not gloat for fear of being thought above themselves and, worse still, if the editor was to see and retract his promise.

'Shall we split up?' Fergus asked in a conspiratorial whisper, clutching his pad and leaning towards Lilly.

'Yes. I have so many thoughts running through my head I hardly know where to start,' she said and exhaled. Lilly looked at her notepad and focussed herself with a deep breath.

'I shall go to the miniatures exhibition and see if I can learn anything,' Fergus said. 'Following that, I will go to the morgue and get an official statement of cause of death from the coroner.'

'Oh yes, excellent thought,' Lilly said. 'I shall see the detectives to get an update and request the sketch so we can run it in the late edition. I will get the sketch to the engravers as quickly as possible so they can begin on it.'

'Right. I shall meet you here in the early afternoon to start writing our story. We will amaze Mr Cowan and our readers, Lilly,' Fergus said with a gleam of ambition in his eyes.

'We will, Fergus.' Lilly said and grinned. 'One day, we will be *The Courier*'s number one reporting team.'

And the newspaper's youngest reporters rushed out to begin their investigations.

Chapter 13

Detective Harland Stone studied his protégé, Detective Gilbert Payne, as they sat in the omnibus with three citizens, pulled by four horses, and travelling to South Brisbane. There, they would alight and walk the short distance to the office of *The Economic Undertaker*. It was a longer process than taking a private hansom cab, but the directive from the superintendent was to reduce costs, which meant, where possible, walking or taking an omnibus. It did not give Harland peace of mind when the omnibus kept stopping and starting, and he was obliged to help ladies on and off as he sat near the entrance step. He liked to use the travel time to think, and studying his frowning partner, wondered if Gilbert thought the same.

'This is not conducive to thinking,' Harland snapped, 'and given I already feel as if we are going from pillar to post on the case, the same can now be said about our mode of transport!'

'I find it very distracting,' Gilbert agreed, 'but I accept I must adapt to change.'

Harland made a non-committal sound as Gilbert continued. 'The Greek philosopher Heraclitus believed the only constant in life is change, and the Russian writer Leo Tolstoy said, "True life is lived when tiny changes occur".' Gilbert looked sheepish. 'I liked that quote, so I committed it to memory.'

Harland gave his protégé a small smile. 'You are reading Tolstoy in your spare time?'

'My mother selects books for me that will broaden my mind, Sir. I must say, she does a reasonable job of it.' The omnibus stopped again. 'Nevertheless, this is most frustrating,' Gilbert added.

'I agree. So, we shall disregard that directive until I get hauled over the coals for being a spendthrift. You can say you were following orders, Gilbert. If the superintendent wants results, he can accommodate our mode of travel.'

'Sir!' Gilbert smiled. 'I have never seen you rebellious.'

Harland chuckled. 'Needs must, and we need to arrive in a timely manner and with time to clear our thoughts.'

The letter from Miss Phoebe Astin burned in his pocket. Harland could not say why he was disappointed. It was a professional letter. Surely, he could not expect her to be anything but formal and business-like, but it was most officious. Perhaps she was writing under duress.

He assisted another lady on board and sat back beside Gilbert, asking, 'It is early days, but have you any thoughts on our two cases?'

'I have thought of nothing else, Sir.'

Harland gave him a surprised look.

'I assure you I have interests outside work, Sir, but I cannot help but dwell on our cases, as I know you do. Last evening, I researched midwives; I have very little knowledge of their work.'

'Nor I, Gilbert. It is not surprising given we are not at that phase of our life yet.'

'True. It was most interesting. The midwives are paid, of course, and some offer an in-home service where the women with children may choose to stay with them or in a dedicated home and have care provided for a period after the birth.'

'Interesting,' Harland said and nodded.

'But not relevant to the women that Nurse Faithful removed children from as we were led to believe, they were poverty-stricken,' Gilbert continued. 'Some midwives advertise in *The Courier*, and many are recommended by word of mouth, meaning they often have areas that become their territory.'

'And if Nurse Faithful offered her services for years, that would be the case. She did relay she saw the children over the years as they grew,' Harland mused.

The omnibus stopped, and they alighted. Again, Harland assisted a lady on board who gave him her most appealing smile and fell slightly, landing right in his arms. Looking less than comfortable with her outrageous flirtation, Harland righted her, tipped his hat, and hurried their pace to *The Economic Undertaker* with Gilbert flanking him.

'My apologies, you were saying?' Harland cleared his throat and resumed his conversation.

'My conclusion, Sir, is that if the wealthier and poorer areas were not that far apart, and Nurse Faithful served them all, is there a chance that the removed children might somehow come across their kin?'

'A very good point, Gilbert,' Harland said. 'What if they looked a great deal like them? I have no siblings, but when I was at boarding school, some brothers looked remarkably alike.'

'Two of my female cousins are very similar; there is no doubt they are sisters... they have a nose shape that is particular to their family. Something more alarming is at play... what if they were to fall in love with their siblings without knowing it?'

'Good Lord, that is an unfavourable outcome. Imagine if they found out later in life.' Harland grimaced.

'It is only a personal observation, Sir, if I may make it, but I don't believe people should play God.'

'As a man of the law, I agree with you, Gilbert,' Harland said and carefully pushed open the door to *The Economic Undertaker,* and the detectives entered.

Julius smiled at seeing his friend, Harland, enter with Detective Payne.

'Excellent timing; two clients have just left,' he greeted them.

'Good morning, Julius!' Harland glanced around with concern. 'Is Mr Astin senior in ill health?'

'No, nothing like that,' Julius assured him. 'Several days a week, I am positioned at the desk. Grandpa is doing charity work and attending to my grandmother; everyone has stepped up. So far, with Ambrose in charge, we haven't lost a body or buried anyone we shouldn't have.'

Harland laughed. 'Well, that is reassuring.'

'Regardless, I think I should like to expire when you are on the job, Mr Astin,' Gilbert added.

'Noted,' Julius said in jest.

'Miss Astin has the sketch ready for us, I believe,' Harland got down to business.

'She does. You know the way.' With a wave of his hand, Julius invited them to take to the stairs, but before they descended, the door swung open way too quickly to be a person in mourning, and Miss Lilly Lewis entered.

'Ah ha!' she said on spotting the detectives and then, with wide eyes, put a hand to her mouth before whispering, 'Oh forgive me, Mr Astin. I've done it again.'

'We are all alone, Miss Lewis, fear not,' Julius said with a small smile. 'There might be a deceased person in the house with Phoebe, but they are rarely offended.'

Lilly gave a small laugh. 'Thank goodness. When I am focussed on a story, I forget you are in mourning.' She turned to the detectives who stood by the stairs. 'I have just been to the police station hoping to catch you both and get the sketch for our edition, and here you are.'

Mrs Dobbs appeared on hearing the voices. 'Detectives, Miss Lewis, good morning. Do you have time for tea?'

'As much as we would like that, unfortunately, no, Mrs Dobbs,' Harland thanked her. 'This is a quick stop on our way to undertake interviews.'

'And hopefully, I will be rushing off with a sketch to the newspaper,' Lilly said, 'as much as I would love a cup of tea, thank you, Mrs Dobbs.'

'Well, do stop crowding my reception area,' Julius said in jest, indicating the stairs. The party quickly departed, Harland calling out politely on the descent.

'Just myself, Detective Payne and Miss Lewis, if convenient, Miss Astin?'

'Of course, detectives and Lilly, please come down,' Phoebe called back, and moments later, they were in each other's company.

A flush of colour appeared on Phoebe's neck at the sight of the detective, and he hoped it might be for the pleasure of seeing him. He felt a restless energy, as he often did in her company, and applied the restraint needed to not stare at her beauty, which served to disrupt his concentration.

'Forgive my abrupt letter, Detective Stone,' Phoebe said after greeting them. 'Claude and Charlie were on hand to take the unidentified lady back to the morgue, and I asked them to drop by your office with my note.'

'It was appreciated,' Harland said, relieved that the note was written under duress and not as a result of a coolness towards him. 'So, she is with Dr McTavish now?'

'Yes. We can collect the body again should we be required to do the burial,' Phoebe said. She gathered her illustrations, handing the face sketch to Harland and a full-body sketch featuring the dress and shoes to Gilbert. Nearby, Miss Lewis looked over his shoulder.

'My, this is excellent. You are a deft hand when it comes to illustrating, Miss Astin,' Gilbert said with appreciation.

'Too kind, thank you, detective. Unfortunately, my talents are limited to drawing,' she said with a self-deprecating laugh, and Harland would have rushed to deny such a notion had they been alone.

'I don't draw or play,' Lilly said in support of her friend and added for Detective Gilbert Payne's benefit, 'Emily plays the piano beautifully.'

'Does she?' Gilbert asked, his interest piqued at the mention of Miss Emily Yalden.

'Yes, and you may get to hear her play,' Lilly started. 'I know you are both very busy, but just a quick mention of a dinner party that the *Vexed Vixens* are hosting at Emily's abode.'

'The *Vexed Vixens*? Will we be quite safe?' Harland asked with a raised eyebrow.

Phoebe laughed and explained, 'It is the name for our intimate group that meets for dinner regularly. Declaring what vexes us takes up only a small part of the evening, but we promise not to do it that evening with the gentlemen in attendance.'

'I make no such promise,' Lilly said with a smile and a defiant rise to her chin. 'The occasion is to test Emily's new dance floor before the students do. We hope you are both free to attend when the invitations are issued.'

'You will not be forced to dance, detectives,' Phoebe added with a glance at Harland, 'but you will be required to be good company,' she said in jest, including them both.

'I would be honoured to attend,' Gilbert said, 'thank you.'

'And I will clear my calendar,' Harland said, barely hiding his smile at the ladies. He was secretly delighted at the thought of attending a small gathering with Miss Phoebe Astin in attendance.

'What more could we hope for then!' Lilly proclaimed, making them laugh. 'Now to business, may I have a drawing for the newspaper? I assure you it will get the editor's attention.'

'I will give you both drawings, Miss Lewis,' Harland said. 'If you could detail the dress, shoes and slippers in your written description, that would be appreciated. Someone may recognise the lady from her clothing. I will need to collect them as soon as possible.'

'Of course, Detective Stone,' Lilly said, thrilled. 'I shall ensure our engravers make it a priority.'

'There is one more thing,' Phoebe said. 'It may be useful, but it has come from my usual sources; thus, you will need to find your own confirmation.'

'Is it in relation to the lady's identity by chance?' Gilbert asked.

'It is, Detective Payne. Shall I tell you?'

'Yes, please, Miss Astin. We have so little to go on,' Harland said regarding her thoughtfully. Her clues in the past had been of great assistance.

She gave a brief nod and hurried on, aware of the demands on all three of her guests and the body waiting for her in the corner of the room.

'Nurse Faithful was shocked to recognise the unidentified lady but left without declaring what she knew. My uncle has assisted me—'

'Reggie?' Lilly asked, having heard quite a lot about him from Phoebe over time.

'Yes, he has not moved on,' she quickly explained to the detectives. 'He spoke with Nurse Faithful for me, and she said the unidentified lady was one of the twins she delivered and re-homed. Her twin is a boy, a man now, and he may not know his sister is dead.'

'That is most helpful, Miss Astin, thank you,' Harland said, running a hand over his jaw as he spoke. 'This is an interesting connection between the two ladies, but it could still be a coincidence.'

Gilbert agreed. 'True, Sir. I don't know the person who delivered me into the world, but were we to die around the same time, I'm sure no one would give it a second thought. Except...' he added, 'that somebody unceremoniously dumped the young lady, and Nurse Faithful claimed to be frightened to death.'

'True. We cannot discount it,' Harland said, and then, remembering where they were, added, 'Please forgive our hasty departure, Miss Astin, but we have some queries to make given what you have just told us.'

'I shall leave with you,' Lilly said and gave Phoebe a quick hug goodbye. The detectives allowed Miss Lewis to take the stairs first; Gilbert followed, and Harland hesitated on the bottom step.

'Am I to ask for an account for the drawing, Miss Astin?'

'Not at all, Detective. My grandfather will send it directly to the station as we have done in the past. I assure you I am most economical,' she said with a smile.

'I have no doubt you are worth a great deal more than what we will pay,' Harland returned her smile.

'Detective, there is one more thing... I hesitate to mention it, especially now with Detective Payne waiting for you upstairs.' Phoebe shuffled, and her doubtful expression made him want to pull her into his arms to reassure her. For a moment, he took a beat to respond.

'Do not concern yourself with that, Miss Astin,' he smiled reassuringly, moving back into the room. 'I am sure Miss Lewis will be questioning Gilbert, saving us some time on the journey. And, as you know, sometimes the smallest thing can make a difference.'

Phoebe nodded and, taking a breath, explained, 'I thought I had seen the unidentified lady before and could not place where I might have met her. But I hadn't met her. I met – this will sound silly, but I met a doll dressed as she was.'

'Oh. May I ask where and when?' he said with genuine interest to encourage Phoebe to continue.

'I was at the *Doll and Teddy Hospital* on Elizabeth Street. I do not collect dolls or teddies,' she assured him hurriedly, 'but I was dropping in a vintage doll for repair. When I went to depart, a package nearly tripped me as it was lying across the doorway. The store was open, but the delivery was not brought inside. The owner, Mrs Crandle, invited me to stay while she unwrapped it, and she informed me that the hospital gets lots of donations that they sell once repaired. Well, it was the unidentified lady in doll format, Detective.'

'The same dress?' He frowned as he contemplated the meaning of what Phoebe was relaying.

'The very same – a yellow dress with cornflowers hand-stitched around the hem. The doll had brown hair, wore white stockings with white slippers, and had a red ribbon tied tightly around the neck, which was cut and needed repair. A note was included, but Mrs Crandle pocketed it rather quickly. One more silly thing happened... when I returned to collect my grandmother's repaired doll, Mrs Crandle was very nervous. She kept looking at the doll shelves, and I saw one doll facing the wrong way. She would not turn it in my company, but I looked back to see her furtively glancing at the doll's face before turning it. It was odd behaviour, as if the doll was sinister; I don't believe I imagined it, as I study faces all day.'

Harland was frowning with concentration as he took in Miss Astin's story, her eyes focussed only on him; her telling of the tale transfixed him.

'I would not have given it a second thought except that Nurse Faithful had said she was scared to her death, and Mrs Crandle looked very frightened,' Phoebe added.

He cleared his throat, realising she had finished speaking.

'And the unidentified lady was found dressed in the same clothing as the doll left outside the doll hospital,' Harland said, thinking aloud.

'I am sure it is a silly coincidence, and if so, I apologise, Detective, for taking up your time.'

'Miss Astin, my time is yours, and I assure you, it is far from a silly observation. We found the body of the unidentified lady crushing Elizabeth Street in the miniature display at the Botanic Gardens.'

'Goodness, that is another interesting connection.'

'Precisely. I am beginning to believe it all may be linked.'

Phoebe smiled with relief. 'That is all I have, Detective Stone.'

'It is most useful. I hope to receive an invitation to Miss Yalden's dinner dance soon. Will you reserve a dance for me? I'll endeavour not to stand on your toes.'

Phoebe laughed, 'That is not the most enticing invitation I have received, Detective, but I have never shirked a challenge.'

He chuckled. 'I ensure you I can dance, but having gone to boarding school, my partners were fellow boys, and thus we were rough and ready. I'll do my best to ensure you don't suffer,' he said, eliciting Phoebe's lovely smile.

Harland glanced upstairs. 'I best go before Gilbert tells Miss Lewis all our secrets, and I'll read about them in *The Courier* tomorrow.' He wished he could sit and have tea with Miss Astin, but the dead needed to be identified, and a murderer might be at large. With that, he bid her good day and departed.

Chapter 14

Lilly Lewis arrived at the office of *The Courier* after midday and hurried to her desk to write her copy; her partner, Fergus Griffith, had not yet returned. She did not bother to check her appearance; after all, she was a reporter, not a fashion plate, and getting the story across the line with Mr Cowan was more important than a hair out of place. The debonair bachelor, Lawrence Hulmes, gave her an indulgent smile, and she saw him catch the eye of his fellow male journalists, indicating a little sport was in order. Lilly braced herself. He was too handsome for his own good and had a long-suffering mistress, or several, truth be known, but Lilly was not in awe of him, nor did she swoon at his attention.

'Just in time for lunch, Miss Lewis. You have only turned me down for dinner a dozen times, but perhaps I will have more luck with a luncheon invitation?'

Lilly settled at her desk and gave him her full attention as he and his band of merry men smiled, ready for a fiery exchange.

'Thank you, Mr Hulmes, but I thought of late that I noticed a few extra pounds on you. I would hate to be the cause of your losing your figure.'

The boys roared with laughter, and Lawrence—always a good sport, which was conducive to his charming the ladies and gents—waggled a finger at her and laughed.

'Very naughty, Miss Lewis. We both know I cut a fine figure, not as fine as yours, of course. Surely an hour or two away from the desk will benefit your writing?'

Lilly bore a second attempt to woo her. 'Right you are, Mr Hulmes, and as I'm just back from an hour or two away from the desk, I'll get to work.' She addressed the gentlemen in the room. 'Sirs, would anyone be available to take Mr Hulmes to lunch? I fear he will fade away with hunger.'

Again, she enjoyed a round of mirth at Lawrence Hulmes' expense, and he play acted that he was wounded to the core. Then, to Lilly's surprise, one of his supporters, a crusty old journalist who had rarely acknowledged her, spoke up.

'Let the young lady be, Lawrence. She's got work to do.'

Lilly gave him a small smile and a nod of thanks, even if her face betrayed her surprise. Lawrence chuckled.

'You're not looking to undercut me and ask Miss Lewis out yourself, are you, Ted?'

Ted scoffed. 'I have a daughter that age, and she's just as clever, not to mention I feel a strong paternal instinct towards Miss Lewis.' He retorted. 'You want to watch that she's not coming for your job.'

The boys in the newsroom all laughed at this, but not as loudly or unconvincingly as they once might have. After all, none had enjoyed Lilly and Fergus's front-page exposure for the past four months.

Ted rose. 'Come on, Lawrence, the pub for an hour. Anyone coming?'

With that, the room emptied except for a couple of sales clerks, and a grateful Lilly got to work.

She closed her eyes to gather her thoughts before she began writing.

UNIDENTIFIED WOMAN FOUND
MORGUE MYSTERY – PUBLIC HELP SOUGHT
BODY FOUND IN MINIATURE VILLAGE DISPLAY

The body of a woman was found on Monday morning in the surrounds of the miniature village display currently showing in the city Botanic Gardens. She remains unidentified. It is our melancholy duty to feature an illustration of the woman, estimated to be twenty years of age. The body was fully dressed with no obvious sign of violence, except for a red ribbon around the neck, tied tightly but not sufficiently to effect strangulation. Despite the location where the body was found and the manner in which the lady was displayed, the coroner, Dr Tavish McGregor, advised the cause of death was by natural causes – tuberculosis.

Our town's leading detectives, Senior Detective Harland Stone and Detective Gilbert Payne, are seeking public assistance. The victim's clothing is somewhat peculiar and in the fashion of a pantomime performer. A yellow dress adorned with blue stitched cornflowers was clean but aged, suggesting the victim lived in humble conditions. White stockings and slippers were in good condition, and the theatre-like makeup on the face of the victim resembled that worn on stage.

Detective Harland Stone exclusively told *The Courier* that it was not simply a failure to establish the young woman's identity that made this case interesting.

'The circumstances of the death are peculiar, and while it is death from natural causes, the external injuries caused by the red ribbon at the throat and the dumping of the body suggest that the woman was mistreated,' Detective Stone said.

There is another twist in the case with the recent death of respected nurse, Charlotte Faithful, from a heart condition. Well-known in the southside community, Nurse Faithful's death was unexpected. It is understood there may be a connection between the two deaths, and *The Courier* will provide further details as they come to hand.

Lilly stopped writing as her partner, Fergus, rushed in.

'You're back,' he said, removing his hat and dropping into the chair beside her.

'Yes, it is really me,' she teased him, stating the obvious. Fergus chuckled. 'My copy for tomorrow is almost done. I have the illustrations too, or rather, the art department has them.'

'Excellent. Let me read what you have, and I shall write up my quotes from the coroner to add,' he said, taking a breath and accepting her copy.

After an hour, their first piece was finished, with Fergus's report included at the end of the story. Lilly quickly read his contribution:

> Coroner Dr Tavish McGregor told *The Courier* that receiving an unidentified woman is a rarity, as most of the unidentified corpses are male.

> 'There are not many dead women taken to the morgue whose relatives, friends, or acquaintances do not come forward,' Dr McGregor said. 'Whereas, there are eight males

presently in the morgue whose names are unknown.'

Dr McGregor believes this is easily understood as 'most women have home ties or domestic associations of some kind. Even the most abandoned have their acquaintances who miss them when they drop out. With many men, it is different,' he explained. 'We have among us many of the waifs and wrecks of other parts of the world. These men have sadly surrendered all connections.'

The coroner said the symptoms the young lady would have been experiencing with her tuberculosis deemed it unlikely that she was in any state to make her way to the miniature display, and the marks on her body indicated she was manhandled.

Management at the miniature display exhibition had not seen the young woman before, and had no knowledge of how her body came to rest on a section of their display.

Anyone who can assist the detectives with information that might lead to identifying the lady in question is asked to contact the Roma Street Police Headquarters.

'Let's file it and plan our angle for tomorrow now,' Lilly said.

'Our story will hinge on the public coming forward to identify her, so an early visit to the police headquarters is vital,' Fergus said.

'Agreed. Plus, I would like to know a little more about this nefarious baby farming business.'

'Baby farming?' Fergus's eyes grew wide. 'Why? Is she connected to that practice? Where did you hear that?'

'A wild theory,' Lilly hurriedly covered up her indiscretion. 'The two ladies might be connected, and I heard a whisper that Nurse Faithful placed babies with desperate parents.'

'Well, that is well-intentioned, is it not?'

'Without the knowledge of the birth mother.'

'Oh.' Fergus sat back. 'Now there's a good story, especially if somehow it involves our pantomime lady. Might she have assisted the nurse?'

Lilly shook her head. 'She is too young. But she may have been one of the placed children. My source wishes me to investigate ourselves and not rely on the information provided.'

'Then we shall,' Fergus said, fired up as Lilly took their copy to the editor to accompany the drawing.

Fortunately, the editor was busy, so she placed their copy in the in-file and hurried back to Fergus. There was a mystery afoot!

Chapter 15

JULIUS WAS STARTLED AS the back door of *The Economic Undertaker* swung open with great gusto. It was early afternoon, and Ambrose hurried in and whisked off his hat.

'Sorry I am late,' he called, coming up the hallway and seeing his brother at the front desk. 'Claude and I are ready to take Nurse Faithful for burial now.'

Julius froze; his eyes widened in shock; confusion and worry fought for position on his countenance.

'Just playing you, brother, do not fear. We just buried Nurse Faithful,' Ambrose grinned and hung up his hat.

Julius's hand went to his heart, and he leaned over, taking a short, sharp breath. The blood rushed from Ambrose's face as he rushed to his brother's side. Julius stood and smiled. 'Just playing you, brother, fear not, you have not given me a heart attack yet.'

'That is not funny at all,' Ambrose snapped.

'Is it not?' Julius asked with a raised eyebrow in his brother's direction. 'And burying the wrong dead party is?'

Ambrose made a huffing sound and walked past his brother, heading to the kitchen to scavenge some leftovers for a late lunch.

'Perhaps you might enter with a little more dignity in case a client is present,' Julius suggested, raising his voice to be heard.

'I will attempt to do so,' Ambrose called from the next room, not making any promises. 'Where is Mrs Dobbs?'

'She has gone to the store to fill her list before our afternoon clients.'

'When is Kate coming to deliver our photos?'

'Kate? Ah, Miss Kirby,' Julius said with interest. 'Tomorrow afternoon. I wanted Grandpa to be here to see them.' He glanced at the diary. 'Oh, sadly, you won't be here then; we have a commitment.'

Ambrose hurried back out of the kitchen with a scone in his hand. 'You are not serious? I must be here.'

'Must you? I'm thrilled you are taking this promotion seriously and are concerned for the company's photographs.' Julius folded his arms and pretended to be none the wiser before adding, 'Ah, this has nothing to do with the photographs, does it? Might you be in love, Ambrose?'

'Why are you so annoying at the moment, Julius? It is like having a little brother.'

Julius laughed at Ambrose's admission. 'Exactly so. Do not fear, little brother; we will all be here tomorrow when Miss Kirby arrives, and perhaps you might escort her home.'

'I will. Do tell, what is the cause of your light-heartedness?' Ambrose asked, sitting in a chair in the reception area and finishing his scone in two large bites. 'Is the cause's name Miss Violet Forrester?'

'Yes. I am going to ask her to marry me this evening.'

The announcement surprised Ambrose as Julius was most candid with his feelings, and his brother coughed and spluttered for a moment before rising with a grin and hurrying to Julius's side, grabbing his shoulders.

'But this is wonderful news, Julius.'

'If she says yes,' Julius said with a smile.

'Of course she will. What girl could resist an Astin?' He pulled his brother in for a rough hug and slapped him on the back before releasing him.

'Not a word until the deed is done. Only our family is in my confidence, and I want it to be a surprise.'

'Phoebe knows?' Ambrose asked.

'I believe she is a family member,' Julius retorted.

'She might forewarn Miss Forrester of your intent; they are friends, after all.'

'Forewarn? So Violet may prepare an appropriate decline?' Julius asked. 'You have little faith in this union, brother.'

'I am joking, of course,' Ambrose said. 'You are perfect together. Both so responsible and sensible.'

Julius gave his brother a wry look before adding, 'I shall be leaving at 5pm to collect Violet next door and depart.'

'Of course. I shall lock up and await the good news at home later tonight. Well, it is a happy day,' Ambrose said, grinning as he returned to the kitchen to reward himself with another scone.

'Let's hope,' Julius said in a low voice and patted his jacket again to feel the reassuring comfort of the ring box in his pocket.

Miss Violet Forrester looked upon the face of the grandfather clock in the corner of the dressmaking store. She had done so numerous times, most of those glances taking place post lunch.

'Well, I believe that is the fifteenth time, not that I was counting,' Mrs Nellie Shaw said with a wink at young Mary sitting opposite.

Violet laughed. 'Forgive me if I have distracted you, Nellie. Mr Astin is collecting me at 5pm for a walk in the gardens, and I have been a little preoccupied.'

'How romantic,' young Mary said with a sigh. 'I cannot wait until I might stroll with a beau through the gardens. Does he hand you out of the carriage, Miss?'

'Of course he does,' Nellie answered before Violet had a chance. 'Mr Astin is a true gentleman.'

'Do you link arms as you walk?' Mary persisted.

'Yes,' Violet said, indulging her with a smile. 'Mr Astin offers his arm, and I place my hand on it or through it depending on the roughness of the terrain or my level of weariness.'

'It's just like in my romantic novels,' Mary said with awe, making Nellie Shaw laugh.

'Your day will come, young lady,' Nellie assured her. 'I might go so far as to suggest you have already caught a young man's eye, but I will say no more.'

Mary blushed furiously, and Violet could not help but chuckle and give a small nod. Her brother, Tom, had taken up the habit of walking his sister home several times a week, and Violet was sure it was only for the opportunity to offer a few words of greeting to the shy and pretty Miss Mary Pollard, with her large brown doe eyes and light brown wavy hair.

Violet glanced at the clock again and then straight at Nellie.

'Goodness, I've done it again.'

'Only ninety minutes to go, my dear,' Nellie said with a smile. 'We'll be sure you are prepared and not late, won't we, Mary?'

'Of course,' Mary said, accepting the responsibility. 'I can see all the comings and goings from here, so if Mr Astin should leave his office, I will warn you immediately, Miss.'

'That is a great comfort, thank you both,' Violet teased. 'What would I do without you?'

'I cannot imagine,' Nellie said with a laugh. 'Oh, straighten up, ladies, a customer approaches.'

The ladies looked their most industrious as two ladies alighted from a hansom and made their way to the door of the *In Mourning – Attire for the Family* store, handkerchiefs at the ready.

With very little to go on until *The Courier* was printed and circulating the drawing of the unidentified lady, and with a verdict of death by natural causes for both the unidentified lady and Nurse Charlotte Faithful, Detective Harland Stone had two options.

'As I see it, Gilbert, I can visit the inspector and ask for a new case to be assigned to us, or we can do a little digging today to see what we might unearth and make a decision tomorrow whether there is a case to be made of it or not.'

'I am inclined toward the latter, Sir. I trust Miss Astin and believe something is amiss about the whole sorry affair, but I will bow to your wisdom.'

'Then we are in agreement. I think an afternoon of investigation to ensure nothing has been missed, and no one has gone unpunished is justifiable. After all, the young lady was dumped and abandoned, so something is not right.'

'The two cases being connected is most interesting,' Gilbert said. 'Surely Nurse Faithful officially registered the children she delivered, and I imagine they were registered with their new parents' names, not the biological parents.'

'I thought the same. I hope she kept a private diary that lists the true heritage of each child.' From his desk, Harland tapped a file in front of him. 'Nurse Faithful's next of kin, a brother, was given her possessions. He has probably already destroyed her work files, given they would not benefit him, but let's call on him and try our luck. I would also like to drop into *The Doll and Teddy Hospital*.'

Gilbert rose and grabbed his pad, pencil and hat as Harland did the same.

'May I ask why, Sir? Do you have a bear there in repair?'

'Very good, Gilbert,' Harland chuckled, and Gilbert smiled at his cleverness. 'No. When I stayed momentarily to ask after her bill, Miss Astin mentioned that something odd had happened there. A doll arrived that was dressed just like our victim.'

'Good gracious, that is odd.'

'And worth a visit to see the store owner. Let us begin with the brother.'

The two men exited their office, and Harland suggested they take the tram – not to appease the inspector but because the tram service regularly ran from nearby their office to Fortitude Valley, where the brother of Nurse Faithful—Samuel Faithful—was postmaster at the Fortitude Valley Post Office in Ann Street. They were there in good time.

'You are in luck, gentlemen,' a mature lady behind the counter said when they requested an audience with him. 'He was not meant to be in today... his sister's funeral, but he just arrived. Come through.'

They were greeted by a man nearing retirement age, small in height with a thin moustache, thinning hair, and a thin build. Neither of the detectives had seen Nurse Charlotte Faithful, so could not say if there was a family resemblance.

'Forgive us, Mr Faithful,' Harland said after introductions. 'I understand your sister, Miss Charlotte Faithful, recently passed away, but we didn't realise the burial was today. Our condolences.'

'Most kind, thank you, Detectives,' he said with a small nod. 'It was a dignified ceremony, but I see no point in staying home. My sister and I were both very committed to our work and the community, and she would rather I was industrious than mourning her, of that, I am sure.'

'If we may impose upon your time,' Harland continued, 'we seek your assistance with a police matter.'

'Gentlemen, do not tell me we are the subject of fraud or something equally nefarious?' he said, sitting behind a large desk and looking at them as if the detectives had been summoned for a work review. He indicated the chairs for them to sit on.

'No, rest assured it has nothing to do with your work. It concerns your sister. Her manner of death, what do you understand by it?' Harland asked, sitting opposite.

'Charlotte's death?' Samuel Faithful asked, surprised. 'The coroner told me it was quick and health-related,' he said solemnly and then frowned as scenarios justifying police involvement dawned on him. 'It was from a heart condition, was it not?'

'So, we understand, Sir, but our investigation into another death of a similar nature leads us to believe further investigation might be warranted,' Gilbert said diplomatically. Harland nodded, pleased with his protégé's discretion. 'Did she have a weak heart to your knowledge, Mr Faithful?'

'Yes. But she had not always been sickly. I believe that because of her line of work, Charlotte was exposed to illnesses and often overextended herself. Her body was weary. This other death – was she a nurse too?'

Harland answered, 'We cannot say anything further at this stage, but I understand you inherited your sister's worldly goods. We are after any paper records or diaries she may have kept about the children she assisted in bringing into the world.'

'Ah, that is an unusual request,' Samuel Faithful said. 'I imagine there is a child who was abandoned or adopted who is now seeking their true origin?' He nodded as if that were a fait accompli. 'I did not like to destroy her life's work, but I had no use for Charlotte's paperwork, so I gave the books to the local parish for safekeeping. St Francis Church, just up the road.'

'Thank you, we will ask there,' Harland said. 'Did your sister ever confide in you about her work or a group of friends called the *Storks*?'

Samuel Faithful gave a small chuckle. 'No, a fitting name though. She loved her work; it was her life, and I never heard her say a bad word about it.'

'Did she mention any fears or concerns to you, Mr Faithful?' Gilbert asked and hastily clarified, 'I ask because there were some break-ins on her street, and violence in our city has been increasing. Nurse Faithful often kept odd hours with her work, which may have placed her in danger.'

Again, Harland was impressed by Gilbert's discretion. The young man was coming along nicely. When they were first partnered, Gilbert would have asked that question directly, giving away the case and panicking the interviewee.

Samuel Faithful shook his head in the negative. 'Charlotte and I only saw each other on special occasions, and we were not close. There is a seven-year age difference between us, and I moved away with work as a young man, only recently returning to my hometown. As a postmaster, I was often asked to oversee agencies or train staff near and far. Charlotte had her work and friends; she would not have confided in me.'

The detectives thanked Samuel Faithful and departed, walking to St Francis' church nearby.

'You did very well, Gilbert, with your questions. Thoughtful and discreet.'

'Thank you, Sir,' Gilbert said with a small smile. 'I hope not to be a disappointment to you.'

'Far from it, Gilbert, we are doing some good work, and your observations are most welcomed.'

'Thank you, Sir. May I offer one then, an observation, that is?'

'Of course, go ahead.' The afternoon was warm but not unpleasant, and they walked on the shady side of the street.

'I wonder if we are best to look for births and deaths on the same date, in the same area, and then determine if there was an insurance claim at that time. Unless she kept a receipt of payment, Nurse Faithful most likely would have handed the insurance policy to the parents to claim. So, if we find a matching birth and death date in her records, we should approach the parents of the deceased and ask for their insurance paperwork.'

'Good thinking, Gilbert.'

'We don't need that paperwork, of course, Sir,' Gilbert continued, 'we are merely establishing if they might have been the victim of a great deception and the recipient of a payout.'

'Exactly so. After all these years, it is unlikely that they might have kept the paperwork, but it may benefit Bennet's case.'

They arrived at the church.

'I almost hope that the unidentified woman—when identified—leads us to a crime of sorts, Sir. This is too interesting to forgo,' Gilbert said.

Harland chuckled. 'Now you are becoming a true detective,' he said, and the pair entered the cool interior of the church, hopeful of retrieving Nurse Faithful's records.

Chapter 16

Mary exclaimed like the town crier, 'Mr Astin is coming, Miss! Oh, he looks most handsome. But he always does.' At the same time, a horse and small carriage pulled up at the front of the dressmaking store, and Claude jumped down, ready to hand the reins to Julius.

Violet rose from her desk. She had freshened up just prior, and accepting the ladies' best wishes for a pleasant stroll, she thanked them and met Mr Astin at the door.

'Good night, ladies,' she called, and Julius paused long enough in the doorway to wish the ladies a good evening after greeting her.

'Are you sure you can leave right on time, given you are at the helm today?' she teased.

'I've left Ambrose to lock up.' He hesitated. 'Perhaps you are right.' Julius glanced at the business and then smiled at her. 'What could go wrong?'

She laughed and greeted Claude, allowing Julius to hand her up into their ride. Julius thanked his stable hand and took the reins as Claude returned to the office next door, leaving them alone. The carriage had been cleaned and smelled fresh, and a bunch of pink roses lay on the seat; Julius had been most thoughtful, she mused with delight.

As they departed, Violet could see Mary watching most intently from the window as if she were storing all the romantic elements to relive later. Violet gave her a little wave, and the young assistant looked away, embarrassed to be caught daydreaming.

'We are lucky to have such good assistants. Nellie and Mary are godsends, and I am sure Ambrose is very responsible when required but plays up on you,' Violet said.

'I suspect you are right, but some evidence of his maturity would be heartening,' Julius said in jest as he nudged the horses. They headed into the moving traffic, leaving South Brisbane and making their way to the Victoria Bridge and then onto the gardens in Alice Street. It was a busy but enjoyable trip, especially across the river.

Once they were moving along safely, Violet studied him discretely. He was such a handsome man; she could not believe the misfortune of her beloved grandmother's death that brought them together and the goodwill that came their way from the union for herself and Tom.

He glanced her way.

'What is wrong? Is my hat crooked?'

She laughed. 'No, you look most dashing. I was musing on my good fortune that I had no other relatives on hand to deter me from dating my manager.'

'My relief knows no bounds,' he said with all sincerity. 'It was hard enough convincing you of my best intentions after your uncle left; should another relative campaign against me, I might have had to start burying a few.'

Violet gasped in surprise and playfully hit his arm. 'What a thing to say! Tell me it never crossed your mind.'

'Only a few times,' he confessed.

'You are incorrigible. I am sure Ambrose, for all his faults, would not have thought such a thing,' Violet teased.

'It was his suggestion and one of his better ones. But luckily, it never came to that.' As their smiles faded, he addressed her soberly. 'I thought all hope was lost.'

Her breath hitched. 'I was despairing. Thank goodness you ignored my uncle and me, Julius. Thank you for knowing my heart better than I.'

He kissed her hand and returned his focus to driving. They were soon in Alice Street, where Violet waited as Julius availed himself of the services of several young men who watered and cared for the horses and stored the carriages and carts. It was a short walk to the entrance to the Botanic Gardens, where it was evident a great deal of work had been done to restore the gardens after floodwaters had caused considerable damage six months earlier. Spring had called forth all the beautiful blooms, and dusk's onset brought a gentle breeze and a perfect temperature for a wander.

Julius and Violet joined the many couples who walked arm in arm or sat watching life milling around them at the end of the business day.

'Where shall we start? At the roses, your favourite, or perhaps a stroll around the lake?' Julius offered Violet the choice.

'Let us stroll around the lake and see the ducks. I have been sitting for some time, and after we get a little exercise, perhaps sit for a moment in the rose garden?'

'To the ducks then.'

Violet noticed Julius slowing his pace to allow for her smaller steps, and they both relaxed, enjoying the burst of colours before them. There were not as many people around the water feature; it was a wide area and not as picturesque as the flower beds at this time of year.

They were halfway around circumnavigating the pond when they heard a shrill scream. Violet turned in haste, Julius pulling her closer lest there be danger, and there was, but not for them. A child had fallen into the water from the rocks near the middle of the path and was floundering. The water was not that deep, but too deep for a young boy. He had floated a little further out in his bid to save himself and, having fallen from the rocks, was well in the middle rather than a few feet from the edge had he waded in.

By now, the youngster's mother was screaming in fright, holding back her two other children who attempted to follow him. The nearest party was Julius and Violet's.

'Good Lord,' Julius said, realising he had to rescue the boy. He hurriedly shucked off his jacket and hat, passing them to a stricken-looking Violet, kicked off his shoes, and waded in.

'Hurry, Julius,' she cried as the boy dipped below the surface.

With Julius's long stride, he was there in moments and had no choice but to splash fully dressed into the waste-deep water to find the boy who had disappeared below the surface.

Violet held her breath, her heart pounding, and the frantic mother and her children raced around to Violet's side of the pond, stopping by her and watching in fear. The little boy's sister called his name as if that might help him find his way back to them. Violet realised the mother was praying – word after word, beseeching God for her son's safekeeping.

Julius surfaced for air and on his second sweep below water, lifted the boy and patted his back to help the lad expel the water swallowed. After some spluttering and coughs, a resounding wail told everyone the lad was alive. Julius hushed and reassured the frightened young boy, who clung to him as if he were a life buoy.

The mother praised the Lord, and Violet slumped with relief, taking a deep breath as she watched Julius stride from the water. He glanced uncomfortably at the gathering crowd. He was now best described as bedraggled. The beautiful shirt she had made was wet and clinging to him; his suit trousers were damp and heavy, with the occasional reed trailing from them, and Julius's hair hung wet in his eyes.

'Oh my, Alfie, oh my, thank you, Sir, thank you. I owe you my life, his life. Are you all right, Alfie? Sir?' the woman wailed, taking her son and holding him despite his struggles to get down and enjoy being the centre of attention.

Julius assured her the boy seemed in good health, and he, too, was perfectly fine, if not damp.

'Oh, Sir, look at you. We have ruined your evening, but I am so grateful. You are a hero.'

'You are, Julius,' Violet said, looking at him with the utmost admiration. Her heart could not be fuller.

People nearby and on the other side of the pond applauded, and others arrived to see what the noise was about. Julius ran a hand through his wet hair and, taking his jacket and hat from Violet, pushed his wet, socked feet inside his dry shoes.

'I am relieved I was on hand and could be of service, Madam,' he said. 'Alfie, stay out of trouble!'

Alfie's mother scolded the lad and hugged him, professing her love and anger in equal measure, and Violet gave a small huff of laughter as the boy nodded solemnly at his rescuer before giving him a cheeky grin.

Then, despite his state of undress and in the excitement of the moment with all ending well, Julius took a deep breath and surprised Violet once more; he dropped to one knee.

At first, she thought he was doing something to reduce the excess water in his clothing and shoes, but then he reached inside his jacket and pulled out a small, dry ring box.

Violet gasped, as did others around them, and there was more applause even before Julius had asked the question. Alfie's mother proclaimed it to be the most unpredictable day.

'Indeed!' Violet agreed, with a look of shock upon her face.

Julius chuckled and, with a small shrug to explain his out-of-character impetuousness, said, 'Violet, I have loved you from the first moment I laid eyes upon you; you have consumed my every thought day and night. At this moment, that ended well, and with Alfie as my witness,' he looked to the boy who gave a solemn nod, 'would you please do me the great honour of being my wife?'

Alife yelled 'Yes,' which had everyone laughing and his mother scolding playfully.

'I believe it is up to the young lady to answer that question, dear,' Alfie's mother said.

Violet wanted to remember every second of the proposal, but she was in haste to say yes.

'Yes, yes, forever and a thousand times, yes!'

They were both grinning and caught up in each other's gaze as if no one else existed. Julius rose from kneeling and slipped the ring onto Violet's finger.

'Oh, Julius, it is breathtaking,' she said and tightened her fingers together, given the ring was a little big and needed to be resized.

Even Alfie insisted on hugging both of them, and given he and Julius were both wet, Julius lifted the boy up to see the ring.

When they were finally alone, walking back to the trap, Julius drying out, he said, 'It was not quite as I planned.'

'I imagine so,' she teased, 'but it was memorable and unique, and I will tell the story of my hero forever.'

Randolph Astin frowned as he saw the curtain moved aside again, as it had been many times in the last hour. His wife,

Marie – grandmother and guardian of Julius, Ambrose and Phoebe, waited with little patience for news of the engagement of her eldest, beloved grandson, anticipating his arrival any moment. Randolph was not impatient with the gesture but worried she might be disappointed.

'Don't be disheartened, dear. They may choose to go to dinner or have some time alone to celebrate before visiting family,' Randolph said from the lounge room, where he enjoyed his nightly glass of scotch before dinner.

Maria shook their head. 'No, darling, I don't believe so. Julius intended to propose after work; he will come by, I know it.'

'I have never seen him like this, so enamoured by a young lady. It is wonderful.'

Maria smiled at her husband. 'It is; I am so happy he has found someone to share his life with. Julius was always so... well, reserved with his feelings. I feared he would be unable to express himself adequately to secure a lady's heart and hand.'

'It's hard to go past the Astin good looks and charm, though,' Randolph said in jest and laughed when his wife of many years shook her head at his playfulness.

'So true,' she agreed and laughed. Then, Maria gave a small cry. 'Here he is now!'

As excited as his wife, Randolph rose and, heading to the front door, called out to Ambrose, 'Your brother is here.'

The pair hurried to the front verandah as Julius handed Violet down from the trap. Only Phoebe was absent, having gone to a play with Emily and yet to hear the news.

Randolph stopped in his tracks. 'Good Lord, what happened?' Julius was damp and dishevelled, his hair slicked back, his jacket, pants and shoes damp.

'Is it official?' Maria asked, clasping her hands together and ignoring Julius's state of dress.

'Yes!' Violet exclaimed, looking up at Julius, her face full of love.

'It is,' Julius said smiling, 'Violet has done me the great honour of agreeing to be my wife.' He held Violet's hand at an angle so they could see the ring that adorned her finger, making it official.

'Oh, this is the most wonderful news,' Marie said, not knowing who to hug first, adding, 'If only your mother and father were here, but we will be happy today on their behalf.'

'How could we not be?' Randolph agreed, shaking Julius's hand vigorously before pulling him in for a hug and kissing Violet's hand.

'My goodness, look at that diamond!' Maria exclaimed.

'But why are you damp?' Randolph asked, 'and smelling, well, like the river.'

Julius casually mentioned the rescue, and Violet proclaimed, 'He was nothing short of a hero, Mr and Mrs Astin; it was amazing.'

Ambrose came out of the house and asked the same questions, and the process was repeated.

'So, you are sure Violet did not push you into the pond in an attempt to escape your proposal, but you caught up with her regardless?' Ambrose asked and added with a wink at Violet, 'You can tell me the truth later.'

She laughed. 'I promise you, Julius rescued a little boy and was a true hero. Everyone applauded him, and the mother was ever so grateful.'

'What a day,' Randolph said, shaking his head, and ushered everyone inside for a toast. He opened a bottle of champagne and poured it into the glasses that were at the ready; Maria handed them around. Randolph could not express how he felt in words—his brother, Reggie, would have made an eloquent job of it—but his heart was filled with joy at seeing the most deserving of his grandchildren so happy. He studied Julius, who was finding it hard to take his eyes off his fiancée, the beautiful woman standing next to him wearing the engagement ring, and Randolph could not be happier.

'It wasn't quite the proposal I had planned,' Julius told them after the toast, peeling a stem of water lily from his trousers and moving to the lounge room window to flick it out of doors, 'but it was eventful, nonetheless.'

'I can't bear to think what might have happened to Alfie if we had gone to the rose garden first,' Violet said now that her mind had had time to think wider than the proposal.

'There were other people on hand; do not fear,' Julius assured her. 'They were a little further away but would have gotten there in time to save him.'

'Will you stay for dinner?' Maria asked. 'Although I think I am too excited to eat.'

'I am not,' Ambrose said.

'We had best not, Grandma, but thank you,' Julius said. 'We need to see Tom and tell him.'

'Oh, yes, you must. Tom will live with you, of course? Oh, I shouldn't ask that. It is none of my business,' she hurriedly added.

'We are family, and it is your business as the matriarch, Grandma,' Julius said. 'He will live with us; I've already discussed it with him.'

'Have you?' Violet turned to him, surprised, her eyes wide with delight.

'Of course. He is the man of your house now, I asked permission to propose and said we'd expect him to reside with us. We negotiated he could come and go as he saw fit,' Julius joked.

Now, she laughed heartily. 'Of course he worked that into the deal.' She softened. 'Thank you for doing that; it was very kind.'

Julius kissed her hand. 'We will all be family.'

Maria gave a small cough to get their attention. 'Perhaps change first, Julius. You have some clothing here.'

'Good idea,' Violet said. 'Your grandmother and I can talk dresses while you are gone.'

'I still have mine. Would you like to see it?' Maria asked.

'Yes, please,' Violet said excitedly, and Randolph smiled, watching the pair hurry off.

'I am going to the club,' Ambrose said. 'Brother, can I tell Cousin Lucian, or would you prefer to do so?'

'Tell away,' Julius said, stopping on the third step as he headed upstairs to his childhood bedroom to change. 'I will tell people as I see them, no big announcements.'

'But will you allow your grandmother and me to put a notice in the engagements section of *The Courier*?' Randolph enquired.

Julius winced.

'It would make her very happy,' Randolph added and laughed at the beaten expression his grandson adopted. 'Good lad.'

Julius groaned and turned, heading upstairs, but Randolph knew his grandson was too happy to let something that small worry him.

'It is a dark day for the single ladies of our town,' Ambrose said to his grandfather, making him laugh. 'Mr Julius Astin and Miss Violet Forrester are to be wed.'

Chapter 17

BENNET MARTIN'S CLERK, DANIEL Dutton, gave a surprised laugh when the detectives arrived on the doorstep at 9am the next morning.

'Forgive me, Detective Stone and Detective Payne. We all work business hours, and I am sure you work longer than that, but Bennet does not. He paints when the inspiration strikes and fits business around that.'

'Of course,' Gilbert said, 'he is primarily an artist.'

'Indeed, and a good one at that,' Daniel said loyally. 'But the private investigator work is the bread and butter.'

'Does he not live on the premises?' Harland asked, recalling Julius had told him so when they were out one evening.

'He does, and he will be up. He rises early and paints with the morning light at its best.' Daniel looked up the staircase to Bennet's room.

'Can you announce us, or can we go up?' Harland asked, now impatient. Police work was more important than putting paint on canvas in his mind, and he wouldn't be asked to come back by Bennet's clerk.

'Of course,' Daniel said, noting the detective's professional demeanour. 'Please wait here for a moment.'

Daniel's aunt and housekeeper for Bennet arrived and offered the men a cup of tea, warning it might take a little longer as she had not yet boiled the water. Both men declined, and Bennet appeared at the top of the staircase moments later.

'Come up, Harland, Detective Payne,' he called down. He was wearing his white shirt, black pants, and a pair of dark slippers. His hair was not as coiffured as they were used to, and Harland imagined Bennet got straight up from his bed and picked up his paintbrush.

The men hurried up, thanking Daniel as he passed them on the way down. Entering the room, the detectives admired the workspace and paintings on display.

'Oh my, you are as talented as they say, Mr Martin,' Gilbert said, looking at the works completed and the one currently in progress. 'Not that I am an expert, but I feel as if these scenes are real.'

'Thank you, Detective. I am vain enough to appreciate all praise, expert or not, and delighted to know people have spoken of my skills,' Bennet said with a grin, wiping his hands on a rag that featured paint blotches of every colour.

'Is that Miss Lewis?' Harland asked, surprised. 'A very good likeness.'

'I hope so. I will gift it to her when done.' Bennet gestured to a table and chairs in the corner. 'Your business with me must be important to call at this hour.'

They sat, and Harland said, 'It is important, but most places are open for business.'

Bennet grinned. 'Of course. How can I help?'

'I think we can help each other,' Harland said. 'You mentioned an insurance agency hired you to investigate what they believe to be false claims for life insurance.'

'Yes,' Bennet sobered, his mind snapping from art to business. 'Claims for deceased children that either did not exist or didn't, in fact, pass away.'

Harland nodded at Gilbert to elaborate.

'The unidentified woman and the death of Nurse Charlotte Faithful may have a tenuous connection to your insurance cases,' Gilbert said. 'Nurse Faithful and a small group of colleagues were taking children from families who could not handle another child and placing them with parents desperate for a child.'

'Good Lord! And you think they might have been declared dead by the biological family and an insurance claim made?' Bennet asked, his interest piqued.

'Precisely,' Harland said. 'As you are privy to Miss Astin's visions, I can share that Nurse Faithful told Miss Astin that her group, aptly named the *Storks*, took out insurance policies for several families, and the parents claimed them once they were advised the child died.'

Harland felt awkward talking about Miss Astin when his own interest was no longer a secret, and the lady had recently rejected Bennet. Fortunately, Gilbert hurried on.

'Nurse Faithful selected the children to remove and faked the children's deaths. She knew the life insurance policy payout would be life-changing for their families,' Gilbert said.

'But surely the parents grieved and wanted those children even if they were financially stretched?' Bennet asked.

Harland bit his tongue; Bennet spoke like a man who had never known adversity or missed a meal. He had no concept of the pain and stress of not knowing if you could feed your child that night or the next.

'They would have grieved in their own way, I imagine,' Gilbert said and diplomatically added, 'As an example, one lady was widowed when she was expecting twins and already had five children. She undoubtedly loved her children, but how could she care for that many? The future was not bright.'

'I understand. So, they were declared deceased to one woman and brought to life by another, none the wiser?' Bennet asked.

'That is what we hope to cross-check with you,' Harland said, 'if you have started your investigation.'

'I have, and your timing is perfect. One moment, please,' Bennet said, rising and going to the door. He yelled out to Daniel to bring up the insurance file and, moments later, re-entered the room with it.

'I met with the client, who gave me a list of claimants they believe have had illegitimate claims. My clerk has provided a little more detail on each family.'

Gilbert placed his hand flat on the file before him and said, 'We found Nurse Faithful's records—her brother gave them to the local parish—and we have birth and death dates of children the *Storks* delivered.'

'Ah. So, a child born on the same day as a child that died may have been substituted, and if I have that same date on any of my claims, they may be illegitimate, and we might have a case.'

'Or thereabouts; the dates might differ by a few days,' Harland said. 'But we are looking at cases from twenty years ago involving Nurse Faithful.'

'Well, that is fortunate. My list of names ranges from historical cases to the present, but only for the southside region. Mind you, the client is more interested in the current cases; they will be easier to prosecute.' Bennet shuffled his papers and perused the dates. 'Yes, a few go back twenty years, and even one or two older than that. Shall we check?'

'Absolutely,' Harland agreed.

Bennet began reading the family name, child's sex, and the date of death. He read four before Gilbert exclaimed, 'Stop, we have a match with that date. A child died, a child was born, and with the same surname for the deceased!'

'That is likely one of Nurse Faithful's deliveries then,' Harland said and exhaled, his cheeks puffed out with the realisation that Miss Astin was right again. They hurried through the rest of the list, finding two more.

'That's the twins,' Gilbert said with excitement in his voice.

'What surname do you have for your claim, Bennet?' Harland asked.

Bennet ran his finger along the line of names, answering, 'Liddle. Mrs Elizabeth Liddle, widowed. She claimed for the deceased twins and was awarded 100 pounds. The twins are not named but listed as baptised, so they were likely to be buried in consecrated ground.'

'If this is Nurse Faithful's doing, she must have told the parents for their peace of mind that their children were baptised. She thought of everything,' Harland said. He looked to Gilbert.

'She meant no harm, as we know, Sir. However, a crime has taken place.'

'I wonder,' Harland mused, 'if both sets of parents were truly innocent or were they aware of this scheme.'

'And is the unidentified lady one of the names on our list?' Gilbert mused. 'She is the right age.'

Bennet eyed their list. 'May I copy the additional names and dates from Nurse Faithful's list to crosscheck if claims were made?'

'I'll leave it with you,' Harland said, providing the list to Bennet. 'If you find matches, can you inform us as soon as convenient?'

'Absolutely,' Bennet said, rising to show them out. 'What will you do in the interim?'

'We shall start with Mrs Elizabeth Liddle if she is still alive. We also have a doll hospital to visit, and we need to get to the office... hopefully someone has come forward and given our unidentified lady a name.'

As they departed, taking the omnibus as it was timely and going the right way, Harland was deep in thought when Gilbert cleared his throat.

'Sir? Might you share your thoughts?'

'I can't claim to have any intellectual thoughts, Gilbert, and certainly not thoughts I should share with a protégé given they are rather selfish, but I shall nevertheless as we trust each other now.'

'Thank you, Sir,' Gilbert said, seeming to rise taller in his seat.

'I mused that we have a case on our hands, but truth be known, fraud or baby farming, or whatever it might be, does not excite me a great deal. Other officers can investigate that, but the connection with the unidentified girl is something again. A dying woman abandoned and left on display is a statement... another woman frightened to death, and a toy store owner possibly being threatened,' he speculated. 'If it could all come together, then we have ourselves a real case.' Harland could not help but smile.

'Yes, Sir,' Gilbert grinned. 'Fingers crossed, even if that sounds a little odd, but the crimes have happened; I am only hoping they are connected,' he justified his enthusiasm.

Harland gave a firm nod. 'Onward then, the threads are unravelling!'

'Congratulations, Mr Astin, well done,' the newspaper seller called as Julius passed the stand on the corner, taking his horse and trap toward the rear of *The Economic Undertaker* business.

Julius frowned, confused, but remembered his manners to thank the man, offer a smile, and move on. Perhaps his grandfather had told the paper seller of the engagement when collecting a copy of *The Courier* for the office, he mused.

He got no further before the fruiterer raised his hand and called, 'I take my hat off to you, Sir, bravo.'

'Well done, Mr Astin, well done indeed,' the fruiterer's wife added, pausing in her arrangement of the bananas to offer her congratulations.

Julius tipped his hat and thanked the pair, appreciating their best wishes but bemused by their comments. People had been getting engaged for centuries, and it was a joyous occasion to be sure, but hardly an achievement of note.

Driving around the back of the business to the stables, he saw his three employees preparing the horses and hearse for the day. He was usually in before everyone, but having taken the small carriage last evening to drop Violet home, he did the collections on the way to work for the business – laundered shrouds that Phoebe used to cover bodies before burials and the mid-week collection of fresh flowers for the meeting room. All three of his staff turned and beamed at him.

'Congratulations, Julius,' Claude and Will said as he dismounted, and a round of handshakes was proffered. Julius thanked them, hoping that would be the end of it now, but knowing he still had to run the gauntlet of his friends—Harland, Bennet, Tavish and Cousin Lucian—not to mention Mrs Dobbs and the ladies next door in the dressmaking store.

'And congratulations from me too, Mr Astin,' young Charlie said.

'Thank you, Charlie. Perhaps you might call me Julius, as we now work together.' He offered, given that Claude and Will both addressed him informally.

'No, Sir, but thank you. My Ma would not like that.'

Julius smiled. 'Very well. Is it working... the new structure?' he asked them, and they all responded positively.

'When you are away for your honeymoon, you can rest assured we will all step up,' Will, the senior of the three, said.

'Thank you. That is a great comfort, especially given Ambrose's tendency to fall asleep in the coffin display room,' he said in jest and departed the group with Will organising to deliver the flowers and shrouds. Entering the back of the building, Julius removed his hat and got halfway down the hallway before Mrs Dobbs appeared.

'Oh, Mr Astin, you have made my day, no, my week, possibly even my month,' she said, and Julius laughed.

'Well, thank you, Mrs Dobbs,' he accepted her kiss on the cheek. 'You will need a bonus to purchase a new hat for the wedding, and we may impose on you to prepare your special fruit cake for our wedding cake,' he said in jest, but the look of delight on Mrs Dobbs's face told Julius the deal was done.

Julius caught his grandfather's attention, and Randolph Astin called out, 'You best come in here, lad.'

He was not one for surprises and entered the meeting room with a look of wariness, especially on seeing his siblings in attendance. Phoebe ran to him, throwing her arms around him and nearly knocking him backward with surprise.

'Oh, so you approve?' he said in jest, one arm around her, the other holding his hat.

'I am so happy. I have already been in to see Violet, and we are all so excited. But I am especially happy for you, Julius,' she said, looking up at him and stepping away. 'You deserve this.'

'You do,' his grandfather said, and Ambrose nodded.

Julius smiled, uncomfortable with the attention, and Ambrose rescued him from replying.

'I am not sure your betrothal will stop the ladies fainting at funerals, but let's hope business does not drop off,' Ambrose quipped. 'Come to think of it, that is how you met Miss Forrester.'

Julius looked surprised. 'I did lift her next to you on the bench seat when she was overcome, but I was taken with her long before then. Perhaps the moment she first appeared on the verandah.'

Phoebe sighed. 'So romantic.'

Julius smiled and shook his head at his sister, and then he saw the open newspaper and the headline. 'Oh no,' he groaned. 'How did they get this?'

'There were many witnesses, I believe,' Randolph explained. 'You are quite the hero, lad.'

'Ah, that's why everyone was congratulating me this morning. I thought you had got around the neighbourhood early, Grandpa.'

'Well, I did that too,' he said with a smile and a pat on Julius's back. 'I am always happy to gloat about my grandchildren.'

'I hope it dies down today,' Julius said with a frown.

'A nice pun, brother, given we have a funeral to deliver now. But this afternoon, no interruptions from four o'clock onwards – Kate is bringing in the photographs.'

'Kate? Not Miss Kirby?' Phoebe teased Ambrose.

'Don't be stealing your brother's moment of glory now, Ambrose,' Randolph chided him.

'Please steal away,' Julius said, encouraging his younger brother. 'Allow me a few minutes to go next door and say good morning to my fiancée, then we will be off.'

'Fiancée, that sounds so good,' Phoebe sighed.

'I will give you fifteen minutes as the ladies will want to fuss over you. If you are not out by then, I shall rescue you,' Ambrose offered.

Julius glanced again at the headline and, with a shake of his head, went to see the face of the woman he was to spend the rest of his days alongside. The day could not come quickly enough for his married life to begin.

HERO RESCUES DROWNING CHILD
DRAMA AT BOTANIC GARDENS' LAKE
HERO PROPOSES TO HIS SWEETHEART

The courage and promptitude of South Brisbane businessman, Mr Julius Astin, on late Tuesday afternoon prevented a tragedy in the making. Young Alfie Redding, aged five, had broken away from his mother and sisters and lost his footing while climbing on rocks near the lake bridge. He found himself immersed in the water and unable to reach the edge.

Mr Astin, with no thought to his own comfort, ran 25 yards to the lake, hurriedly removed his jacket and shoes and waded in to assist the boy.

Witnesses said Alfie disappeared for a moment below the waist-deep water, and Mr Astin had to immerse himself to find the boy when he did not surface.

He effected a gallant rescue, and we are pleased to say Alfie is no worse for wear, except for further punishment metered out by his mother for her suffering during the ordeal.

On exiting, Mr Astin went ahead with what was a planned proposal as he was bearing a ring on his person and dropping to one knee, with Alfie as his witness, proposed to Miss Violet Forrester. Young Alfie said yes before the intended, to everyone's amusement.

Mr Astin is well known around town as the successful proprietor of *The Economic*

Undertaker funeral business. Miss Forrester is an accomplished dressmaker.

Mrs Redding, Alfie's mother, said she was grateful beyond all measure for Mr Astin's quick actions and wished the couple every happiness.

A happy ending prevailed from what might have turned out very differently.

Mary exclaimed excitedly, 'Mr Astin is coming, your fiancé, Miss!'

'Oh good, we will have a chance to congratulate him,' Nellie said, looking up from her work.

Violet's heart skipped a beat as her eyes went to the windows, and she saw him approaching. He opened the door hesitantly, as he always did for fear of distressing a customer. Several racks of clothing hung near the door awaiting collection, and rolls of fabric were on the table in the process of being cut. Violet was standing behind the desk, scissors in hand; Mary was cutting a pattern, and Nellie was sewing.

'I am sorry to interrupt when you are so busy,' he said. 'I was just wishing to say good morning to my fiancée.'

Violet came to greet him, seeing how self-conscious he appeared, wearing his heart on his sleeve, and the other two ladies rose.

'Good morning,' Violet said, allowing him to kiss her hand.

'Congratulations, Mr Astin,' Mary said, dropping a curtsy. 'It was an exciting proposal.'

'Thank you, Miss Pollard, and yes, it was not quite how I planned it,' he said with a smile, addressing Mary, who flushed red, resumed her seat and continued work.

'And my congratulations too, Mr Astin,' Nellie Shaw said. 'To say I am delighted is an understatement.' She clasped her hands in front of her in delight.

'Thank you, Mrs Shaw. As am I, delighted that is.' Julius suddenly noticed all the flowers, at least a half dozen bouquets. 'Is it someone's birthday as well?'

Violet laughed. 'No, these are bouquets congratulating us on our engagement. Six already this morning, and we've been open but an hour.'

Julius frowned, confused.

'From people in business with you, Mr Astin, wanting to acknowledge your lovely fiancée,' Nellie clarified.

'Really?' he asked, surprised.

Violet nodded. 'They are beautiful, and I'll send thank-you notes and ensure the ladies here and next door all take a bouquet home with them tonight.' She pointed to each one, 'From the florist *The Economic Undertaker* frequents, the fabric store, grocer, make-up supplier, launderer, and from your cousin, Lucian, welcoming me to the family.'

Julius looked surprised and impressed.

'Shall we give you both a moment?' Nellie asked.

'No, but thank you, Mrs Shaw. Ambrose is waiting for me. Perhaps you might walk me to the back area?' he asked of Violet.

'Of course.' She looped her arm through his, and they walked through the lunchroom to the back door and stairs.

'I did not sleep a wink last night for excitement,' Violet said, followed by an embarrassed huff.

'Nor did I, so if I fall asleep today on the job and tumble headlong into the dug-out grave, I have you to thank for it.'

She laughed, and for a moment, they looked at each other before Julius cleared his throat and said, 'I best go.' He opened the back door and stopped again on the lower step, turning.

Ambrose called out his name and a greeting to his future sister-in-law, and Julius turned to indicate he was on his way. Turning back, Violet was now at eye level with Julius and desperately wanted to touch him.

'I never thought I could be this happy,' she whispered.

'I hope you remember that when Grandma and Phoebe visit to discuss the wedding date, guest list, dresses, flowers, and sorry, but Mrs Dobbs might be making the wedding cake.'

Violet's expression relayed her delight. 'Oh dear, I shall start thinking of all that then.' She hesitated, her face falling slightly. 'There is only Tom and me; I won't call on my distant uncles or aunts to attend.'

'We are a small family too, but we both have friends and staff who will want to attend. A small but intimate wedding, then?'

'Perfect.'

'That you are,' he said, kissing her hand and turning. He hurried down the stairs before Ambrose could bellow his name again.

Chapter 18

Mrs Crandle's heart skipped a beat with fear as she saw two gentlemen standing outside the *Doll and Teddy Hospital*, waiting for her to flip the sign on the door to "Open". She rarely received male customers, let alone professional-looking gentlemen, and she feared it was related to the recent threats.

Schooling herself to stay calm, she opened the door to them. 'Good morning, gentlemen. Do you wish to enter?'

'Yes, thank you, Madam. Detective Harland Stone and Detective Gilbert Payne. May we have a moment of your time, please?' Harland asked.

'Yes, of course, do come in.' She was about to turn the sign to "Closed" to deter customers from overhearing any conversation that might be unsavoury but thought better of it. A customer might hurry the men out of the store quicker.

'It is Mrs Crandle, is it not?' Harland asked.

The lady nodded in agreement.

'Is Mr Crandle in attendance?'

'He has gone out for the mail,' she said, relieved. 'How may I be of assistance?'

'Do you both repair the dolls?' Harland asked.

'No, Mr Crandle is our repairer. I run the business. Is this about a repair?'

'This is a call of concern, Mrs Crandle,' Gilbert said, and she allowed herself to exhale a little with relief. 'We understand you have been receiving some strange, uh, donations of late. A threat perhaps, or something untoward?'

'I can't imagine what might make you think that, Sir? We are gifted donations and are always delighted to receive a doll or teddy into which we can breathe new life.' She moved behind the counter to look official and busy, hoping they might depart sooner. 'May I ask who told you this?'

She studied the tall detective with his rugged looks, educated speech, and neat, smaller partner – an odd pairing.

'Oh! You are the detectives who recently solved the kidnapped child case; I read about it in *The Courier.*'

'Yes, Ma'am,' Gilbert said. Neither detective answered her question as to its source of information.

'We believe you might have a connection to a crime we are investigating.' Gilbert continued, not revealing too much for fear of earning his superior's disapproval.

'Goodness, how is that so? No, I am sure you are too busy and important to waste your time with me,' Mrs Crandle said, flustered and portraying a surprised demeanour. In all her years in business, she knew how to handle people from all walks of life.

'I believe you received a doll recently with a red ribbon around the neck. The doll wore a dress of yellow with blue flowers around the border,' Harland said.

'Cornflowers,' Gilbert said, filling in the finer details. 'The doll has brown hair and is possibly wearing white shoes.'

'As pretty as that doll sounds, I can't recall it. We do receive quite a few dolls and teddy bears,' she said with a frown.

'It was Monday last week. We can wait for Mr Crandle if you prefer. He might recall repairing the doll,' Harland said, and she could hear a hint of impatience in his voice as he looked around the shelves to see if he could spot it.

'I will check his workroom. Is there some reason this doll interests you, detectives?'

'Yes. When we see it, we will explain if our assumption is correct,' Harland said. 'Please, Mrs Crandle, we are busy, as are you.'

She gave a curt nod and disappeared behind the curtain into the workroom but hesitated, watching them as both detectives quickly studied the surroundings.

She returned to the room a moment later, announcing, 'I believe it has been returned to its owner after Mr Crandle repaired the doll's neck.'

'I was reliably informed it was donated,' Harland snapped.

Mrs Crandle's surprised look gave her away. She had not expected the heavy hand of the law, but it was just about to come down on her right then and there.

Detective Harland Stone did not like being played for a fool, and he was a man who could sense an untruth before it was uttered. He took a breath to ward off his anger.

'Is there some reason you are hesitant to discuss this with us, Mrs Crandle?'

He saw her eyes flit to the door and back to him as if she feared her husband's return.

'Sir, we repair many dolls, and often they will come in with cuts and tears inflicted by brothers, rough play, or wear and tear. Many, as you can see,' she said, waving her hand toward the shelves, 'have a similar appearance – why, I have half a dozen with brown hair.'

'I understand,' Harland said. 'We shall wait for your husband then and see if he recalls the doll.'

'Or perhaps we might have a quick look around your workspace and find her ourselves,' Gilbert suggested.

'I think that is better,' Harland said, and ignoring her protests, he asked to be admitted to the area.

'This is highly unconventional, detectives. You are making me feel like a criminal,' she said indignantly.

'Madam, if any danger were to come to you because of our negligence, then we would be remiss in our duties. Your workroom, if you please.'

Mrs Crandle's lips tightened, and she moved the curtain aside, admitting them. The doll was not on display, but Harland imagined she had quickly hidden it, and as Gilbert looked on the shelves under the workbench, Harland opened a large cupboard. Her protest told him he was right.

'Ah, this is the doll in question,' he said, pulling a large doll off the shelf. 'It appears no work has been done on her yet.'

'My husband has a backlog and is very busy,' she said.

Harland placed the doll on the workbench. It was, as he expected, an imitation of the unidentified lady, as Miss Astin had said.

'The red ribbon, Sir,' Gilbert said under his breath, and Harland nodded at the tightness and location around the neck.

'Did a note accompany the doll, Mrs Crandle?' Harland asked.

She shook her head in the negative, and again, he did not believe her.

'It is not in your best interest to hinder a police investigation, Mrs Crandle.'

She became most indignant. 'How is the donation of a doll a police investigation, I ask you, Sir? I would expect to see you here daily if that were the case.'

'May I ask what was your profession, Mrs Crandle, before the doll hospital?' Gilbert attempted to keep the peace.

'Why, I have been here for as long as I can remember,' she said, and again, Harland felt she was side-stepping the truth.

'Mrs Crandle, you will tell us if you feel threatened, won't you? We can increase patrols in this area. I am guessing you live above the shop,' Harland said, glancing at a staircase that led upstairs.

'Yes. But that won't be necessary, thank you, Detective. A doll and bear hospital is not of great interest to criminals, and we have had no trouble before.'

'Yet,' Harland said, prepared to lay down his cards to gauge her reaction. 'It is odd, is it not, that this doll should be dressed in the same manner as a young lady found murdered recently?'

Mrs Crandle gasped. 'Oh, that is ghastly! Was she strangled with a red ribbon?'

'No, but it was made to look so,' Gilbert said. 'You have no idea who might have dropped this into your shop or its significance?'

She shook her head most vehemently. 'I cannot imagine unless the person who harmed that young lady felt guilty and returned her doll for repair. Was it her doll?'

'We do not know that as yet,' Harland said. 'May we take this?'

She nodded. 'I shall wrap her in paper for you.'

'Would you have the packaging the doll arrived in?' Harland asked.

'I am sorry, Detective, but no. It was discarded.'

They waited while Mrs Crandle wrapped the doll, and thanking her, departed, Gilbert carrying the bundle under his arm.

'What do you make of that, Gilbert?' Harland asked as they walked back to the station.

'I think she would be a terrible poker player, Sir,' Gilbert answered, and Harland chuckled.

'Agreed.'

'I think she is hiding a secret and is frightened to speak of it.'

Harland mused about his partner's thoughts. 'Yes, and I suspect her husband may not know her fears. I know extra patrols were increased in that area a month ago at the behest of the inspector. There had been a few break-ins, and the wealthier shop owners protested directly to him. It might benefit us to chat with the constable on that beat to see if he has had any trouble or sightings of interest to us in the last few weeks. Let's see what we might unearth.'

The detectives were halfway down the hallway to their office in the Roma Street Police Headquarters when John, the desk sergeant, waved them down.

'Detectives, I believe your unidentified lady has been identified,' he pronounced, waving a note at them.

Harland reached him in a few quick strides. 'I hope you have not been inundated on our behalf.'

'No, surprisingly. A few offerings, but this is the only firm identification we received,' the sergeant said, handing over the note.

'Thank you, Sergeant. Can you send the constable on the city night beat to see me when he is next in the office? Specifically, in the Elizabeth Street precinct. As soon as convenient would be good, with his notebook.'

'I shall indeed, detective.'

Not opening the note, Harland waited until they entered their office, and taking off his hat, he unfolded the scrap of paper.

'Well, this is interesting,' he said, reading the note and turning his attention to Gilbert. 'It appears the matron from the Goodna Asylum for the Insane can identify our young lady as Miss Jane Dellow, a patient who never returned when taken out on a day trip by her brother, James. Fortunately, she has left us an address for James.'

'I wonder if they are twins, Sir, Jane and James. I believe it is common for parents to alliterate with twin names.'

'We shall soon find out. Let's hope the address is up to date, and we find the brother in residence.'

'Why would he dump his sister's body at the miniature display... if he indeed he did,' Gilbert mused.

'It is an act of defiance, but against whom... his sister, authority, an enemy, or maybe the asylum?' Harland suggested. 'I want to go via the coroner's office first and take the doll with us to compare with the lady we now know as Miss Jane Dellow. Let's see if the doll is a message of sorts or if it is just a strange coincidence.'

'Sir, while you do so, and now that we have a name, shall I see if the parents of Jane and James Dellow are still alive and if Mrs Elizabeth Liddle, the mother of the deceased twins, is still with us? I can also see if we have any information in our records about the brother, James.'

'Good idea, Gilbert, thank you. I shall return for you after I visit Dr McGregor.'

Grabbing the wrapped doll, Harland departed, walking to the nearby coroner's office and going over all aspects of what they had to date in his head, which was very little. He was pleased to find Tavish in attendance.

'I prefer my gifts in a bottle,' Dr Tavish McGregor said in his Scottish brogue, looking hairier than usual as if a shave and haircut had eluded him. He eyed the package in the detective's hand.

Harland chuckled. 'I'll remember that.' He shifted the wrapped parcel to his other side. 'I hoped to see the unidentified lady, who, mind you, is now identified. We believe she is Miss Jane Dellow of the asylum. Next of kin is a brother, James.'

'Ah, well, that's good if there is kin. She needs to be buried and very soon,' Tavish said. 'We are coming up to a week now, and without embalming...' his voice trailed off.

'We are looking in on her family today; Gilbert is on the job.' Harland started unwrapping the package under his arm, revealing the doll. 'I had hoped to compare the victim with the doll.'

'I have seen stress affect men in different ways, but never have I seen a detective driven to doll collecting.'

Harland gave the coroner a wry look that caused Tavish to erupt in laughter as he pulled the lady from her storage cabin and revealed her. Sobering, he said, 'Well, look at that.'

'Yes, it appears to be a match. This doll was left at *The Doll and Teddy Hospital* anonymously on the morning when the body of Miss Dellow was found.'

'A deathly doll,' Tavish said.

'Why would you say that?'

'Well, did it warn of a death to come, or did it warn there were more to follow? Or perhaps it blames the owners of the doll or the store owners for the death.'

Harland thought about this for a moment. 'The doll was left anonymously, so there is little hope of tracing the owner without a witness. Miss Astin was in the store at the time and did not see who left it on the doorstep, nor did the store owner.'

'Ah, the lovely Miss Astin. She did a fine job on that illustration.'

'Indeed,' Harland agreed. 'But thank you for your musing, Tavish; all insights are welcome. Gilbert and I believe the shop owner, Mrs Crandle, knows more than she is saying.'

'Is she frightened?'

'Hard to tell with all the bluff and bravado she displays.' Harland frowned as he re-wrapped the doll.

'What are you pondering?' Tavish asked.

'Your words – the deathly doll. I am wondering if there is more than one, doll that is.' He could not mention Miss Astin had told him that Nurse Charlotte Faithful had seen a music box and a doll outside her home the night of her death. Where was that doll?

'Funny you should mention that. A doll was brought in recently.' Tavish tapped his chin while he thought. 'It was found next to a victim, retrieved, and added to the personal goods box. It is most likely collected by the family by now.' Tavish's eyes narrowed as he thought. 'It will come to me who the victim was, and it was not a child. I have had no young ones this week thus far.'

'Was it Charlotte Faithful, the nurse, a mature lady who had the heart condition?'

'I believe that is the one.' Tavish said, looking relieved. 'You asked about her last visit, did you not?'

Harland nodded. 'So, that doll found by her side is definitely not here?'

Tavish shook his head. 'No, I'm sorry to say. The nurse has been buried, and the personal goods were collected when the body was retrieved.'

Harland gave a huff of impatience. 'I recently saw Nurse Faithful's brother and secured her midwife records. I imagine he has disposed of the doll, but I shall try there, just in case. Tavish, thank you.'

'Always a pleasure to see the living,' he said in jest. 'Ah, wait up.'

Harland moved to the door as Tavish returned to his desk and waved a card at him.

'Did you get invited? I imagine you did, as it is from the very same ladies who organised the table at the hospital ball – the *Vexed Vixens*. I hope I have the chance to vex them all!' he grinned, making Harland chuckle.

'I have been invited verbally, as has Gilbert, but we have not received our formal invitations as yet.'

'The lovely reporter, Miss Lilly Lewis, will be there,' Tavish said with a tip of the invitation and a wink. 'I shall look my best.'

Harland smiled and shook his head. 'I fear you have lost her to Bennet. You may have to accept the fact.'

'That rogue,' Tavish said in jest. 'How can that be? I need to see the evidence for myself.'

'It is unbelievable, I know,' Harland played along. 'Right then, I shall send word on the collection of Miss Jane Dellow for burial as soon as possible if you are ready to release her?'

'Thank you, my friend. She is all yours.'

With that, Harland hurried back to the office, hoping to visit James Dellow and revisit the brother of Nurse Faithful.

Chapter 19

Detective Gilbert Payne was sitting forward in his chair, making notes and referring to a file beside him.

'A young lady to see you, Detective,' Sergeant John announced with a quick rap on the timber office door. The sergeant departed, tipping his hat to the young lady.

Gilbert could not get to his feet quickly enough, astonishment registering on his face. It took him a moment to speak.

'Miss Yalden. This is an unexpected pleasure,' he said, gathering himself and running a hand down his jacket to ensure he was respectable. Before him was the woman who had been in his thoughts a great deal of late, most often last thing at night and first thing in the morning.

The charming and attractive Miss Emily Yalden—Phoebe's dear friend—flushed at the sight of him, but of course, she knew what to do; Emily was, after all, the proprietor of *The Emily Yalden School of Deportment*.

They were as neat and respectable as each other. Gilbert pressed and polished to within an inch of his life, and Emily's dark hair was respectably pinned back, her dress a picture of elegance, and her deportment second to none.

'Detective Payne, please forgive this interruption to your day; I imagine you are very busy.'

'Not at all. Well, yes, we have a murder—forgive me—a crime on our hands, but that is always the case.' He stopped talking too fast and took a deep breath. 'It is lovely to see you again, Miss Yalden.' He moved from behind his desk to stand closer as she came in from the doorway.

'And a pleasure to see you, too, Detective.'

'May I offer you a seat or a cup of tea?' he asked. 'We do not produce the best tea here, as you can imagine, but it is sufferable if parched.'

She gave a small laugh. 'As enticing as that sounds, Detective, I will decline, but thank you. I won't hold you up for more than a few minutes. My students are at a debutante rehearsal this morning, so I am taking the opportunity to deliver invitations to a small dinner party I am hosting.'

'Ah, yes, Miss Astin mentioned it to Detective Stone and me.'

'There is no obligation to attend,' she hurried on.

'I can think of nothing that would give me more pleasure,' Gilbert said with no self-consciousness or restraint. Given that he was training himself to reflect before speaking, as requested by his superior, that lesson left his mind at the sight of Miss Yalden.

Emily was smiling at him before she remembered herself. 'Ah, yes, so please do accept these two invitations – if you would be so kind as to give Detective Stone his as well. I will understand if you must decline with work or other commitments.' She handed him two small envelopes, their fingers not touching as appropriate.

'I assure you, Miss Yalden, the city's best criminals will not keep me away.'

Emily laughed. 'I look forward to seeing you then, Detective.'

'Allow me to walk you out.'

She nodded her thanks, and as Detective Gilbert Payne escorted Miss Emily Yalden down the hurried hallways of the police headquarters, he had never felt so passionately in love or such a need to protect a lady as he did in those few moments. It was a new sensation that he found most satisfactory.

One hour later, barely recovered from the unexpected shock and pleasure of seeing the woman he most admired at his place of employment, Detective Gilbert Payne was en route to the postmaster's office with his superior, Harland Stone. He relayed the bad news – Jane and James Dellow's parents were deceased. And the good news – that Mrs Elizabeth Liddle was very much alive.

Arriving at the postmaster's office, the visit to Nurse Charlotte Faithful's brother proved fruitful.

'Ah, yes, Detectives, I have kept the doll. Most odd your enquiry though,' Samuel Faithful said, as he went to a cupboard behind his desk and, selecting a key that hung from a chain on his waistcoat, opened it.

Harland breathed a sigh of relief. 'Excellent, thank you, Mr Faithful. It may seem an odd request, but we are undertaking a line of investigation whereby several citizens have been harassed or frightened—'

'But why would my sister be harassed?' Samuel interrupted Harland to ask as he hesitated in front of a cupboard filled with an odd assortment of items most likely lost in the post.

'That is the question we want answered, Mr Faithful,' Gilbert said.

The older postmaster regarded them both briefly before returning his attention to the cupboard and finding the doll. He placed it on the desk in front.

Before them lay a doll with brown hair, a red ribbon around its neck, and wearing a yellow dress with blue cornflowers around the hemline. Small white slippers were on the doll's feet. Gilbert shuffled from foot to foot, and Harland gave him a small shake of his head, reminding his protégé that his body actions were as readable as his mind for some people. Gilbert stilled.

'I was going to send it to my cousin, who has a little girl,' Samuel Faithful added.

'We shall endeavour to return it to you, but can we take it for now?' Harland asked.

'Of course.'

'Perhaps you might wrap it?' Harland asked, indicating the roll of brown paper in the corner.

Samuel laughed. 'Yes, I imagine the sight of two well-dressed gentlemen with a doll might raise some eyebrows.' He took the doll and tore some brown paper off the roll, hurriedly wrapping it and securing it with string.

'Thank you, Mr Faithful, you have been most helpful again. I assure you we will update you when we have consolidated our line of enquiry,' Harland said, accepting the doll. They departed to visit James, the brother of the deceased Miss Jane Dellow. Once far enough away from the postmaster's hearing, Gilbert exhaled.

'Sorry, Sir.'

'Not at all. You did not say anything, but some signs give away our reaction. Now, there is no doubt we have a connection between the cases – the doll found beside the deceased Nurse Faithful is identical to the one deposited at the doll hospital and replicated in the dress Jane Dellow wore. Fascinating,' Harland said, his voice betraying his enthusiasm.

Gilbert agreed enthusiastically. 'And we might never have made the connection had it not been for Miss Astin,' Gilbert added as they hailed a hansom.

'There is no chance we would have unless Nurse Faithful's brother had claimed she was being threatened. The deathly dolls are our only connection.'

Gilbert gasped. 'The deathly dolls! That is very good, Sir, and sounds terribly sinister.'

'I cannot take credit for it. Tavish—Dr McGregor—used the term,' he said, stepping into the hansom and shuffling over as Gilbert entered.

'Miss Lewis would love that angle, Sir.'

Harland groaned, as he often did at the mention of the ambitious reporter. As they travelled silently, preparing for their interview with the deceased young woman's brother, Harland eventually said, 'Perhaps, Gilbert, it might be a good idea to give the doll story to Miss Lewis. We might flush out someone else who is being harassed.' Then he shook his head. 'But then again, we might create a panic, and dolls would appear all over town with deformed faces and sinister intent. We would never hear the end of it.'

'I imagine you are right, Sir. Some people do love the macabre. But someone must have seen the dolls delivered or prepared. Or perhaps someone sells that doll, and there are more with yellow dresses and blue cornflowers,' Gilbert said.

'Or could they be two of the original dolls that the *Storks* gifted to families? I shall see if Miss Astin can ask Nurse Faithful to describe the doll if the chance arises.' They rode silently for a short time before Harland suggested, 'Perhaps you might discuss it with Miss Lewis and promise her the deathly dolls story once we have our killer in hand, but see what might be done to flush out witnesses without terrifying the city, children especially.'

Gilbert was pleased with the responsibility placed on him. 'I shall follow it through after we visit Mr Dellow.'

'Excellent,' Harland said. 'When did the parents of James and Jane Dellow pass away?'

'Some five years back now, Sir. Natural causes.'

As the hansom pulled up at a respectable townhouse in Milton, and a young male could be seen entering via the gate, Harland said, 'That is most likely the man in question.'

'He has the same colouring as Miss Dellow; perhaps they are twins, but I would say definitely siblings.'

'And I suspect this house has been left to them by their parents.' Harland alighted and paid the driver. 'Let's get to the bottom of this, Gilbert.' He strode towards the townhouse with renewed purpose. 'I have a report to file to the inspector, who is impatient for an update.'

Gilbert hurried to catch up. Nothing could dampen his mood after the visit by Miss Yalden, not even a case with many balls in the air.

Julius felt his brother's stare and glanced at Ambrose as they sat on the bench seat of the hearse, driving slowly despite the fact they were alone with the corpse and no mourners followed.

'Is something amiss?'

'Not at all,' Ambrose said. 'I am imagining you married, coming to work daily with a lunch packed by your lovely wife, wearing a shirt made by her, and maybe—oh, the joy—sporting baby food stains on your suit. Imagine!'

Julius gave him a dry look. 'Fortunately, the occasion restrains me from laughing.' Ambrose quietly chuckled.

'Will you be my best man, brother?'

Ambrose groaned. 'Now I feel terrible for making fun of you,' he grumbled.

Julius flashed him a quick smile, the most he dared under the circumstances and most out of character amid a funeral procession. 'Will you?'

'Of course. I would be proud to stand with you. And after all, I am the best man for the job.' He nudged his brother in jest. 'No one knows all of your annoying habits nor tolerates them as I do.'

'A blessing I am thankful for every day.'

They sobered at the sight of half a dozen mourners at the gates to the South Brisbane cemetery, ready to follow the mourning coach to the final resting place.

Today's funeral was different from most. The mourners were not known to the deceased, the Police Magistrate had been called upon to pay for the burial expenses of the destitute middle-aged man, and it would not be the first funeral where the priest and the Astin brothers were the only people in attendance had it not been for the local church ladies. In return for a small donation to the local parish, the ladies of the church committee who were available on the day would attend the funeral in black mourning dresses to see the soul off to the next life with humanity.

Julius greeted and thanked the committee ladies for their compassion as they affectionately responded to the Astin brothers, even congratulating Julius on his heroics and engagement. Underway again, the small party walked behind the mourning coach, arriving at the gravesite in moments. Julius stopped the hearse, and the brothers dismounted. There was no family to act as coffin bearers, so the Astin men and two gravediggers—who were on hand to fill in the burial plot—assisted. Julius was pleased to see Father Morris in attendance.

'No kin?' Father Morris asked Julius.

'Sadly, no.'

'I'll keep the prayers brief then and send him off with the bare necessities to get into heaven,' Father Morris said with a wink.

'I wish you would do that every time,' Julius said in jest as they had officiated over a dozen funerals together.

Father Morris chuckled as they settled the coffin for the prayers. 'I hear congratulations are in order. Do let me know if you need a priest. It would be my honour.'

'Thank you, Father,' Julius said sincerely and stood back as the ladies gathered near and Father gave his blessing.

'Eternal rest grant unto him, O Lord...'

And in that moment of death, Julius turned his mind to the next chapter of his life.

Chapter 20

DETECTIVE HARLAND STONE'S EYES narrowed as he studied the young man before him, concluding that if he were acting, he was very good at it.

'I returned Jane to the asylum after our outing,' he said, looking up from the chair he had dropped into in shock when the detectives told of his sister's death. 'How did this happen? How could she be at that miniature show in the Botanic Gardens? It is impossible.'

Gilbert nodded sympathetically. 'That is what we are trying to find out, Sir, for your and Miss Dellow's sake.'

'Why didn't the asylum send me a telegram to say she was missing?' he said, throwing his hands up. 'Sorry, please sit if you wish to. I should offer you a drink.'

'No need to, thank you, Mr Dellow,' Harland said, and the detectives sat opposite on the couch.

'You did not see the illustration of your sister and the request for identification that we ran in *The Courier*?' Harland asked.

'No. I don't read the newspaper. I work the night shift at the Grand Hotel and sleep most of the day when I get home. I didn't know she was missing, so didn't know she needed identifying.'

'How often did you see your sister?' Harland continued his questioning.

'Once a week, every Sunday. I collected her from the asylum, and we went on an outing.' James Dellow hesitated and then, in a choked voice, added, 'I loved my sister, Detectives. Of our family connections, we are all that are left in the world. Just the two of us.'

'I am very sorry, Mr Dellow; it is dreadful to lose your siblings. Were you twins?' Harland asked.

'Yes, and very close, even when she had to be committed.'

'Can you tell me about your life... your childhood? For example, were you the only two children, and please explain why your sister was in the asylum facility?' Harland asked.

James nodded and, taking a deep breath, told of his family. Gilbert jotted down the salient points.

'Yes, we were the only children. Our mother could not have more, which saddened her, but she always said we were a blessing from heaven. As for our father, he was very strict, and it is fair to say Jane and I were frightened of him, as was our mother. He would go away on business—he worked in sales—and for those brief weeks, we breathed.' James's lips thinned and his jaw tightened, recalling his father. 'I am not ashamed to say I wished him dead. I hoped one day he would have an accident on his trip and never return, but evil people always live on. It's the gentle souls that suffer.'

'That is often the truth, Mr Dellow,' Gilbert said sympathetically.

'He drove my mother to an early grave; she was weak and did not survive the smallpox outbreak... or perhaps she lost the will to live under his iron rule. He caught smallpox too and died not long after Ma. I wish he'd suffered more. I imagine my heartlessness shocks you both.' James looked from Harland to Gilbert for a reaction.

'We both understand what cruelty can drive a man to do and feel,' Harland assured him.

'Yes, I suppose you have seen the worst of mankind in your work,' James said.

'Your sister did not catch the disease?' Gilbert asked, bringing James back to the story of his family life.

'No, but only because she was in the asylum, and we did not allow her to come home when Ma was ill. Despite how much Ma called for her in her last days, Jane never got to say goodbye. It was safer that way.'

'Pray tell what brought on your sister's confinement?' Harland asked.

'My father, it was his doing. My sister was all nerves, and at his threat to marry her to a man who could ensure her spiritual education continued, a man twice her age, Jane collapsed. She could not speak in our father's presence and shook violently. The asylum, oddly, was preferable.'

'And on the Sunday just past, you collected her and returned Miss Dellow in the usual manner?' Gilbert clarified.

'Yes, I signed the book to say she had returned, and I watched her enter. She turned and waved to me.'

'Was an orderly or nurse in attendance to oversee her return?' Harland asked.

'Normally, that would be the case, but as Jane is no threat to herself or anyone else, I often just return her, and she enters of her own free will.'

'And you have no idea how your sister might have left the asylum, or with whom, and ended up at the miniature display?' Gilbert asked.

James shook his head. 'I cannot imagine.'

'Did she not want to come live with you once your father had passed?' Gilbert asked.

'My sister felt safe where she was, in a familiar routine.'

'You knew of her illness, Mr Dellow?' Harland asked.

'Yes. Tuberculosis. But yet, I didn't catch it from her; we had been together many times before her diagnosis. She was very tired and weak, so we had curbed our outings to little more than taking tea and being in each other's company. The asylum doctor did not want me to take her out,' he added as if admitting the doctor was right and he should not have done so.

'You know of no other visitors your sister might have received?' Gilbert asked.

'No one. My sister was nervous and unsocial. There is no one alive who would call on her.'

'Might she have a friendship that you did not know about? Something she kept private?' Harland pushed.

James vehemently shook his head in the negative. 'We are twins, were twins. Our lives are entwined. There is no one.'

Harland waited a beat, but the young man added nothing further.

'Miss Dellow was found dressed in a manner as if in a pantomime—'

'What do you mean?' James cut Harland off, and Gilbert explained with care about the make-up and doll-like dress.

'Is it not enough she is dead without being mocked?' he said, his voice choking.

'Thank you, Mr Dellow. Do you have someone who you might lean on?' Harland asked.

He nodded. 'I shall go to friends.'

'Please let us know if you think of anything.'

'I will. Can I collect Jane for burial?' His voice faltered, and James cleared his throat.

'Yes, now that she has been identified. I shall let the coroner know you will collect the body,' Harland said.

'This will be the third burial I have organised for my family.'

'I imagine burying your father was bittersweet,' Gilbert said.

James nodded. 'I used *The Economic Undertaker* and chose their cheapest package.' He huffed, amusing himself. 'I heard the cheapest package was the one the hospitals, churches, and the police selected for the deceased with no kin or who are unclaimed. It was too good for him.'

The men excused themselves, and Harland asked James Dellow to not leave town until the investigation was complete, lest he was thinking of leaving. As they walked up the street to hail a hansom, Harland asked, 'Your impressions, Gilbert?'

His protégé thought momentarily and answered, 'Even though Miss Dellow died of natural causes, I can't help but think her brother is not telling us something. He is an embittered man.'

'My thoughts exactly, but I found his reactions convincing, especially to the manner of dress in which his sister was found.'

'Just a thought, Sir, but a boy growing up with a violent father has most likely learned to hide many truths and to act as necessary to please.'

'Yes, I imagine skilfully with years of practice. I wonder if his bitterness extends to Mrs Crandle or Nurse Charlotte Faithful.'

Reporter Lilly Lewis entered the newsroom and fell into her chair, throwing her notebook on the desk.

'A detective was asking for you at the front desk, Lilly. What have you done?' Ted, one of the senior reporters, joked.

'A detective! He may be my source,' Lilly said hurriedly, rising.

'Too late, you missed him by about ten minutes,' Ted said. 'His name was Pain.'

'Detective Gilbert Payne! I shall head to the police station. Thank you, Ted,' Lilly said as everyone in the newsroom was on a first-name basis, and she would not be treated differently from the men. She scribbled a note to Fergus advising of her destination and moments later was rushing up the stairs, not caring for her state of neatness, but only for the story.

On arriving at the roadside, she raised her hand to call forth a hansom; one pulled up, and Bennet Martin leaned out.

'I was coming to see you about my research. Are you off somewhere?'

'Yes, to see the detectives, they have an angle.'

He jumped down. 'Allow me. We shall go together if no objections?'

'None whatsoever. Most timely you are.'

He offered his hand, and Lilly accepted it, levering herself into the hansom while instructing the driver, 'To the Roma Street Police Headquarters, please.'

Bennet jumped in beside her.

'Have you discovered something of interest, Mr Martin?'

'I am very well, thank you, and yourself?' Bennet teased, and Lilly could not help but laugh.

'Forgive me. I can be singularly focused on a story with a deadline, which always seems to be my state of late.'

'I admire that very much,' Bennet said.

'Do you?' Lilly asked, surprised.

'Absolutely. When I am painting, I wish for no interruptions. In fact, I don't even hear or see that going on around me without some prompting, usually from my annoying clerk, Daniel.'

'A very patient clerk, I imagine.'

'He is excellent, and I could not do without him, but do not tell him I said that. He already believes he is indispensable and thus gets away with murder,' Bennet said in jest. 'What have you got, or are you racing to see the detectives to curry up a story?'

'Detective Payne dropped in less than a quarter of an hour ago to see me, and I missed him. So, they must have an angle they want me to promote. Very exciting. What are you currently painting?' Lilly asked, doing her best not to be too work-focused.

'Well, if you must know...'

'I must.'

Bennet grinned. 'You.'

'Me!' Lilly looked at him, actually looked at Bennet Martin. Until now, her mind had been racing over the story while she was half present – enough to carry a conversation.

'Really? A portrait without me sitting?'

'Yes, I'm quite good at remembering details. It is why my father wanted me to follow in his footsteps and become a detective.'

She suddenly became more aware of her appearance.

'Goodness. It has been hours since I consulted a looking glass, and I have been rushing around like a charwoman. Given you only see me during my working hours, the portrait is bound to look somewhat bedraggled,' she said.

Bennet laughed. 'I beg to differ. You look flushed, excited, alive!'

She mused on his words before asking, 'I am very flattered, but why? That is, why am I your subject?'

'Because you are enchanting, Miss Lewis. I thought I would challenge myself to see if I could capture that on canvas. Relaying one's personality with the hint of a smile or the tilt of an eyebrow is most difficult,' Bennet said.

Lilly frowned. 'I wonder, do you paint every young lady who crosses your path.'

'Wonder all you wish, but I will tell you the answer is no. I have painted Miss Astin, but you are my new muse.'

'Goodness, I never thought I would be someone's muse. That is exciting.' Lilly glanced out as they drew up beside the police station. 'You are very honest, Mr Martin.'

'Is that refreshing or confronting?'

'A little of both.'

He laughed at that, adding, 'I shall pay the driver or rather my client will,' he said, leaping from the hansom and offering her his hand for dismounting. Despite her impatience, Lilly waited long enough for Bennet to settle with the driver, and they hurried into the station together. The afternoon was pressing upon them, and the evening paper deadline was looming.

Chapter 21

Miss Kate Kirby had a two o'clock appointment with her client, *The Economic Undertaker*, to deliver the photographs she had taken of the front of house with staff, and of the dressmaking store and ladies next door. She hoped they would be happy with the result and felt confident in her work. The photographs, framed, were lovely and dignified, and as for her appearance today, Kate had spent some time on her preparation to her mother's great delight. She was wearing a pale lime dress that was particularly flattering but not too revealing given Mr Astin senior and Mrs Dobbs would be in attendance. The colour was most becoming with her auburn hair, which her mother had put up with small braids that highlighted Kate's cheekbones. The final touch was a light dab of lilac fragrance that did not detract from the fact that she was a professional photographer, and that was the purpose of the visit.

Despite the many photographs Kate had taken, it always amazed her to see people she knew in the images, captured forever. In the top drawer of her desk was the image she had taken with Ambrose recently when they were both being silly – Kate wearing a top hat and Ambrose holding an umbrella over her that he had secured from the props' cupboard. Truth be told, she pulled that drawer out and looked at the image regularly; sometimes, she even touched his face. It would be on display, but she did not want to encourage people to think her business was frivolous.

Kate looked at the last photograph before sealing it in brown paper. The horse-drawn mourning carriage looked dignified in the centre of the image, with Ambrose seated holding the reins. My, he was handsome; she mused. It was appropriate for a business image, and she hoped the viewer would be drawn to the centre and the sign above the business first and foremost. In the front doorway was Mr Randolph Astin looking resplendent. Next to him was the eldest Astin brother and business owner, Julius. To Julius's right stood beautiful Phoebe, her presence gracing the image. Another shot featured all the staff, including Mrs Dobbs and Will, Claude and Charlie from the stables, all polished and buffed in suits and hats. She glanced at the large grandfather clock in the corner, hurriedly wrapped the image, and tied it with string.

With one last check of her appearance—ridiculous fussing, she scolded herself—Kate took the stairs, carefully carrying the photographs to a waiting hansom cab and gave the driver the address. Seated, she fussed once more over her appearance. It was not so much the client that was making her nervous, but one gentleman in particular – Ambrose Astin. Long had she read of love and romance and dreamed and hoped for it, but she felt this was different. It was not the crushes experienced in the years following her debut, but something more intense. More frightening in its possibility of heartache, and at twenty-two, she wanted to know real love.

That dreadful debutante had rudely remarked on her auburn hair, and Kate knew she wasn't a striking beauty, but her father, not given to flattery, said she had a well-constructed face, and her mother claimed her to be lively of nature. Surely, that must hold some appeal to a gentleman. Then a thought occurred to Kate: what if Ambrose Astin was off burying someone? She would be most cranky. Calming the restlessness rising in her, Kate took a deep breath, put her chin up and smiled.

'It is a business meeting,' she reminded herself, 'and you will do well to remember that, Kate Kirby.'

The hansom arrived at *The Economic Undertaker*, and her concern for the acceptance of her photographs took precedence over her romantic notions.

Pulling up out front, the driver peered down. 'Are you sure this is where you want to be, love?' he asked, concerned that she looked very much alive and not in mourning.

'It is indeed, thank you kindly.'

The door to *The Economic Undertaker* opened, and Ambrose Astin presented himself to assist as if he had been waiting inside for her arrival at the prescribed hour.

'Miss Kirby, you are looking particularly becoming today. May I be of assistance?' he hurriedly paid the driver before Kate could fetch the amount owning and offered his hand to assist her.

'Why, thank you, Mr Astin. May I say you are looking particularly dapper yourself?'

'You may,' Ambrose said with a smile, making her laugh. They looked at each other for a moment before Ambrose added, 'What can I carry, Kate?'

Kate took the larger framed and wrapped photographs from the seat and carefully handed them to him. She picked up a couple of smaller framed images that remained. Thanking the driver, they moved to the store, where Randolph Astin held the door open.

'Good afternoon, Mr Astin,' Kate greeted the senior Astin. 'I hope you will be happy with the photographs.'

'Miss Kirby, good day to you. I have no doubt we will be delighted,' he said with the Astin charm she believed ran in the family; although it was often harder to see in the eldest Astin but his manners were always impeccable.

Ambrose led Kate to the large meeting room and placed the images he held down on the table. Behind them, Phoebe and Julius entered, and greetings were exchanged.

'Of course, if you are not happy, I will re-do the photographs at no charge, Mr Astin,' Kate said, offering her usual terms and conditions to Julius, who insisted it was time he called her by his Christian name and she reciprocated.

As she unwrapped each image, their exclamations of delight and wonder put her fears to rest.

'These are wonderful, Kate,' Julius said, moving from image to image and studying each in depth.

'Oh, Kate, how marvellous,' Phoebe said. 'I love them. Is it not peculiar to see ourselves like this?'

'I am much more handsome than I thought,' Ambrose said in jest, enjoying the reaction from his family and Kate's laugh.

She watched Julius as he studied the photograph of the ladies in their dressmaking store and saw the slight smile ghost his lips at the sight of Violet. Kate exhaled with relief.

'I shall leave you with the photographs then and to your work.'

'Kate,' Julius began, and her breath hitched, wondering if he had found something not to his liking. 'Could I commission you to do a wedding portrait of Violet and me?'

Kate clapped her hands together. 'Oh, I would be delighted to do so; thank you, Julius.'

'What a great idea,' Ambrose said, beaming at his brother and hitting him on the back.

'Your grandmother and I would love to purchase that photograph, too,' Randolph said.

'My clever friend,' Phoebe teased.

'Now, may I walk you back, or do you have something pressing this afternoon?' Ambrose asked. 'I am not in demand, as unusual as that is.'

Kate laughed at Julius's roll of his eyes, Phoebe shook her head, and Randolph sighed.

'Now that I am much lighter, having deposited my photographs here, I am at leisure for the rest of the afternoon and would welcome the escort,' Kate said.

'That is decided then,' Randolph said. 'Miss Kirby, our sincere thanks. Please provide me with your invoice and take my restless grandson away with you,' he joked. 'He has been watching the clock for hours.'

Ambrose groaned, and Kate looked at him with delight.

'I will take the photographs next door to show the ladies,' Julius said, lifting the framed images with the photograph of the dressmaking staff in their place of work on the top. 'I am sure they will be fascinated to see it.'

'I shall see you soon, Kate,' Phoebe said, kissing her cheek.

'Come then, we don't have a moment to waste,' Ambrose said.

'Haven't we?' Kate looked confused.

'No. It is several hours until sundown, and I walk very slowly.' He offered his arm and bade everyone farewell. Kate left with a flush of happiness after an afternoon well spent.

Harland Stone was impressed that Lilly Lewis agreed not to mention that the doll delivered to the doll hospital had an uncanny likeness to the deceased young lady identified as Jane Dellow.

'We do not know how the doll hospital is involved yet, but should you write of it, you will shut down our investigation before it starts,' Harland said. 'I am merely flagging it, so if you should hear it elsewhere, you can alert me, and I will give you the facts before rumours are in earnest.'

'I agree, Detective, but it is a story that will sell many copies of my paper, so I will champ at the bit to write it.'

'Of course. But remember, you would not know about this story if I had not informed you first.' Harland reminded the ambitious reporter. 'I will ensure you get it exclusively.'

'Agreed. And there were two dolls?'

'So far. One was found next to Nurse Faithful's body, and the second we collected from the *Doll and Teddy Hospital* and is in our possession. Will you show Miss Lewis the deathly doll, please, Gilbert?'

'Oh, that is a headline!'

'You will have to thank the coroner for that,' Harland said with a smile.

'Clever, Dr McGregor,' Lilly said. 'I shall have it drafted, ready to release the moment we know enough not to panic the doll-owners of the city!'

Harland nodded, and while Gilbert unwrapped the paper for Lilly to view the doll, Harland turned to the private investigator. 'Did you have something of value that might help us, Bennet?' He paced his office as he often did when thinking.

'Yes, and no. I requested from my client data for historic payouts on the southside only, in the five years you claimed Nurse Charlotte Faithful and the Storks did their work. There appear to be fifteen claims with matching birth and death dates, give a day or two,' Bennet Martin told them of his findings.

'But they cannot reclaim the funds, surely?' Lilly asked. 'It was decades ago, and the claimants most likely did not know that their child lived and had been swapped.'

'That is the dilemma,' Bennet agreed. 'My client is of the mind that they will have to write them off as bad debts. Thus, for now, he wants me to focus on the recent cases while he meets with the board to discuss what to do.'

'So you are, in effect, off our case?' Harland asked.

'Unless you can use my services to investigate for the purposes of prosecuting a historic crime?'

Harland considered this for a moment. 'Most interesting and very possible. Let us see what else we uncover, and then if Nurse Faithful's colleagues are still alive and can be charged, there may be grounds for your appointment, thank you, Bennet. But if we are to believe Nurse Faithful, and she has no reason to lie now, then no fee was paid, so it is not technically baby farming. However, there were false insurance claims.'

'And what a terrible scenario to think that more than fifteen children were removed from their rightful parents and brought up by other families, all none the wiser,' Lilly said, jotting down notes.

'If we believe Nurse Faithful, then both parties were unaware of the swap,' Gilbert said, 'and it might have benefitted the children sometimes, but not always.'

'Why do you say that, Detective Payne? Have you discovered something?' Lilly pushed.

'No, but Detective Stone and I met with James, Miss Jane Dellow's brother, today,' Gilbert said. 'Mr Dellow said they had a terrible childhood; their father was strict. So, I had been musing that the children might not always go to a better home. They may not have grown up in poverty but ended up in a strict or unloving home.'

'Very true. So, you are telling me that Jane and James Dellow are two of the placed children?' Lilly asked enthusiastically.

'Not that we are aware of yet,' Harland said, keeping some of his investigation up his sleeve.

Lilly sighed with disappointment. 'I want that doll story... the deathly dolls,' she said, running her hand through the air as if the words were up in lights.

'Yes, I can see your headline,' Harland said with a small smile. 'It will come, I assure you. Tomorrow, Gilbert and I will visit the asylum where the young lady was a patient and see what comes to light.'

'Oh, that will give me a good angle for the next day. Is it the Goodna Asylum for the Insane? May I come, Detective?'

'It is, and could I stop you?' he asked with a small smile.

'Hopefully not. Shall we say nine o'clock then at the asylum?' With that, she rose. The detectives bid the reporter and private detective good day.

No sooner had Miss Lilly Lewis and Mr Bennet Martin departed than a constable entered the detectives' room, knocking lightly on the ajar door.

'Sir, the sergeant said you wished to speak with me. I'm Constable Jackson; I do the night beat in the city, Alice to Elizabeth Streets, and the cross streets – George and Edward,' the tall, gangly police officer said to Harland. Jackson glanced at Gilbert with a look that could be nothing but disdain. Harland knew those in the lower ranks believed the younger detective should not be where he was, and they did not attempt to hide their dislike for the favoured ones.

'Ah, thank you, Constable Jackson. We believe a crime was committed and hoped you might have seen and noted something on your beat. Gilbert, was that last Monday?'

'Last Tuesday evening, Sir, close to midnight,' Gilbert said, 'at *the Doll and Teddy Hospital* in Elizabeth Street.'

'There's often people hanging around the city at odd hours, Detective Stone, but I didn't hear of that location being disturbed.'

'Could you consult your notebook for that evening and let me know what you might have observed then and on the day prior?'

Jackson nodded, retrieved his notebook from his pocket, opened it, and thumbed through the pages until he found the days in question.

'Well, Sir, I saw two young men dressed in dark clothing walking down Elizabeth Street around 11pm the night prior, the Monday, but nothing came of it. I had several drunk men I moved along that same night. There was a bit of a rowdy street fight outside the Prince of Wales Hotel on the corner of Edward Street, and we took a few into the watch house to sleep it off.' He flicked the page. 'On the Tuesday you asked about, it was a quiet night. There was a homeless man who had imbibed too much, and there was a loiterer in Elizabeth Street at about 11.30pm, but I moved him along. He was near *your* doll store,' he said directly to Gilbert, making it clear he thought the junior detective weak. Constable Jackson returned his attention to Harland and said, 'The pub was nearby, so I suspect the loiterer had come out of there.'

'I understand you were doing extra patrols around the doll store and business area at the inspector's request?' Harland asked.

'I was, Sir, and still am.'

'Good, thank you. Did you record this loiterer's name?' Harland asked.

'No, Sir, I just asked his business for being in the area.'

'And did he tell you why he was loitering?'

'He said he was strolling, clearing his head, and was happy to move on. I watched him until he reached the end of the street, and then I continued on my beat.' Flicking through the pages, he added, 'That's about it, Sir. The other entries are drunken brawls or homeless vagabonds that I had to get out of doorways.'

'And you've had no complaints of break-ins by any of the store owners in that area?'

'None, Sir, not since we've been doing the extra patrols. Ah, there was one – a few weeks back, the tobacconist's window was broken, but we got the man who did it with his pockets full of smokes.' Jackson looked at Gilbert again; his sneer was more pronounced as if explaining the real work the foot police were doing daily.

'Thank you, Constable. Could you describe the man you saw near the doll store that evening at 11.30pm?' Harland asked.

Constable Jackson referred to his notes again. 'He was tall, with dark hair and a medium frame. Haven't seen him around since.'

'Is that the extent of your notes and recollection of this man?' Harland asked.

'Yes, Sir. As I said, he was happy to move along.'

'You had a suspicious male loitering in the area of interest; that should warrant more detail. Are there any more physical details you can recall about him, Constable? It is important to our case.'

'I only saw him for a few minutes at most, and he didn't appear to be a threat.' The constable shrugged.

Harland turned to Gilbert. 'Detective, would you please stand and turn around?'

Gilbert looked surprised, as if he were being made an example of in front of a junior, and Constable Jackson's smirk said he would enjoy whatever the senior detective had in mind.

Gilbert rose. 'Yes, Sir,' he said, turning his back to the constable and Harland.

'Gilbert, have you met or seen Constable Jackson before?'

'No, Sir. We have not met before this day.'

'Constable Jackson,' Harland continued, 'would you say you were in the man's company in Elizabeth Street for about the same length of time you have been in Detective Payne's company just now?'

'I'd say so, Sir,' Jackson answered, standing taller and pleased to be asked. 'The light is better in here.'

'But you had a conversation with the man in Elizabeth Street?'

'I did, Sir.'

'Gilbert, if you please, from your observations in Constable Jackson's company today, please describe him to me without turning around.'

'Yes, Sir. The constable is approximately five foot ten, of thin build, and gangly. He has dark brown hair, cut short at the sides and longer on top, brown eyes and thick eyebrows. His nose is narrow and angular. He has a crooked front incisor tooth, top row, left, I think, Sir. He is sporting a bruise on his right cheek, and there is a scar on his right hand from the wrist to inside his sleeve. The constable's uniform is well pressed, but his third and fourth buttons are tarnished, his shoes are shined on the top but neglected at the sides of the shoe—'

'That will suffice, thank you, Detective. Please turn again.' Harland looked at Constable Jackson. 'Your observations may have assisted our case if you had recorded a name, address, or even a notable feature. Have you anything further you can add about the man you spoke with that night?'

Constable Jackson looked displeased, as if he were about to remonstrate about the lesson he had just received.

'Constable?' Harland asked again, unimpressed with the junior's attitude. He would never have been disrespectful on the beat in his early days, even if he could have taken on all his superiors and won hands down.

'No, Sir, but it was dark, and we meet types like that every night, all the time. My notebook would be filled with scribblings if I wrote every name and description.'

'But he was neither drunk nor on business, and likely loitering with intent. Was he not?'

'Yes, but he said he was just clearing his head.'

'That is why we ask for notebooks to be kept, as memory does not serve us well. Your notes do you no credit, Constable, and I will be speaking with your superior to understand if this is the standard of work we expect these days. Discipline, Constable Jackson, starts with the uniform and is reflected in your actions. You may return to your beat.'

'Yes, Sir.' Constable Jackson exited hurriedly with a sneer at Gilbert but did not see Harland shake his head in disappointment.

'Well, Gilbert, the man who broke into the doll store could well be James Dellow, but he could be a thousand other men too.' He reached for his jacket on the back of his chair. 'Did he really have a crooked incisor tooth?'

Gilbert smiled. 'Yes, Sir, but the fourth button on his suit wasn't as tarnished as I thought. Thank you, Sir.'

'Every dog has his day, Gilbert. Shall we?' He strode to
the door and lifted his hat from the rack. Gilbert grabbed his
notepad and hat and followed.

Chapter 22

DESPITE NOT WANTING TO tell the police about her fears, Mrs Frances Crandle of *The Doll and Teddy Hospital* was relieved the senior detective had allocated extra patrols in the area of her shop-home in Elizabeth Street. Not even her husband, Frank, knew of what she had done. He believed the *Storks* were a harmless group of ladies taking tea to discuss the babies they brought into the world.

Unbeknown to the other ladies, Frances Crandle had skimmed the cream off some inheritances—an administration fee, she called it—and charged some of the wealthier families double for her services. In the latter years of their marriage, Frances and Frank had spoken of starting a doll and teddy hospital, the idea coming from the wet nurse's husband, George Stockton, who made the dolls and tin soldiers the

Storks gifted. He claimed he was always offered money to repair other people's toys.

Mrs Crandle's husband believed their new business venture had come about with an inheritance from a great aunt, not the stealing of pounds and shillings that the *Storks* did not miss. But now, she feared past crimes were catching up with her.

Even more worrying was the unexpected death of Charlotte Faithful. They had stayed in touch, meeting once a year for a Christmas drink. She wanted to ask Charlotte if anything untoward was happening in her life, but now, it was too late.

Someone was watching her; Frances was sure of it.

'We should be rewarded for our good deeds,' she muttered. 'Saving babies from families that could not feed another mouth and placing them with families who could provide a good life. It was better for everyone.' Nothing would convince her otherwise. But somehow, these threats were related.

'Did you hear me, love?'

Frances jumped, startled, and turned to her husband.

'Sorry, my dear, I was miles away,' she said with a small laugh. 'You are off then?' Frances returned the broom to the closet.

'Yes, the card sharks await,' Mr Crandle joked. 'Do not wait up; I might be late if I'm on a winning streak, and give my best to the craft ladies.'

She chuckled at the thought of her husband and his mature-aged friends in their smoky room playing to win.

'I will be home before you and most likely be reading. You have your key?' Frances asked.

'I do.'

She kissed him goodbye and locked the door behind her husband. Observing the street through the shop's darkened windows, she saw people heading home at the end of their day and nothing untoward. But that did not stop the ill-feeling from rising within her. The feeling that someone was out there, watching.

Frances Crandle took the lamp and, satisfied the shop was clean and secure for business tomorrow, headed upstairs to freshen up. On the nights Mr Crandle played cards, Mrs Crandle joined her craft group. Not a great deal of craft was created, but wine and sweets were enjoyed, and laughter ensued. They met at Betsy's place, a brisk walk to Petrie Terrace that normally took only twenty minutes if Frances chose to walk. Tonight, she did, but she would accept the offer of a ride home later in the evening in one of the ladies' traps.

As the evening progressed, among some of her oldest friends, Frances almost forgot the nagging feeling that her past was catching up with her. She had a brief reprieve from remembering the recurrent nightmares – the dolls crowding her, forcing her into a corner, their eyes accusing, and her own scream frozen as they crushed the air out of her.

Suddenly, a thought occurred to her, and Frances gasped. *Was her good friend Charlotte Faithful murdered?*

'Are you alright, Frannie?' Betsy asked, hurriedly filling the glass of water in front of Frances.

'Yes, sorry, silly me. I just remembered an order that must be delivered tomorrow. I will get Mr Crandle onto it first thing.'

'At least you remembered before it was too late,' Betsy said, and the other ladies nodded.

Now, Frances was impatient to get home and look again at Charlotte Faithful's death notice. Did it say anything that might imply an unnatural or sudden death? The clock was as if it had stopped, and finally, an hour later, Frances Crandle secured a ride and was home, unlocking the door of her shop to enter.

Pausing, all seemed well. It was quiet within; everything was in order. Frances hurried in and locked the door behind her; she was home, safe. There was enough light from the gas streetlight outside the store to allow her to find the matches in the drawer near the cash register and light the lamp. She found Charlotte's death notice by searching through the same drawer.

'Sudden and unexpected death!' she read, her hand going to her throat. *What does that mean? Unexpected!* She threw the notice back in the drawer and slammed it shut.

'Silly, you are being silly, Frances,' she told herself, putting her shoulders back, but the bravado was short-lived.

Taking the lamp, the former midwife, now doll hospital matron, made her way up the stairs, stopping long enough to glance around the room and satisfy herself she was safe. Frances had always enjoyed her time alone, but now she wished Frank was home; she would not sleep until he was beside her.

Undressing, she prepared for bed and was soon comfortable below the covers. Listening again – no, all was quiet, all was well. Frances extinguished the lamp and soon gave in to exhaustion. It felt like she had just closed her eyes when a voice startled her awake.

Did she imagine it?

'Who is there?' Her voice quavered despite her attempt at bravado.

Frances sat bolt upright, her book falling to the floor with a thud and startling her.

'Frank, is that you, dear?'

And then she heard the thinnest of whispers coming from the staircase. 'Frances, Frances, come out to play.'

A cry of fear escaped her lips. 'Go away, whoever you are, go away!'

'Come out to play.'

Then, the figure appeared. It was not so dark that she couldn't see the strange figure at the top of the stairs – a toy soldier. No, a man dressed as a toy soldier, and then he began to march to her bed, laughing at his own actions, a laugh that ended in a growl.

'Go away, go away! Please,' she begged and cried in terror, but before she could utter a scream, he gave her a malevolent grin and covered her mouth.

Frances kicked and fought but was no match for the large man dressed in the toy soldier uniform. His eyes filled with hate for her, and in a low, gravelly voice, he said, 'I know what you did, Frances, we all do,' and his gloved hand remained across her mouth, stifling her scream.

Frances' dream—the dolls, the toys, coming for revenge—had come partially true.

The terror... Frances' heart gave way, and she did not live to see the tin soldier march away.

Chapter 23

ON ARRIVING AT WORK, Violet Forrester's first desire, as it was most days, was to see Julius. She heard the men's voices out the back of the store and, opening the door, glanced out to see her fiancé talking with Ambrose and the stable lads. The men were about to depart for a funeral, and Julius was doing his final checks. Soon, they would come to work together as Mr and Mrs Astin unless she chose not to work, but Violet could not imagine being idle. She was confident Julius would not want her to stop working until she wished to or was with child. The thought excited her. Julius employed his sister after all and was quite modern in his outlook.

Violet watched as he easily stepped into the cab, took the reins, and then glanced her way as if thinking of her. Their eyes met, and she smiled and gave a small wave; his face lit at the sight of her. Ambrose looked to see what had gotten his brother's attention and grinned, offering his own wave. After a moment, Ambrose nudged Julius and tried to take the reins, snapping his brother back to the job at hand. Violet laughed at the brothers' antics as they moved the hearse from the yard.

She closed the door and returned to her sewing desk, where her two staff were already working. Mrs Shaw measured their first client of the day for a mourning dress, and Mary cut fabric.

They worked in companionable silence for a while, just the sound of Nellie Shaw's sympathetic tone and the bereaved's voice speaking softly in the background.

'Miss,' Mary whispered.

'Yes, Mary?' Violet looked up at the young lady seated by the window.

'I was thinking last night, and I understand you may already have a wedding dress or you might want to make it yourself or use a senior dressmaker; that would be very sensible, but...' she took a breath, 'I designed a dress that I feel would suit you beautifully and it would be an honour to make it for you. But I don't expect to, of course; I was just thinking of you and—'

Violet cut her off. 'Mary, what a truly lovely idea and so very kind. I do not have a dress I wish to wear and had contemplated making it, but I would be thrilled to see your design.'

'You would?' Mary coloured with pleasure. 'Thank you, Miss.'

'No, thank you, Mary. If you might show me during our lunch break, I would be most pleased to see it.'

'I will, Miss, thank you.' Mary beamed and returned to her work, her smile not fading for a long time.

Such a gentle, kind girl, Violet thought, glancing occasionally at her young seamstress, and knowing her brother Tom was taken with the young lady was a happy thought. Violet hoped that now the dress design was not too outlandish. It was a comforting thought that Mary was so skilled and, even at her young age, was the best dressmaker among them.

'How thoughtful,' she said again with a smile and heard Mary laugh with delight.

It was an early call out for Detectives Stone and Payne, who soon found themselves detoured from their Roma Street headquarters and on the way to *The Doll and Teddy Hospital* on Elizabeth Street. However, it was not as early as it might have been; Mr Frank Crandle did not realise his wife was dead until the morning. He had got in late, not lit the lamp for fear of waking Frances and being so well familiar with his surroundings, Mr Crandle undressed in the dark and crawled into bed beside her, quickly succumbing to sleep. The shock in the morning and the thought that he had laid beside his dead wife all night was a torment that would remain with him for the rest of his days. But on this morning, the cause of his wife's death was the main concern.

'Miss Lewis will wonder what became of us,' Gilbert said as he strode beside his superior, the store now in sight. Two young constables stood outside, moving the public along.

'If she is a reporter worth her salt, she will be waiting for us at the doll hospital,' Harland said, and as they neared, he saw the lady reporter waiting.

'Right you are, Sir,' Gilbert said with a smile and a nod to Lilly.

'I heard from our early roundsman that there was a crime afoot, and once I knew the location, I assumed you would both be here,' she greeted them without thinking to say good morning.

'Good morning, Miss Lewis, very astute of you,' Harland said. 'We must ask you to wait here until we inspect the scene.'

'Of course,' she said, clearly frustrated, but as Harland moved away to speak to the constables, he saw Lilly approaching a couple of the adjacent store owners to see what they knew.

'Good morning, Constable Wright,' Gilbert said, recognising the policeman with the happy countenance who had no ambitions to rise above his rank and liked the street beat.

'Hello again, Detective Payne, and to you, Sir,' he said, addressing Harland as he joined them.

'What have we here, Constable Wright?' Harland asked in a low voice, his back to the gathered crowd.

'A lady dead in her bed, Sir. Her husband, Frank Crandle, has confirmed it is his wife, Frances. She has no obvious marks upon her and is fully clothed, but she wears the most fearful look. Mr Crandle did not find her dead until this morning.'

'Why would that be?' Harland asked, frowning.

'It was his card night, Sir,' Constable Wright said. 'I have several names of his fellow players so that you can check his alibi. He came in late; his wife was in bed, the lamp off, so he did not wake her.'

'Quite a shock, I imagine,' Gilbert said with a sympathetic look.

'Yes, he realised at first light. Apparently, she is always up early, and Mr Crandle was surprised to wake before Mrs Crandle.' Constable Wright nodded toward his fellow constable. 'We have secured the area, Sir, and had a rudimentary look. There appeared to be no windows ajar or broken. However...'

'Yes?' Harland asked, wary.

'I am assuming it is not normal, but there was a tin toy soldier halfway up the stairs as if it was on its way to rescue the lady, and there is a doll perched on the counter with a red ribbon around its neck pulled very tight... quite odd.'

'Did you have the chance to ask Mr Crandle if the doll and toy soldier were there before his departure last night?' Harland asked.

'I did, Sir, and he said they were not. When he came in late without the lamp, he saw the doll's silhouette but thought his wife had left it there to remind him to deliver it. He said she did that sometimes. And as he did not trip over the tin soldier, he didn't notice it.'

'Excellent work, thank you, Constable Wright. Come then, Gilbert, let us see Mrs Crandle for ourselves. If you can manage the crowd, Constable Wright, will you send your colleague for the coroner?'

'Done, Sir.'

With a nod of thanks, the detectives took a moment to study the outside entry of the store to confirm Constable Wright's observations, then proceeded inside to inspect the murder scene. They started up the stairs and stopped where the tin soldier lay to study the toy. There was nothing out of the ordinary about it.

Harland continued, 'This must be connected... the *Storks* gifted tin soldiers and dolls. If our first assumptions were correct, then Mrs Crandle was frightened and threatened, and knew more than what she told us. She would not elaborate on her past line of work, but I would not be surprised to learn she was a *Stork* and is likely Nurse Faithful's colleague.'

'I agree, Sir, and her past has caught up with her.

The detectives made their way to the bedside. Constable Wright was correct; Mrs Crandle wore a look of terror.

'Oh goodness,' Phoebe exclaimed with surprise on turning and finding a lady standing nearby; she was rarely frightened by the dead appearing. 'Forgive me. I don't have any bodies at present, so I was not expecting anyone.'

'The apology is mine to make, Miss,' the lady, who looked around the same age as Phoebe, with a small, round attractive face, said. She wore a simple pale blue dress with a white apron over it, as nurses wear. 'I should have gently coughed, but I find I can't do everything I once did.'

And then she was gone again.

'Hello?' Phoebe looked around. The woman reappeared.

'Forgive me. I have never appeared to anyone before and am clearly not good at this.'

Phoebe laughed. 'I am sure there is no rulebook for it, so please do not apologise. I am Miss Phoebe Astin. May I be of assistance?'

'Oh yes, please.'

She was gone again, and Phoebe couldn't help but smile. This might take some time, she imagined.

'I am Mrs Esther Banes,' a voice said, and Phoebe turned to find the spirit near the window. 'That is better; I feel a little more stable now. I am one of the *Storks*... one of the three deceased.

'Oh, the *Storks*! Nurse Charlotte Faithful's group. So, you must be the wet nurse.' She stopped suddenly to ask, 'Three?'

'Yes, three of us have passed over.' Esther relayed the fact quite casually, as if death was inevitable and no one should be surprised by it. 'My, this is quite a lovely room you have here.'

'Thank you, but... my apologies, Mrs Banes, I thought only you and Nurse Faithful were on the other side.'

'Frances joined us last evening. Frightened to death in her bed upstairs from the doll hospital. But she is safe forever now.'

Phoebe could not hide her shock. 'Mrs Frances Crandle, from *The Doll and Teddy Hospital*, is dead?'

'The very same. I do hope you don't have a doll in there for repair; it might take a while now. Poor dear Frank. That's her husband.'

'Goodness, this is a shock.' Phoebe sat down on the chair underneath the window; Esther sat in the chair opposite.

'I am very sorry, Miss Astin, I didn't know you were acquainted; I should have been more sensitive in my delivery.'

'Barely acquainted, please do not be concerned, Mrs Banes,' Phoebe said. 'It's just she was very much alive only a day ago when I collected my grandmother's doll, and I didn't know Mrs Crandle was a *Stork*. Nurse Faithful did not tell me the names of the living members.'

'Oh dear.' Esther thought for a moment, then shrugged. 'It matters not now that she is dead. Charlotte told me she spoke with you; she was always most discreet by nature.'

'Yes, Nurse Faithful believed a crime was afoot, and that she didn't die of natural causes. And you are saying Mrs Crandle's death was unnatural? So sudden,' Phoebe said again, processing the news.

'Death is funny like that. Some get time to plan; others, like myself, have no time to say goodbye. I died in childbirth, ironic for a wet nurse, would you not say? But twenty-three years have passed. My husband remarried, and my daughter, who survived when I did not, has her own children. Such is life.'

'Nevertheless, I am sorry to hear that, Mrs Banes. I have no doubt your husband's pain has dulled in time, but he still carries it, and I am sure your daughter would have loved to have known her mother.'

'Especially as I weaned so many babies but not my own. But to the matter at hand,' she said most practically, and Phoebe could see why she would have fitted nicely in a working party with Nurse Faithful and Mrs Crandle.

'Charlotte and Frances did not want me to speak of this, but I shall. Two *Storks* remain, Miss Astin, and their lives could be at risk. May I give you their names so you can warn them of what became of us? I am sure you will find a way without saying it is a message from the dead.' Esther gave a small laugh. 'Who would believe that?'

'Some might,' Phoebe said. 'There is no doubt in your mind that Nurse Faithful and Mrs Crandle were harmed because of the work of the *Storks*? Do you know by whom?' Phoebe asked.

'No, Frances said her murderer was a man dressed as a tin soldier – dressed like the gift we used to give to boy babies. Charlotte's heart gave away after several terrible frights... especially when the doll left in her back garden was one of the dolls we gifted.'

'The very same?'

'Without a doubt. So you see, it is connected to the babies we re-homed. Maybe one of those children themselves. They would all be nearing their third decade. I cannot imagine how they came by the news, but please, Miss Astin, warn the two remaining *Storks*.'

'I shall, I promise. Tell me their names then, Mrs Banes, if you would be so kind?' Phoebe rose and, going to her desk, collected her notebook and pen.

'Mrs Louise Killick, a former midwife,' Esther said and waited for Phoebe to jot down the name, 'and another wet nurse like me, Mrs Winifred Stockton. Please help them so they do not join us before their time.'

Phoebe frowned. 'I will, of course, but what if this is their fate?'

'What if their fate is that I should warn you to warn them?'

Phoebe chuckled. 'Yes, who is to say? Rest easy, Mrs Banes; I shall do my best.'

'We are all very grateful, Miss Astin.' Esther Banes departed with a small smile and bow, and Phoebe exhaled. Now, she mused, should I tell the detective which ladies might be next... he is likely to be at the scene of the crime. Or should I tell Lilly and ask her to investigate subtly? Phoebe trusted her friend would never put her at risk or expose her secret; nonetheless, she thought it best to tell the detective first, and he could determine if Lilly might have the information at no risk to his investigation. Perhaps they were both together, given what had just happened, and Phoebe decided a trip to the doll hospital was in order. She had made a promise, after all.

Chapter 24

HAVING FINISHED THEIR CURSORY examination of Mrs Frances Crandle's body and the surrounds, Harland and Gilbert waited on the coroner's thoughts as Dr Tavish McGregor proceeded to study the body on the bed. Glancing out the bedroom window to the street below, Harland summoned Gilbert to his side.

'Is that James Dellow?' They looked at a man in the crowd gathered outside the *Doll and Teddy Hospital*.

'It does look like him. I shall ask him his reason for being here, Sir,' Gilbert said, hurrying to the stairs. Harland followed him to the lower level, curious as to why James Dellow would be at a doll store when his sister was found dead in doll-like make-up. He watched the interaction from within the store.

Surprisingly, the man did not run as Gilbert approached. A few minutes later, Gilbert returned inside.

'Sir, a remarkable resemblance, but that man is not James Dellow and does not know of him. His name is Nathanial Liddle.'

'Liddle, that name sounds familiar,' Harland said, noting the man had now moved on and then, to his surprise, he saw Miss Phoebe Astin outside talking with reporter Lilly Lewis. The two were close together, as if sharing a secret, and Miss Lewis was scribbling in her pad. His anger rose. Whether or not it was irrational, he expected Miss Astin to provide information to him first and not fuel the fire by providing the newspaper with red herrings. Nor should she be here at a murder scene.

'Miss Astin is here!' Gilbert said, surprised, following his superior's gaze. 'Shall I see if she is after us?'

Her eyes met his through the large store window, and she gave a small, respectful nod, which he reciprocated and quickly turned away. 'Yes, thank you, Gilbert. I shall see if Tavish has any insights.'

He took the stairs to the Crandles' accommodation and felt ridiculously churlish as he did so. Miss Astin owed him nothing, and he was privileged that she chose to share her gift with him when it put her at risk to do so. Perhaps they were speaking of Miss Yalden's dinner dance while they waited for him; maybe she was on a work errand and saw Miss Lewis. By the time he had reached Tavish's side, he was angry at his quick temper, which Harland thought he had curbed long ago. In his early days of training, his superior had warned him many times about the consequences if he did not manage it; that was why he took up boxing after his school years.

Would he have felt that anger if it were anyone but Miss Astin? He asked himself. Was this some sort of possessiveness he felt towards her?

Was he angry because she was at a crime scene, and he did not want her there in that murderous environment?

If he were honest with himself, he knew that was a justification he could use, but Phoebe was no stranger to death. He wanted to be her first and only contact for information and for her not to risk his case by talking to Lilly. Pure and simple. Not that she ever had, he had to admit, and her friendship with Lilly went back much longer than his association with her. His mind was going around in circles, full of self-justification and anger at himself, at Phoebe Astin, and back to himself again.

'Right then,' Tavish said, getting his attention. 'The victim appears to have died from heart failure, and her expression would indicate she was terrorised prior and saw her killer. Her pillow was askew and may have been used over her mouth and nose; Mr Crandle said he did not touch it. But there are no bruises on her arms, neck or face, and no broken nails; thus, there is no sign that she struggled. Her heart gave way.'

'Most peculiar. Thank you, Tavish. We are finished if you wish to have her removed.'

'Right then, I shall tell you if I discover more once she is on my table.' Tavish sighed. 'A nasty business to attack a harmless elderly lady managing a doll shop.'

'I am not sure she has always been harmless,' Harland said low enough for only Tavish to hear. The two departed together, Tavish allowing the men with the stretcher to remove her and bidding Harland goodbye.

Gilbert and Miss Lewis approached.

'Was Miss Astin wishing to speak with us?' Harland glanced around to glimpse her but could not see the beautiful mortician.

'Yes, but she left the details with me,' Gilbert said, waving a note.

'I did my best to get it out of her,' Lilly said with a roll of her eyes, 'but Phoebe said she was not confident enough to give me unchecked information and lead the press astray.'

Harland felt a wave of shame for his judgement.

'Miss Lewis, I shall give you an overview of this morning's crime as I believe it is connected to the death of Nurse Faithful and Miss Jane Dellow. Your report may draw out witnesses.'

'Thank you, Detective,' she said, surprised, pad at the ready. 'So, Jane and James Dellow were delivered by the *Storks*?'

'Let's travel to the asylum and discuss it on the way,' Harland said, giving her a brief nod to her question. The party departed, with Harland glancing around once more in the hope he could see Miss Phoebe Astin and make amends.

Phoebe felt humiliated. Detective Harland Stone had looked at her as if she were a pest. It was a look he often gave Lilly but unkinder because Phoebe had started to believe her contribution was of value. He did not even offer a small smile, raise his hand, or take a moment to join them. Harland, in fact, scowled. Of course he was busy, and it was a death scene, but his expression was far from subtle when their eyes locked. She was a nuisance and a fool to believe otherwise.

The mortification made her cringe, and she hurried back, happy to see the sign for *The Economic Undertaker* and to open the door into the safe world she knew, closing it quickly behind her.

'That was quick,' Julius said as he stood talking with their grandfather.

'An errand, nothing more.'

'Are you all right, Phoebe?' Randolph asked, studying her. He knew his grandchildren and their mannerisms better than they knew themselves.

She stopped and took a breath. 'I think I have seen too many people of late,' she said, offering her grandfather a small smile to not worry him or be interrogated further. 'I need the solitude of my room and my family.'

Her excuse did not appear to work as both men studied her, and Julius moved the curtain to look outside before returning his attention to her.

'What happened?' His expression left no doubt that he would pummel anyone who had caused her distress.

'Nothing, I assure you.' Her shoulders slumped at his fierce look, and Phoebe shared one reason she was distressed. 'It is Mrs Crandle, the store owner of the doll hospital where I had Grandma's doll repaired. She has been murdered in her bed. I saw Lilly outside the store, she told me.'

'Good Lord,' Randolph said.

'I believe it is connected to Nurse Faithful's death and—'

'Were you seeking Harland to tell him?' Julius cut to the chase.

'Yes, but I... I was most uncomfortable at the death scene.' She looked from Julius to her grandfather. 'I know that must sound silly when I see death all day.'

'It doesn't sound silly at all,' Randolph assured her. 'We are in the business of seeing people respectfully to the next life and helping their families with the transition, not with the violence of death, even if we get victims who need a little help to look their best.'

'Thank you, Grandpa, for understanding. Would it be too disrespectful to ask not to see anyone for a while?'

'Of course not. You give a great deal of yourself. But not even the detectives?' Randolph asked.

Phoebe shook her head in the negative and then relented. 'I will see the *Vexed Vixens*, should they come by, but I am not expecting them, and perhaps Detective Payne.'

'Detective Payne?' Julius asked, thinking he had misheard. Then she saw him make the connection – a connection she did not want him to make. 'Did Harland say something to offend you?' he snapped. 'I will—'

'Of course not,' she hurriedly assured him. 'I didn't speak with him; he was busy inside the shop.'

'Only Detective Payne then,' Randolph agreed.

She could feel Julius studying her, and then he agreed, 'I think that is a sound idea, Phoebe. Rest in the quiet of your room, and we shall keep the world at bay.'

'Thank you,' she said gratefully and hugged him before taking to the stairs and disappearing to her room below. Phoebe felt she had overstepped her mark and told herself it was best to remember her core work and get back to doing it. If spirits insist on her help, a note to the detectives via Julius might be best in the future. She had given Detective Payne the names of the two *Storks* in danger, so her duty was done to the spirit, Mrs Esther Banes. If Detective Stone wanted to seek her counsel, she would assist, if possible, but she would not pursue him again in the future.

Despite making her plan and feeling better for it, Phoebe could not forget the detective's look nor ignore the quiet conversation her brother and grandfather continued in her absence that filtered down the stairway in their concern for her.

Waiting until she was well down the stairs, Julius said to his grandfather, 'What do you make of that? I can't imagine Phoebe would have gotten close enough to the death scene to be distressed by it.'

'Odd indeed. I have always admired both detectives, but do you think Detective Stone dismissed her while he was on duty?' Randolph asked. 'You know him reasonably well.'

Julius's jaw locked as he thought. 'I would like to give him the benefit of the doubt, but we witnessed how indifferent he was to Phoebe's wellbeing in the interview room on the debutante case.' He hurriedly added, 'I don't believe he would ever do anything to distress Phoebe intentionally, but he is very focused when working and unaccustomed to working with ladies, I suspect.'

'And Phoebe is a sensitive soul. I wish she would confide in me what distressed her.' Randolph looked to Julius. 'She is closest to you; perhaps she will tell you more when she has time to calm herself.'

'He may be a boxer, but if Harland has done or said anything to distress her, God help me; I will not be responsible for my actions.'

'Steady, lad. I suspect you and the detective are both hotheads if pushed hard enough,' Randolph held up his hand to stop Julius from protesting and added, 'even if you have worked very hard at not being that fiery young man anymore. Besides, there might be another reason for Phoebe's reaction.'

Julius studied his grandfather. 'She is in love with him.'

'It can make you act out of character, or so I hear,' Randolph teased him, and Julius gave his grandfather a look that only brought on laughter.

'Nevertheless, I shall get to the bottom of it.'

Randolph placed his hand on Julius's arm. 'But go gently, lad.'

Julius sighed. 'Yes. You are right, Grandpa. And if he has slighted her, then I will bury him myself.'

Chapter 25

IT TOOK SOME TIME to reach the asylum, which allowed Lilly Lewis to get all the information she needed for her news piece. Throughout the entire trip, Harland berated himself for his behaviour. He asked Gilbert for the note Miss Astin gave him and read two names on it – living *Storks*, Mrs Louise Killick, and Mrs Winifred Stockton. These women were in danger, but he could not ask Gilbert for more details without arousing the reporter's interest.

Why did I not give her the benefit of the doubt?

Why am I such an idiot?

'Oh, it is so foreboding,' Lilly said as they approached the dark, gloomy Lunatic Asylum.

'If you want me to wait, it'll cost you extra,' the driver called to them.

'We'll pay,' Harland assured him. He turned to Lilly. 'There is every chance the matron will not wish to speak with you present. If so, we will have to conduct our interviews separately.'

'I am hoping she may relent because I am with you.'

The driver stopped near the entrance stairs, and the detectives alighted. Gilbert offered his hand to Lilly, who accepted.

Harland went through the motions, but his mind was only half on the job, and whether his protégé realised it or stepped up because Harland was deep in thought, he appreciated Gilbert doing the introductions. Given the matron's affection for the deceased, the matron saw no harm in allowing Miss Lewis to stay. They sat around her desk in stiff timber chairs that did not invite loitering.

'Jane was special,' the matron said, her severe countenance softening. 'She came to us on her 21st birthday and has been with us for these seven years now. A gentle soul and no trouble whatsoever.'

'Did she need to be here then, Matron?' Gilbert asked.

'I raised that topic with her brother several times, Detective. You have met James Dellow?'

'Yes, we spoke with him, and he was unsure how his sister found her way to the miniature display at the Botanic Gardens,' Harland said.

She scoffed. 'Because he did not bring her back. I wouldn't believe a word he said, detectives. It is easy to sign someone in when you sign them out; it has happened before, and I can tell you, Jane did not return.'

'Were you not concerned then?' Lilly asked.

'No,' the matron shook her head. 'With some patients, including Jane, we have an agreement with the family to allow them to stay out longer if their risk is low. Jane was definitely that, and occasionally, her brother took Jane away to the beach or on small trips, returning her two or three days later. For patients who were a danger to society or themselves, then they could not leave, or we would sign them out and back in ourselves.'

'That is a relief,' Lilly said.

'But to your earlier question,' she turned to Gilbert. 'I don't believe Jane needed to be in an asylum. However, she felt safe here. She was frightened when out in the world, rarely leaving her room or eating. It was best Jane stayed here where she could walk in the garden, paint and eat well.'

'You knew of her tuberculosis, Matron?' Harland asked.

'Of course. I didn't want her to go out this time, nor did our doctor, but Mr Dellow wanted to have the time with her to revisit some places sentimental to them both, or so he told me.'

'Did you meet her parents, Matron?' Lilly asked.

'Yes, her mother several times. She was not dissimilar to Jane in nature... a slight, nervy little woman, but they looked nothing alike. It would not have surprised me to find her as a patient. Mr Dellow senior, well, he was a nasty one. Rude to the staff, demanding, and insisting no one spoke of Jane's admittance.'

Harland saw some patients walking across the grounds with a man in white, an orderly, accompanying them. He returned his attention to the matron. 'Did you ever hear of the Dellow twins being adopted or given up at birth?'

She shook her head in the negative but added, 'Although her father would have been happy for that excuse. I recall the time he looked at Jane in disgust and said he could not believe she and her brother were from his family line, and he would not have put it past his wife to have cheated and trapped him. The horror on that woman's face told me everything I needed to know. He was a cruel and unchristian man.'

Harland continued, 'Did Jane have any friends or other visitors, Matron, that might have called on her and taken her out?'

The matron shook her head and answered firmly, 'No one but her family came here in the many years she was with us, and she only ever left the premises with her brother.'

With nothing further to add, Harland thanked the matron for her time, and they resumed their journey. He was uncharacteristically distracted most of the way back to the station, and on arrival, Harland alighted, and Miss Lewis continued in the hansom, accompanied by Gilbert, whom the detective sent onward to the morgue to see if there were any further revelations from Tavish, concerning Mrs Frances Crandle.

Harland strode down the hallway to his office, hat in hand, his mind processing a thousand thoughts, and when he looked up, he stopped in his tracks. Julius Astin waited in the doorway.

Violet always looked forward to luncheon at the *In Mourning – Attire for the Family* office. When the shop was clear of customers, the three ladies would take their lunches and sit together, enjoying each other's company. Violet set aside her lunch of an apple and biscuits with a cup of tea as Mary presented her designs for the wedding dress. Nellie looked on from where she was seated opposite, keen to see the young girl's vision.

'If you don't like it, Miss—'

'I am very keen to see it, Mary, and I am grateful that you would take the time to think of me, let alone design me a wedding dress.'

Mary gave a small shrug of embarrassment. 'But if you don't like it—'

'Then Miss Astin will thank you and commend your design for another lucky young lady,' Nellie said, stepping in.

'Would you like to design dresses, Mary?' Violet asked.

'Wedding dresses, yes, Miss. My dream is to one day have a bridal shop.'

'Then it shall be, as you are very talented, Mary, is she not, Nellie?' Violet asked the senior seamstress.

'Absolutely,' Mrs Nellie Shaw agreed. 'And when you are in a position to have your shop, you can be sure that Violet and I will recommend you to everyone we know seeking to wed.'

Mary flushed with pleasure and could not help smiling. With a little more confidence, she undid the string on her folder, removed the sheets of paper, and pushed the design towards Violet. The drawings showed the front, back and side details.

'Oh my, Mary, this is a stunning dress,' Violet said delightedly.

'It will suit your shape, Miss, as you are slim with a lovely swan-like neck and a good bust line.' She flushed again at having said the words.

'Mary, you have a gift,' Nellie said, dunking her biscuit into her tea and studying the designs.

'You do, and I am honoured to be the recipient of your talent,' Violet said. 'I will pay for your design, of course.'

Mary looked horrified. 'No, Miss, you mustn't. It is a gift, and seeing you in it will be worth all the pounds in the world.'

'I am sure we can access the fabric wholesale,' Nellie said. 'Mr Astin might help us with his business contacts,' she added with a wink.

'And I will make it for you, Miss, after hours.'

'Oh, Mary, I don't expect that,' Violet said, delighted with the design.

'But I must, Miss. To be a bridal dressmaker, I must bring my designs to life. Will you allow me?'

'Then yes, absolutely, but you will quote me on making the dress, and I will pay. Yes?'

Mary shook her head in the negative. 'No, Miss. I know you could make your own dress for free, so you must not outlay money for me to do so.'

Violet looked at all three designs again, admiring them. 'I promise you, Mary, I had not considered making my wedding dress. With our day jobs here taking up considerable time, I intended to hire a dressmaker to fit and make it for me, and I have found her. So, I shall pay you the going rate; I insist upon it.' She added, putting Mary's mind at ease, 'Julius has given me a generous allowance towards my bridal expenses, and I have accepted it knowing I must look the part for him.'

Mary grinned with pleasure. 'Well then, Miss, I shall quote you fairly, thank you. I promise you it will be beautiful, Miss.'

'I know,' Violet said with a small laugh. 'It already is.'

Harland extended his hand, and the two men shook without speaking. Of equal height and build, a current of friction ran between them. Julius followed Harland into his office, and the door was closed. He had hoped his sister might fall in love with Bennet Martin. She would want for nothing, be cherished, and Bennet would be home with her, even if he were working in his studio. Harland's work would always see him out of the home at all hours and at risk; Phoebe would never be his priority. But there was no dictating what the heart wanted, and it appeared she had her heart set on Detective Harland Stone.

'I deserve your censure,' Harland said, raising his hand before Julius could speak, taking the heat out of Julius's argument. He strode across the room, throwing off his coat and hat and running a hand through his short hair. He stopped when he had returned and was opposite Julius.

'What did you do?' Julius asked him.

'Nothing, that is the problem. The look I gave your sister was discouraging... it was a crime scene, and... I was surprised to see her there; it registered on my face.' He stopped abruptly. 'Why are you here? What has Miss Astin said?'

'Not a thing. Phoebe entered the workplace and asked not to be interrupted by anyone except her girlfriends and Detective Payne.'

'Gilbert!' Harland looked as if he had been hit.

'Naturally, I concluded you had offended her,' Julius said, his eyes narrowing. 'You cannot imagine what it takes for her to tell you of her visions and trust you. The risk to her and us in doing so... it could ruin our livelihoods. Phoebe seeks little company besides her inner circle and has now retreated.'

Harland exhaled and looked ashamed. 'I would never speak about your sister to anyone. I know you barely know me, but know that I am trustworthy.'

Julius considered this and nodded. 'If you need her help in the future or if she has anything for you, I shall pass it on in note form.'

'No, Julius, do not do this,' Harland hurried to assure him he would not hurt Phoebe. 'My intentions towards your sister have always been honourable. I held her in high regard from the moment I met her, but I knew of Bennet's interest, so I withdrew. Please do not stop me from getting to know Miss Astin better now that I have the opportunity. I hoped it might be encouraged.'

'But your work is your focus.'

'My work is one of my priorities, and I will not make the mistake of putting it before your sister's comfort again. That day previously with the debutante case, I was on the clock, surrounded by people distracting me, and I don't hear the spirits, so I am not as capable of judging when Miss Astin is overwhelmed, but that does not apply this time,' he hurriedly added before Julius suggested the same.

Julius studied Harland, getting the measure of the man he had welcomed into his social circle these past few months. 'I know you are a clever man, Harland, an educated man, and I know you think I am just a funeral director.'

'I think no such thing,' Harland said indignantly. 'I know you went through school on a scholarship you earned. I know you have grown your business into one of the town's most successful. I have nothing but respect for you.'

'Then you must know that you and I deal in human emotions daily. You try to read your suspects. I spend hours watching all the emotions of those acquainted with the dead play out. Heartbreak, greed, relief, admiration.'

'Yes, I agree with that.'

'Then, if you saw my sister and were concerned about her being at a crime scene, your expressions and actions would have relayed that. I suggest you looked at her as if she were a hindrance.'

'No, I—'

Julius cut him off. 'And for fear of being accused of the same, I will take my leave. Stay away from her, Detective Stone.'

Harland moved quickly to the door to stop Julius's departure. Phoebe's eldest brother could not know of the hours Phoebe had filled Harland's mind and disturbed his sleep, and he could not stay away from her now.

'You have come this far, Julius, do me the courtesy of hearing me out,' he begged. 'This is a matter of my and your sister's future happiness.'

Julius stopped and stepped back. He considered Harland and nodded, re-entering the room and seating himself on the edge of the desk.

Harland took a deep breath. He was not adept at expressing his emotions; most men weren't, but having been raised in a boarding school, and with no sisters, Harland had less experience than most.

'In my defence,' he began, 'when I saw your sister, she was talking to Miss Lewis. I experienced a range of emotions – initially delight, concern, fear for her, anger, and even petty jealousy.' Harland kept talking, more than he usually did for a man so well put together. 'I was worried about Miss Astin with the people around her; one might be a killer. I wanted her to talk with me and me alone. I don't want her at death scenes, and I would have come to your office in a heartbeat if she summonsed me.' He stopped and took a breath. 'Gilbert offered to go to her, and I allowed it and went inside to the death scene. I quickly felt remorse for my actions, and she was gone upon my return.'

Harland threw his hands up in the air as if defeated. 'Make of that what you will, but surely you understand those emotions better than most, Julius.'

'How so?' Julius asked, surprised.

'I have learnt to manage my recklessness, as I believe you have as well.'

'I don't know what you heard, but that was long ago.'

'I like to think my hot-tempered days are long gone, too,' Harland said. 'But this is new to me, having to consider someone else under my protection.'

'I find wanting to protect somewhat instinctive. Surely, in your role, it is more so.'

Harland looked defeated, and he nodded, accepting Julius's logic. There was truth in that.

'But,' Julius conceded, 'in a developing relationship, it is difficult to know how much and how little to give.' He said in a conciliatory manner.

'Yes, and your sister is a unique mix of strength and vulnerability,' Harland said, adding, 'That is my observation from what little time I have spent in her company.'

Julius sighed. 'It would not be the ideal life being in love with a detective.'

'No, but I hope Miss Astin will take the time to know me and decide I am worth the risk. I am not saying I won't make the same mistake again, Julius, but I know that if I am given the chance to court your sister, nothing will come before her, and I will treat her as she should be treated.' He had offered all he could think to say, having not had time to prepare for the confrontation with Phoebe's brother.

Julius stood to go and turned at the door. 'All right then, but know this, Harland, if you hurt her, there will be a six-foot plot with your name on it.'

'Are you threatening an officer of the law?' Harland asked with a small smile and an obvious look of relief.

'Yes,' Julius said, allowing himself to smile as well.

'Fair enough then.'

Harland approached, and the men shook again, cordially this time.

'Will you tell her what I said, explain it?'

'If you wish me to?' Julius asked.

'Yes.'

Julius agreed and departed, and Harland felt the weight of the world falling off his shoulders. Now, he just had to hope Miss Astin would be as understanding.

Chapter 26

AFTER VISITING THE CORONER, Dr Tavish McGregor, who had little else to add to the death of Mrs Crandle that would assist in a criminal conviction, and seeing Miss Lilly Lewis back to *The Courier* newspaper office, Detective Gilbert Payne decided to investigate a thought that had been buzzing in his mind since departing from the doll hospital this morning. He knew his superior had a report to do on the progress of the case, which would be a challenge to write given they now had three suspicious deaths linked to a group of women who, over two decades ago, played God, and no culprit in mind. He did not envy Detective Stone.

Gilbert shunned the hansom cabs and took the omnibus, not as confident as his boss nor willing to disobey the orders from above to start cost saving. He was on his way to where the James Dellow look-alike lived. Despite the man's protests, Gilbert had taken his name and address after speaking with him in front of the shop and murder scene. He assured the man, Mr Nathanial Liddle, they would take everyone's name and address who was present that morning.

Feeling the heat in his grey suit on a warm afternoon, Gilbert descended from the omnibus at the top of the street in South Brisbane near the man's residence and, remaining at the stop, took the opportunity to observe the comings and goings. This was Nurse Faithful's area, where she looked after the mothers before and after birth. It was a respectable working-class area and may have prospered a little since Nurse Faithful serviced it twenty years ago.

He wandered down the street, finding the further he walked, the closer he got to the wharves and fish markets, the shabbier it became. Gilbert saw the dilapidated state of houses, emptied his pockets of a few coins to barefoot children tugging on his jacket before running off, and saw the neat, clean, but lean women as they swept their paths or pushed prams. The occasional male sat outside a house. Maybe they worked the night shift or were unemployed. He nodded to one man wearing trousers, no shoes and a white singlet and was greeted with a wave of the hand.

Finding the numbered house he was looking for—that of Nathanial Liddle—Gilbert had no expectations of seeing him as the man was most likely at work. There was, however, a mature lady sitting on the front verandah, knitting: Nathanial's mother, no doubt. On reaching the corner, his luck changed; Gilbert ran headlong into the man himself.

'You again,' Liddle said with displeasure. He wore overalls that had seen better days and had a streak of grease on his right cheek.

'Mr Liddle, I was hoping to have a word, but I wasn't expecting to find you here. I thought I'd try my luck since I was in the area.'

'I do shifts. Only a few hours today. Did you speak with my mother?' he asked, glancing at the house and seeing her at work in her chair on the verandah.

'No, I assumed you would be at work and did not wish to startle or interrupt her. Had she not been there, I would have knocked.'

Liddle nodded his thanks. 'What do you want to ask me then?' He folded his arms across his body as if it were armour, and he was expecting to be accused of something.

Gilbert sensed he was up against a man with little regard for the law, in or out of uniform, and was wary. But the resemblance to James Dellow and his twin sister, Jane, was remarkable and could not be denied. They shared distinct features – slightly hooded eyes and mouths that were thin-lipped. Nathanial Liddle had a habitual look that was neither a sneer nor a smile; Gilbert would classify it as ridicule; he had seen it often enough in his past, and there was no mirth about it.

'Do you know Mr James Dellow?'

'Is that the man you thought I was this morning at the shop?'

'Yes.'

'Can't say I know him. Why? What's he done?'

'Nothing, he is related to a victim of a crime. Do you know a Nurse Charlotte Faithful?' Gilbert asked.

'Yeah, everyone from around here knows Nurse Faithful. She delivered most of us. Mum thinks she's a saint. She's dead now.'

'Yes—' Gilbert's next question was cut off by Mrs Liddle, who had approached the fence of her home and called out to her son.

'Is everything all right, Nat?'

'Everything is fine, Ma; I'll be there in a moment. It's just a detective asking after Nurse Faithful.'

Mrs Liddle opened the gate and walked towards them. The men met her halfway. Gilbert observed in her the thin lips but not the hooded eyes. Perhaps Mr Liddle had that feature of the face.

'Good afternoon, Mrs Liddle, I'm Detective Gilbert Payne. Your son was helping me with some enquiries about Nurse Faithful.'

'Hello Detective. The woman's a saint, what she did for us.' Mrs Liddle shook her head. 'Delivered all my children and helped me with an insurance policy when my husband was killed at work.' She looked at Nat with great affection. 'I wouldn't have been able to continue to pay our mortgage or feed the family without it.' She returned her attention to Gilbert. 'You won't hear a bad word about her in this neighbourhood.'

And then, James Dellow rounded the corner.

Ambrose and Will lowered the coffin into the earthy plot, and the family present said their last farewells. One person remained – a young woman of slim build, with fair hair tied in a neat bun at her nape and a light black veil covering her heart-shaped face. Ambrose and Will finished their duties and moved aside. With a subtle nod, Ambrose authorised the men waiting nearby to come closer with their shovels.

'Would you like us to wait, Madam?' Ambrose asked the young lady in black, who looked particularly beautiful and vulnerable as she stood by the grave.

She looked up at Ambrose as if seeing him for the first time. Clutching a white lace handkerchief, she looked down into the grave at the coffin within and sighed. 'No, please go ahead.'

'Some people find it distressing to see the grave closed in,' he said. 'Might I suggest you leave now if you are ready.'

'Thank you for your concern, but I am here for the whole journey to see my mother to her final resting place.'

Ambrose nodded and authorised the men to shovel the dirt into the grave as she stood back and watched it being filled in. He could not take his eyes off her. There was no doubt she felt the loss keenly, yet she would not leave her mother's side. He wished someone stood beside the young woman to support her. His colleague, Will, must have thought the same thing and moved to stand near her, clasping his hands behind his back. She looked up at him and nodded her thanks.

As the men shovelled the earth, Ambrose thanked the reverend, who departed after a kind word to the young lady. Ambrose and Will waited. *The Economic Undertaker* usually left once the fill-in began, but no customers remained.

It was as if she realised she might be holding them up and said, 'Oh please, do not stay on my account; I prefer to be alone.'

'It is no inconvenience, Madam,' Ambrose assured her. 'Perhaps we might offer you a ride home afterwards to your residence or the wake.'

She smiled, and then in one swift movement threw herself into the grave. Will snatched for her, his fingers brushing the fabric of her black mourning gown, but he was not quick enough; the men had shovelled a load of dirt upon her before they realised what had happened. She gave a small cry as she fell on her knees and hands.

Ambrose leapt down into the grave beside her. She scratched and thrashed at him as he attempted to lift her out.

'I will go for a doctor or an ambulance,' Will said from above, leaving the two men with shovels to help haul Ambrose and the woman out.

'Leave me. I am staying here with my mother. Leave me!' she demanded, shrieking at Ambrose.

'Madam, we cannot leave the living to lie with the dead,' he said, trying to hush her as they stood amongst the fresh dirt in the cool of the grave. 'I am sorry for your loss and pain, but your mother would not want this for you.'

'I took her life; I deserve no better than to die with her,' she wailed hysterically. Ambrose froze. Should he send for Detective Stone?

'You took her life? Are you saying that you killed your mother?'

'Yes. I eloped, and the agony brought about my mother's demise.'

Ambrose exhaled. 'I see. Where is your husband, then? He should be here comforting you.' He wanted to keep her talking until help arrived in case she did something else to harm herself, and gave thanks that the coffin lid was nailed down lest she try to climb in.

'My mother despised him, so I thought it disrespectful to bring him to her funeral.'

With that, she pulled away and threw herself upon the coffin again, dirt and all, and began to wail.

Ambrose groaned and looked at the two men above. One looked away, and the other gave a small shrug, unsure what to do.

'Come then,' Ambrose tried again. 'If you loved this man enough to elope with him, you must have the courage to stand by your decision. I am sure your mother will forgive you. Your love for each other will surpass this obstacle.' He clutched at any platitude at his disposal in the hope she might rise. Where was Julius when he needed him; why couldn't this happen on his watch?

'I thought she would come around,' she sobbed, rising slightly, and he offered her his hand. She looked at it before accepting it and rising to her feet. 'But she never did; she hated him and was broken-hearted by my actions.'

'Your workmate is back with help,' Mr Redford, the senior gravedigger, informed him.

Ambrose looked up and gave a nod of thanks. Finding his footing on the dirt, he said, 'Come, let me help you out of here now. I am sure she is as regretful as you that you could not reconcile.'

Will looked down upon the two of them, and Ambrose gave him a pleading look, hence the young man added, 'Ma'am, we all have regrets. Perhaps try to remember all the good times with your mother. Let me help you up.'

'Very well said, Will,' Ambrose added, and she allowed herself to be lifted from the dirt plot. Steady hands pulled her up, and she administered herself to the doctor and his assistant. Ambrose looked expectantly at Will. 'Well, don't just stand there, help me out.'

Will turned to the two men with shovels. 'It is mighty tempting, and if you were to say nothing—'

'Very amusing,' Ambrose smirked and held up his hand, his impatience beginning to show.

Will laughed, gripping it, and with the help of the younger Redford grasping Ambrose's other arm, they hurled him out.

Ambrose moved away from the hole and brushed down his suit. 'It would happen on Julius's day off.'

'She still would have done it,' Will said with a shrug.

'Yes, but I would have ensured he went into the plot. He likes to be gallant. Look at me,' he grumbled and continued to do so all the way back to the office.

Chapter 27

JAMES DELLOW TOOK OFF as if he hadn't seen Detective Gilbert Payne, Mrs Liddle, and Nathanial.

'Was that young James?' Mrs Liddle said, looking back to catch a glimpse of him.

'Was he coming to see you, Mr Liddle?'

'No doubt,' Mrs Liddle answered for her adult son. 'He is a lovely boy and the spitting image of my boys. If I did not know better, I would say my husband had been playing around, but James comes from a well-to-do family, and my husband would not have had entry there,' she said with a knowing chuckle.

Gilbert studied Nathanial. 'So you do know him?'

'James, yeah, I didn't know that was the James you meant.'

'I see,' Gilbert said, less than impressed at the time wasted by Nathanial Liddle's denial. 'How did you meet then, as I imagine you didn't go to the same school?'

Mrs Liddle laughed. 'No, James went to one of those expensive private schools,' she said, pushing her finger below her nose in an uppity motion.

'We met at the pub. I beat him at darts, and after a while, we became friends. Mainly because people kept calling me James and him Nathanial.'

'Like brothers,' Mrs Liddle said again. 'It makes me a little sad, I have to confess.'

'Why is that, Mrs Liddle?' Gilbert asked sympathetically.

'It does sound silly since I have five children all out in the world, but I always birthed healthy babes, but my last two didn't make it. Twins, and they would have been James's age.' She sighed at the thought. 'It's a long time ago. It would have been a younger brother and sister for you, Nat.'

'It would have, Ma,' he agreed.

'I believe the stress of my husband's death brought about their deaths,' she continued. 'I was without a penny to my name and five young children to feed. I loved them and could not imagine breaking up our family, and with two more babes on the way,' she shook her head at the memory. 'The poor little darlings probably didn't feel welcome.' Her voice hitched as she spoke.

'It was the stress, Ma. I know you would have loved those babies and found a way to keep us all.'

She gave him a grateful smile, and Gilbert had the feeling the Liddle family had spoken of this subject before today.

'It was, as you said, Ma, a long time ago, and you were not to blame, never you,' Nathanial said, his voice laced with anger.

'Was anyone to blame?' Gilbert asked a question he thought only Nathanial would understand, and the fiery look he was given answered his question. 'I thank you both for your time.'

'Did you get an answer to your question, young man? Whatever you wanted to know about Nurse Faithful?' Mrs Liddle asked.

'I believe so, Ma'am, and thank you.'

Gilbert tipped his hat and turned to leave, glancing back to see Nathanial leading his mother inside and looking back at him. He felt he was in dangerous territory. Was James Dellow waiting for him? Would Nathanial return and corner him? The two men were connected, and three women were dead. They would not hesitate to keep their secret if they were brutal enough to harm women.

He hurried his steps, making his way up the long street to the crossroads where the omnibus would get him safely back to tell his superior what he had learnt. Before he reached the end, James Dellow reappeared.

Julius re-entered the office of *The Economic Undertaker* through the back door after checking with the stable lads that all was well and that Will had stepped up and taken his place at the funeral with Ambrose. It was not Will's day to do so, but Julius was pressed to see Harland and would not be distracted.

'How did it go, lad?' his grandfather asked as he appeared in the reception.

'Good, I shall speak to Phoebe. I was prepared to ward him off, but Harland stopped me before I could speak, telling me of his failures.'

'I am glad he was remorseful; I believe he is a good man,' Randolph said. 'We have to make some allowances for his profession.'

'I am not keen on it. I wish Phoebe had feelings for Bennet. Her future would be secure,' Julius said and exhaled with frustration. 'I am, however, prepared to make allowances for Harland's upbringing. He explained he spent most of his childhood and adolescent years in a boys' boarding school, and having no sisters and little contact with females, he is unaccustomed to the sensitivities required.'

'Sounds reasonable,' Randolph agreed.

'Yes, but I would have thought his protective instincts would come to the fore with his profession. I told him we will not have Phoebe distressed.'

They turned sharply on hearing a noise on the stairs and found Phoebe behind them, looking aghast.

'Tell me you did not accost Detective Stone on my behalf, brother?' she said in a low and mortified voice.

'I spoke with him,' Julius said, clearing his throat as he saw her anger rising. 'I should, as your protector. He wishes me to relay our conversation—'

'Julius! How could you without speaking with me first?' Phoebe said, cutting him off, her face flushed and voice shaky with fury. She turned and stormed down the stairs.

Julius turned to his grandfather, and his shoulders slumped. 'Well, that did not go as planned. I shall talk with her.'

'Perhaps leave it a little while,' Randolph suggested. 'Phoebe is slow to anger but quick to get over it.'

'Yes, if you think that is best.'

The back door opened, and Ambrose stormed in, his face, hands, and suit covered in dirt and his hair dusty.

'What on earth happened to you, lad?' Randolph asked.

'You are filthy. Did you fall into the grave?' Julius said and groaned. 'Tell me everything is all right with our clients?'

'Fear not, brother; it went well. There was a distraught daughter who stayed behind on her own and decided to follow her mother into the grave. You would know if you had attended as you were supposed to. I need to change,' Ambrose said, storming off to clean up.

Julius looked at his grandfather. 'It appears I am not very popular this afternoon.'

Randolph chuckled. 'I still like you. Perhaps drop in next door and take this paperwork to Miss Forrester. I'm sure she still likes you, too.'

Julius smiled, took the paperwork and hesitated. 'I'm not sure I should risk it, given my luck today.'

'Be brave, lad,' Randolph teased. With a small laugh, Julius checked his appearance. He exited, heading next door to his successful mourning wear business managed by his fiancée, Miss Violet Forrester, soon to be Mrs Julius Astin.

James Dellow smirked. 'So you worked it out then, did you?' he asked, appearing quite different from the man they had interviewed to tell of his sister's death.

'Worked what out?' Gilbert played along.

James scoffed. 'That Nat and I are brothers. Blood brothers. Wouldn't take much to work that out, yet we were raised with different parents.'

'He's smarter than he looks,' Nathanial Liddle said, coming from the other direction.

Gilbert stepped back and held up his hands. 'Now listen, gents, you might look alike, but it's a big claim to say you have the same parents. Mrs Liddle was just saying she didn't believe your father would have met Mrs Dellow,' he said to Nathanial.

'Maybe he isn't smarter than he looks after all,' James said.

Gilbert would have loved to prove them wrong and fire question after question:

Why was your sister made up to look like a doll, James? Why abandon her in death?

What did you discover about your origins? Do you know of more children taken? Have you met them?

What were you doing at the doll shop this morning, Nathanial? Making sure Mrs Crandle was well and truly dead?

But his self-preservation kicked in, and stepping back further, he continued to play ignorant. 'I've got to get back to the office. I came to ask you about Nurse Faithful, Mr Liddle. We think she made false insurance claims. I wondered if you'd heard anything in the neighbourhood. Don't worry, your mum's claim is safe; they can't ask for any money back for historic claims.'

'She wouldn't have known anyway. She's not a thief,' Nathanial Liddle spat.

Gilbert nodded. 'Nor were any of the other beneficiaries, we believe. Good day, then.' He saw the look they exchanged, silently asking each other if it was safe to let him walk away, but he started to depart, regardless. Then he saw Constable Jackson and called to him.

The cocky constable, who had not hidden his disdain for Gilbert in the office earlier in the week, smiled as if he had found a fly in his web.

Gilbert heard one of the men mutter, 'It's Jackson.'

'Well, what do we have here – a tea party?' Constable Jackson said with a sneer to match his mocking voice.

'The gentlemen were helping me with my enquiries, but we are finished now.'

'*The gentlemen*,' Jackson mimicked but did not get any laughs; it was apparent James Dellow and Nathanial Liddle had little time for the young police officer.

'I thought you were on the night shift in the city,' Gilbert said, studying Constable Jackson and noticing his shoes were shinier and his uniform more presentable.

'I got relegated thanks to you and your boss. Now I'm walking around this dump putting up with imbeciles like this,' he said with a wave of a hand at the two men.

'Be very careful, Jackson,' James Dellow said in a threatening voice that was more educated than Jackson and Liddle. 'My friend, Nat here, knows a lot of people in this area, and we'd hate for you to have an accident.'

'Good day,' Gilbert said again and began to walk up the street as fast as he could without running. He glanced back to see Constable Jackson watching the other two men walk away. Before he reached the end, he heard footsteps hurrying towards him and turned alarmed. It was Constable Jackson.

'What did you want from them?' he demanded.

'Some information for a case we are working on.'

'Tell me, and I'll get it out of them,' Jackson said. 'This is my area now; you wouldn't survive a day here.'

'Maybe not, but I have all I need, thank you.' Gilbert had reached the corner and saw the omnibus coming down the street. He exhaled with relief. It was a close call and a mistake he would not make again.

'You don't belong in the detective ranks. You haven't got the street smarts or done the hard yards,' Jackson scoffed. 'We all know how you got there.'

Gilbert studied him and nodded. 'You are right, but nevertheless, I am there and have to work twice as hard for a modicum of respect and to prove myself. What would you have done?'

Jackson looked surprised. 'About what?'

'If you had been given the chance, offered the role, even if you knew it was a shortcut. Would you have taken it?'

Jackson's eyes narrowed, and as the omnibus pulled up, the constable walked away without answering, kicking a stone and not looking back.

'I thought so,' Gilbert said under his breath and boarded, never so pleased in his life to be on a vehicle moving away from Nurse Faithful's neighbourhood.

Chapter 28

MID-AFTERNOON, JULIUS PROGRESSED SLOWLY down the stairs to Phoebe's room. He stopped halfway and asked, 'I have a white flag. Should I wave it?'

'I would take cover if I were you,' she retorted with a hint of a smile.

Encouraged, he continued down the stairs and made his way to her workbench, where Phoebe styled an elderly lady's hair in a dignified manner.

'I am sorry, Phoebe,' he said in the quiet manner in which they spoke to each other. 'Not for speaking with him and calling him to task for distressing you, but for not waiting until you were ready to tell me the full story. I was…'

'Angry? Impatient? Impetuous?' she offered some words.

'No,' he pondered her words, doing his best not to bite and give credence to them. 'Protective, concerned and yes, a little angry that he might not treat you as you deserve.'

'Oh, Julius,' Phoebe sighed and stopped her work to look at him. 'You are the dearest of brothers, and I am grateful for your protection, but I'm embarrassed that you accused him of something he did not do.'

'And yet, before I had said a word, Harland confessed he was at fault. He said he did not acknowledge you kindly nor send you home to ensure your safety.'

'Did he?' she asked curiously. 'Tell me how your conversation went then and do not favour yourself.'

Julius faked indignation. 'As if I would. I entered his office, grabbed Harland by the throat, and pushed him against the wall. I told him if he came near you again, I would bury him.'

Phoebe gave her brother a wry look, making him laugh. 'And do not paint yourself as a villain. I know you would not do that, although you once might have.'

'True.' He told her about the conversation. When he had finished, Phoebe waited a moment, during which he held his breath.

'I see. That sounds rather rational,' she said, and Julius exhaled in relief at her calm tone. The siblings had rarely fallen out, and he was not of a mind to do so. 'Thank you for not forbidding him to see me. I might have had to sneak behind your back if you did.'

'Yes,' he said, narrowing his eyes, 'the thought had crossed my mind. I wish you had fallen in love with Bennet.'

'I know.'

'But I do like Harland. He is a man of integrity.'

'Let us have our chance, brother. It may amount to nothing, who is to say?' she said and reached for his hand. 'I feel better for knowing why he reacted as he did and that he felt remorse afterwards, thank you.'

Julius kissed her hand and left her to her work. Now, to check on Ambrose.

Harland looked to the ceiling as if he could see the heavens beyond and sought strength before returning his attention to Gilbert.

'There's a reason why we are always paired, and that is one of them. You are not to place yourself in danger again. Do you understand, Detective Payne?'

'Yes, Sir,' Gilbert said and swallowed at the use of his full title. 'I knew you were report writing, and I had visited the coroner, so... I didn't expect danger, but it presented itself.'

'Assume that any foray into an area where a crime might have taken place could be dangerous,' Harland said before sighing. 'Well, at least Constable Jackson has been of some use, even if unintentional.'

'His uniform and shoes were in better condition, too,' Gilbert said, sitting behind his desk.

After taking a minute to rein in his anger rather than take it out on the irresponsible act of his protégé, Harland added, 'Your research is most inciteful.'

'Seeing them together, Sir, there is little doubt they are siblings. But how do they know for sure unless one of the *Storks* confessed to them?'

'They may be making assumptions and are hellbent on taking revenge. But why would they care?' Harland mused. 'Nathanial Liddle might begrudge the better life James Dellow had, but surely Dellow is not angry to have missed out on a life of struggle—' he stopped. 'Ah, but of course. Dellow's father was an angry, violent man who terrorised the family, whereas Liddle's father had passed, and his mother was loving.'

'I understand James Dellow's anger, especially with his sister committed to an asylum. The love of siblings and a family environment vastly differs from the violent home he and Miss Dellow grew up in.'

Harland shrugged. 'Easy for Dellow to say when he's never been without. Nathanial Liddle might have preferred to attend an elite school, wear better clothes, and know that good food would always be on the table.' He stopped pacing and sat behind his own desk. 'I don't know how Dellow persuaded his so-called brother to seek revenge. What is in it for Liddle? Did the man seem impressionable?'

'No, he was wilful enough but was good to his mother.'

'Hmm. So, was it a statement then that Dellow made by abandoning his sister in death for us to find? We know the *Storks* gifted the dolls, and Dellow dressed his sister similarly and left her on display for all to see.'

'Why not leave her outside the doll store?' Gilbert asked.

'Too many eyes or police patrols, whereas the miniature display was locked up, and he did place her upon the relevant city block. Assuming of course this was his work.'

'I can't imagine it is anyone else's work, Sir, or a motive for doing so,' Gilbert said.

'Nor can I,' Harland agreed. 'We will get James Dellow and Nathanial Liddle in for questioning one at a time, but for now, I shall assign a senior constable to keep an eye on both. If anything should happen to the remaining *Storks*, I want to catch them committing the crime.'

'That would make our case easier to prove,' Gilbert agreed. 'The report from the coroner is no more enlightening; Dr McGregor had nothing to add, and sadly, the shops on either side are not residences, so, at that hour of the night, there was no one around.'

Harland sighed and sat back, looking at their board with very little detail on it. 'Those two names on the list Miss Astin gave you—the remaining *Storks*—we need to track them down and warn them. If Dellow and Liddle believe we are onto them, they may become desperate and act more quickly to harm the ladies.' He remonstrated again, adding, 'It would have been more useful and safer if you had sought the remaining *Storks'* addresses than ventured into a shady neighbourhood.'

'I have done that too, Sir,' Gilbert said, opening his notebook.

'Of course you have,' Harland said under his breath, and as Gilbert gave him a sheepish look, Harland rolled his eyes, and it appeared the lecture, for now, was over.

Lilly Lewis had little regard for her skirts or their state as she strode through the cemetery. Grass, dirt and weeds snagged her, but she hurried on. Lilly had filed her story earlier—that of the death of Mrs Crandle with comments courtesy of Detective Harland Stone—and in the last light of the day, she sought to investigate the life insurance crime a little closer.

Across the path, her partner, Fergus, was walking along, muttering a name and looking at headstones.

'Lilly! Found them,' his voice carried, and she hurried over to his side. 'The church records weren't far wrong, just other graves had obscured them in time.' He pointed to the one headstone with two inscriptions.

'That is them,' Lilly said and read it with great interest.

Infants Liddle

Mordecai and Edie.

Lost but loved, taken above.

12 February 1862.

'That is the same date that James and Jane Dellow were born. It is too much of a coincidence when Nurse Faithful was the midwife,' Lilly said, looking pleased.

'So, who are the poor babes abandoned and buried here if not the real Mordecai and Edie?' Fergus asked.

'Well, if the detectives and Phoebe are correct, they are the deceased twins of Mrs Dellow. In return, she received the living Mordecai and Edie and named them James and Jane.'

'Poor little ones,' Fergus said, his tone reflecting his sorrow.

'You are sentimental about this,' she studied him, surprised.

'I am a father of a young boy; it is hard not to be saddened by it. I believe what you say, that the women's intentions might have been good, but would Mrs Liddle agree if she knew her twins were alive?'

'Given she had just lost her husband and had no family support, it is likely Mrs Liddle would have had to farm all her children out to charity or orphanages. This way, she kept all five and never knew of the two young ones.'

'That doesn't mean she did not think of them often. You will feel that one day, Lilly.'

'I feel it now, Fergus. I don't need to be a mother to understand the pain it would cause to lose or be separated from a child,' she corrected him indignantly, and he held up his hands in a peace-making gesture. 'I am human. I am only saying that five saved is better than all lost. The insurance money from these babes kept the family together.'

'And perhaps it would not have been so bad if James and Jane Dellow had experienced happy childhoods, but clearly that was not the case from what the detective told you.' Fergus looked around. 'I wonder how many more are buried in this infant section that are not who they are as claimed on the headstone.'

'We should get the sketch artist to draw this headstone in its surroundings. It would be poignant with our story when the detective gives me the nod to publish it,' Lilly said and exhaled.

'Yes, that is a good idea. Did the detectives appear to be any closer to closing this case this morning when you were in their company?' Fergus asked.

'I believe so, not that they would admit that to me,' Lilly said as she established her bearings to instruct the illustrator, and they started their walk out of the cemetery grounds. 'There was a resolute look about Detective Stone, as if Mrs Crandle's death confirmed he was on the right path. I would not be surprised if he finds her murderer this very day.'

'Then our report tomorrow will be the lead story,' Fergus grinned. 'I shall never tire of it.'

'Nor I,' Lilly said with a grin, appreciating her partner and good fortune. 'It is a great day to be alive,' she said, departing the cemetery.

Chapter 29

Mrs Louise Killick had not told the police the truth; how could she? Adjusting the curtain, she watched as the two detectives departed in the dusk light. With her sixtieth birthday but days away, she found she was more easily startled these days. Perhaps because she could not run as fast as she once could or protect herself if need be. If she had admitted to having received some frightening messages, then she would have had to admit why, and that part of her life was a closed book. All the *Storks* had sworn to secrecy; too many lives were at risk, too much could be undone.

Louise quickly checked the house – the windows and doors were locked. When her husband was alive, they never bothered with locking the house. No one did. But times were changing; it was a decade until the start of a new century, and the population and crime were on the increase. She began to hum a hymn to stop herself from overthinking.

No more than three streets away in the suburb of Woolloongabba, another *Stork*, former wet nurse, Mrs Winifred Stockton, 48, was returning from work. Her nursing days were long over; she worked as a cashier these days. Her husband would not be home from his night of drinking until much later, and Winifred was grateful for the reprieve. Alarm had her heart racing when she saw the note in the letterbox asking her to contact Detective Harland Stone at the Roma Street Police Headquarters.

What now?

First Charlotte Faithful, then Frances Crandle. Was it more than a coincidence?

Her alarm turned to rage. Winifred Stockton would not be intimidated. If someone has something to say to her, they can march up the stairs, knock on the door, and lay out their grievance. With that sorted in her mind, Winifred set about preparing her dinner. On her bed sat a gift that she was yet to discover – a toy tin soldier like the one her husband used to make for the *Storks* to gift to new mothers. Harmless enough, some might say.

'Beer?' the coroner, Dr Tavish McGregor, asked.

'Yes, thanks,' Harland said, letting Tavish order while he viewed the competition. He would take on a couple of men in his weight category; he just had to be careful not to get too many hits to the face. It didn't look good for a senior detective to look like he'd been accosted on the job.

Harland needed to fight; he recognised the signs within himself and knew if he did not release some steam, he would do so at an inopportune time, having to apologise later for his actions. If not for the fact that he had been hot-headed on seeing Miss Astin at the doll hospital and reprimanded by her brother, he most likely would have been angrier with Gilbert for his potentially dangerous act today. Harland was frustrated and struggling – with the case, in love, in general.

For that reason, he found himself at the Brunswick Club – a bar and boxing club in Fortitude Valley. Harland was not convinced that everything that went on here was legitimate, but given he had won several boxing bouts at the club since arriving in Brisbane and there was nothing obvious amiss, he was prepared to ignore that which happened behind closed doors.

He accepted the beer and nodded towards a large man in the corner, who was about to enter the ring. 'He might do for a bout if he's still standing by the time I'm ready.'

'You could start with someone more your size,' Tavish said, and Harland raised an eyebrow, turning to study the man again.

'I thought he was my size. I'm obviously not as big as I thought,' he said, making Tavish laugh.

'I'm just having a joke at your expense,' Tavish said, his Scottish accent stronger as he relaxed and drank his beer. 'He'd be about your match. Have a few drinks first; you might feel more relaxed and not need to take to the ring.'

Harland grunted, believing that scenario to be unlikely.

'Ah, here's the rest of the lads,' Tavish said, and Harland followed his gaze to see Julius and Bennet enter. Julius could hold his own but rarely fought, and Bennet liked a bet, so they were no strangers to the venue. Harland stiffened. After this morning's awkward encounter, he wondered how Julius would react when they were out socially together, and Miss Phoebe Astin was not the reason for their meeting.

'Get off early tonight?' Bennet asked Harland, shaking hands.

'I don't think I'm ever off the clock.'

'That's what my father says,' Bennet recalled of his serving detective father.

Harland shook Julius's offered hand, and the two looked elsewhere. Julius had always welcomed and encouraged Harland to join the group, even though Tavish introduced the men. They had found common ground and interests – business, human nature, and sport. He felt Tavish studying them; not much got past him.

Harland cleared his throat. 'I needed to do a few rounds.' He looked at the ring and turned to the group to find Julius studying him.

'Ah, what is going on with you two?' Tavish said, looking from one man to the other.

'Nothing—'

'Not a thing—' They both answered quickly and in unison, making Tavish laugh.

'Something then,' the coroner said with a raised eyebrow in Bennet's direction, who gave a small shrug.

'I am oblivious,' Bennet offered.

'Well then, Harland, Julius, will you take on each other?' Tavish asked.

'Definitely not,' Julius said. 'I'd be whipped.'

'I'd put money on you,' Bennet said and added so as not to offend Harland, 'I like an underdog.'

Harland scoffed. 'I cannot imagine I would be welcomed at *The Economic Undertaker* by Mr Astin senior or Miss Astin if

I did any damage to the proprietor. Not to mention your stab wound would not be fully healed yet?'

'It is considerably better but still burns like hell,' Julius agreed.

'I will get a round,' Tavish said. 'Bennet, give us a hand.'

'Right, yes,' Bennet hurriedly answered and gave Julius a look of interest on departing.

'Apparently, we've been left alone to sort out our differences,' Julius said with a smile.

'Should we put on a show for them? A bit of head shaking, fist waving and a threat or two?' Harland suggested, and Julius laughed.

'Tempting.'

'Should your sensible sister reject me, I hope it will not change our friendship,' Harland said and saw Julius's barriers go down.

'If she has any brains, she will,' Julius said and grinned at Harland's smirk. He added, 'I think our friendship can withstand your rejection, should that happen.'

Harland exhaled and looked away. He thought the odds of Miss Astin walking away from him were reasonable. 'I am going to take him on.' He sized up an opponent and took off his jacket.

'Now?' Julius asked, surprised.

'Right now. Let him do his worst, then I can relax or lick my wounds, or both.'

Harland left his jacket with Julius, his tie long since removed, and heading to the ring, he began rolling up his sleeves. He needed this, and if nothing else, he would prove to Julius that his sister would be safe in his care. Harland would always protect her.

Tavish placed Harland's drink on the table as the men watched him enter the ring. Julius accepted the beer with thanks.

'He looks fit enough,' Tavish said.

'He can hold his own,' Julius agreed.

'Must feel good to let off a bit of steam,' Bennet said, 'although I prefer to do it with my paintbrush. I'm going to place a bet.' He took the odds from Julius and Tavish and left them to put the bet on before the official fight began. Harland was now pacing around the ring, as was his opponent, waiting for the call to start, for the bell to ring.

'Are Ambrose and Lucian coming?' Tavish asked above the rising noise of interest in the fight about to start.

'No, Ambrose is annoyed with me, I believe,' Julius said.

'And you've had a fallout with Harland?' Tavish stirred. 'You've had a successful day.'

Julius gave a huff of laughter. 'I can't have offended Harland too much, or he'd be taking me on instead of that poor sod.'

'Ah, but he loves your sister, so he won't do anything to harm her precious brother.'

Julius turned to Tavish. 'You don't miss much, do you?'

'I spend my day looking for signs and markers on the dead; sometimes it transfers to the living,' he said and chuckled as Bennet rejoined them. 'Here he goes.' Tavish cupped his mouth and shouted, 'Knock him out, Stone!'

The fighters were well suited in build, and it would be skill, not strength, that would most likely find the winner; Harland Stone looked more determined, and Julius understood where it came from. Waiting for Violet and feeling like he might lose her pushed him to the edge, and Harland had been waiting long enough. He imagined Harland might suffer if his affection for his sister was half as strong as Julius felt for Violet.

And then the first blow was struck.

At 10pm, retired nurse Louise Killick turned in. She carried a small lantern to the bathroom and performed her nightly ablutions before retiring to her bedroom.

On entering, her breath hitched. The window was open; the breeze moved the curtain, and it was pitch black outside. Frozen, Louise backed slowly out of the room. She would leave the house, even if it meant standing in the middle of the street until she thought about what to do next, but something caught her eye as she turned. A doll sat in the middle of her bed, nestled on her pillow – a doll she knew only too well from her *Storks* days.

With a scream of terror, Louise dropped the lantern, the flame licking the curtains and rug, and they blazed like a torch in the night. A firm push on her back saw her tumbling into the room. The door slammed behind her. Louise struggled to her feet and grappled for the door, but the rug in front of it was aflame, and she pulled away in fright. The only exit was through the window, where the curtains were ablaze. Moments later, the window slammed closed from outside, and Louise Killick was trapped in the room, a fire burning, a doll smiling at her as she collapsed in terror.

Several streets away, Winifred Stockton was pleased to hear her husband's footsteps on the internal stairs.

'Is that you, love?' she called out.

There was no answer.

Chapter 30

IT WAS NEARING MIDNIGHT when Ambrose—who had been in bed for less than thirty minutes but had fallen into an easy sleep—called out in fear.

Phoebe sat bolt upright in the room across the hallway from him, woken by her brother's cry in the quiet of the night.

Downstairs, Randolph Astin, a light sleeper before he and Maria became the carers of their three grandchildren and was even more so once they came into his care, awoke. Even though his grandchildren were adults, he heard every sound under his roof. Beside him, Maria slept soundly; she had always done so.

He shrugged on his dressing gown and hurried up the stairs, telling Phoebe all was well and sending her back to bed as they met at the top of the staircase. But Ambrose's cry of fear was loud enough to cause him alarm. Knocking, Randolph did not wait for an invitation but barged straight in.

'Grandpa!' Ambrose said between gasps, gripping his heart.

'What on earth is wrong, lad?' he dropped onto the bed, grabbing Ambrose by the shoulders.

'I was buried alive; I couldn't breathe,' he gasped.

'It was a dream. You are above ground and breathing. We would not abandon you to be buried, Ambrose,' his grandfather soothed him. Even though he was an adult now, both men had fallen into a familiar routine; there were many nightmares after the death of the children's parents, especially for Julius.

Ambrose hurriedly regained himself. 'Of course. I am sorry I woke you, Grandpa, a stupid dream, that is all,' he said, his breathing steadying.

'I was awake, do not worry. Do you want to come downstairs for a cup of tea or hot chocolate?'

'Yes,' Ambrose said without hesitation. 'I need to put the dream well behind me.'

Randolph waited as Ambrose rose and donned a dressing gown to ward off the midnight cooling of a spring night. As they took to the stairs, they heard Phoebe talking.

Randolph hurried to her door and knocked.

'Come in,' she called, and the two men tentatively entered. 'I must tell someone, but whom? Nurse Charlotte Faithful is here and tells me two former *Storks* are in danger now!'

'I will dress and ride to Harland's place,' Ambrose offered.

'Thank you, Ambrose. Nurse Faithful is saying the name Louise Killick. Please hurry, but be careful.' She nodded as the spectre they could not see spoke to her, and Phoebe responded.

'I will change and come with you, Ambrose,' Randolph offered as the two men exited Phoebe's room.

'No need, Grandpa. If I need backup, I shall go via Julius's house.'

Appeased, Randolph agreed, and Ambrose was dressed and out the door quickly. Phoebe came downstairs to the kitchen, where her grandfather was making a pot of tea.

'I fear it is too late to help them,' Phoebe said suddenly.

'Why do you—' Randolph stopped. 'Oh, do you see them?'

Phoebe shook her head. 'Thankfully, no. But Nurse Faithful just came and went; she told me Mrs Louise Killick had now passed to the other side.'

'What a burden that is for you, child.'

'I truly don't feel it is so, Grandpa.'

Randolph sighed and glanced to the window, fearful for his grandson. He would wait up until Ambrose returned.

Harland was not long in bed when he was awoken by banging on the front door of his residence.

'It's the women, the remaining *Storks*,' Ambrose panted as Harland opened the door. But before he could finish, Harland had rushed to his room to dress, being proficient at doing so quickly. Racing out of the house, he joined Ambrose in the Astin's small trap, and they hurried to Louise Killick's address, which Harland had visited early that evening.

'What happened? What do you know?'

'Nurse Faithful appeared to Phoebe and said the two *Storks* were in danger. She gave Louise Killick's name. Do you know who the other one is?' Ambrose asked.

'Yes, thank you for coming to alert me. Please thank Miss Astin for me as well.' Harland groaned as the house came into sight.

They could see the small crowd in the street and smell the smoke as they approached. It was soon clear that the fire was out, but not before it had destroyed over half of the timber house.

Harland leapt down and hurried over to the constables at the scene.

'Dead, Sir,' the young man told him. 'The lady who lives here... the fire was in her bedroom.'

'Did you see anything, constable?'

'No, Sir. I kept an eye on the place as directed, but no one came in the front or side while I was here. They must have climbed over fences if they came in via the back.' The constable looked at one of the firemen. 'They think she tipped over her lantern, and the flame caught the curtain.'

'Thank you, Constable. Take another constable with you and go as quickly as you can to the home of Mrs Winifred Stockon.' Harland told him the address. 'If she is well, and all seems in order, you can resume your duty. When you wake tomorrow or after your night shift, please see me at Roma Street to report in.'

He left the constable and approached one of the firemen rolling up the hand reel out the front of the home. Harland identified himself.

'The body is in there, waiting for you and the coroner,' he said with a nod to the house. 'We got here pretty quickly, but...' he shook his head. 'She would have breathed in a lot of smoke with the windows closed.'

'Did you see anyone loitering or leaving the house?'

'Yes, all the neighbours were out and about with buckets of water by the time we arrived, and several had braved the house to try to rescue her. But no one looking guilty, if that's what you mean?'

Harland nodded. 'Can I enter?'

'Yeah, the fire is extinguished if you want to go in,' the man said, allowing Harland entry.

Harland thanked the fireman and went to enter but remembered Ambrose was still waiting nearby. He returned to him.

'Mrs Killick is dead. Thank you, Ambrose; I will be here a while if you want to head home. My thanks to you both.'

'You will not check on the other lady?'

'I've sent two constables, and I will follow when I am finished here.' He bid Ambrose good night, thanked him again, and entered the premises. The smell of the burnt timber filled his lungs, and he quietly cursed himself for not doing more to protect the woman. Louise Killick was adamant she had not been threatened when he spoke to her earlier, but if she did not want to admit to being a *Stork*, she likely concealed the truth from him.

He stopped in the hallway, seeing her burnt remains, and then looked around the door, keen to establish one thing. A doll was on the bed. The face remained, surprising Harland that it did not crack, given its thinness. Perhaps the firemen put out the flames before it got too hot in the room. The rest of the doll's body had burned, but there was no doubt it was the same face and doll. The deathly doll had struck again.

Phoebe and Randolph waited and met Ambrose at the door on his return.

'What happened?' Phoebe asked, not waiting for him to enter.

'Louise Killick is dead. I do not know about the other lady; Harland will go there next.'

Phoebe exhaled; her shoulders slumped. 'We knew as much. Nurse Faithful said she had joined her, but Mrs Stockton had not yet. Thank you for delivering the message.'

'You are welcome, and Harland said to thank you; he was grateful for the information.' Ambrose entered and followed Randolph into the kitchen, where a pot of tea remained on the warmer. Phoebe poured him a cup.

'How did she die, do you know, lad?' Randolph asked.

'A fire. It destroyed half of her timber cottage, including the bedroom where she was sleeping. Before I left, Harland confirmed she was dead.'

'What a terrible job he has,' Phoebe said sympathetically.

'And comforting him and bearing the hours he worked would be the lot of his wife,' Randolph said gently, his message not going astray.

'We shall all be weary on our feet tomorrow,' Phoebe said, sitting beside Ambrose. 'Only Julius will be bright and cheerful.'

They all smiled at the thought of Julius being cheerful.

'Well, he'll be awake,' Ambrose said, and they allowed themselves a small laugh to chase away the glumness of the evening.

Chapter 31

DETECTIVE GILBERT PAYNE ARRIVED at the office the next morning, having earlier called on the last of the living *Storks*, Mrs Winifred Stockton. He was pleased to find she was as alive this morning as last evening when the constables woke her and Mr Stockton from their sleep.

Now, on arrival at his shared office, Gilbert found Detective Harland Stone sitting at the desk with his head in his hands.

'Sir?' he said concerned, entering and removing his hat.

'Ah,' Harland looked up, 'you are back.'

Gilbert saw some bruising and swelling on the senior detective's face. 'Did that happen last night?' He indicated the eye area.

'What? Oh, the bruising, no. I had a few rounds in the ring earlier in the evening. I do my best not to wear my sport on my face. What have you then?'

Gilbert went to his desk and sat down. 'Mrs Winifred Stockton is still alive and well, and so is her husband, I am pleased to say.'

'Well, that is a relief, at least,' Harland said, sitting back.

'You have some bad news, Sir?'

'I have no news, so yes, Gilbert, you might say that. I will catch you up shortly. Tell me then if anything suspicious happened to them last evening?'

'Nothing, Sir. She was surprised by my visit and assured me she got your card yesterday and intended to drop into the station today. She was also most upset to hear of the passing of Mrs Louise Killick.'

'Yes, she is the last remaining,' Harland mused. 'If the deaths are natural or accidents—which I don't believe they are—she has nothing to fear, but I believe Mrs Stockton knows better.'

'I think you are right, Sir. The neighbour pulled me aside as I was about to depart,' Gilbert said, 'and told me he heard Mr and Mrs Stockton having a ferocious fight late last night. Supposedly, from what the neighbour overheard, Mr Stockton did not announce himself on the stairs and scared Mrs Stockton "into next week", Sir, her words, I believe.'

Harland scoffed. 'I bet he did.' He rose, closed the door, and began to pace. 'We have nothing. No one was seen going into Louise Killick's house or leaving, but the doll was left on the bed, and the windows were sealed, almost as if glued into place, but had no obvious obstructions. It is possible she dropped her lamp in fright, and it set the room alight.'

'What of our two suspects, Sir, Liddle and Dellow?' Gilbert asked, looking to the board and back to Harland, who shook his head.

'At the time of the fire, Liddle and Dellow were together at the pub on the corner and in perfect sight of the constable I assigned to watch them. They could not be in two places at once.' He threw up his hands in despair. 'We need to start from the beginning. Let us do so now, Gilbert, and go back over every piece of evidence we have. We may unearth something.'

Gilbert rose, grabbed several folders from the shared table, and returned to his desk. 'From the beginning,' he said and would not admit it out loud, but he did enjoy raking over cases and hoping something would fall into their laps. On this occasion, hopefully before the last of the *Storks* met her end.

Julius glanced to his left at Ambrose, who stood some distance from the grave and not in the customary position beside him to see the coffin into the earth. He noticed his brother looked weary and heard of his late-night ride to get Detective Stone. He raised a questioning eyebrow at him, and Ambrose gave a small shake of his head. Julius returned his attention to the grave, and once the blessing was done and the body lowered in, he stepped back with the priest to allow the family to say their final farewells.

'What is the matter?' Julius asked, now at his brother's side.

'Nothing, all is well. Just a little tired.' Ambrose tugged at his suit jacket and straightened.

'Falling in the other day has you rattled,' Julius said and could see his brother was about to deny it, but instead, Ambrose gave a small, indifferent shrug. Julius reassured him, 'In all the years we have been doing this, it has only happened once, so the odds are good it won't happen again, brother.'

Ambrose nodded but did not take his eyes off the gravesite.

Julius continued in a low voice. 'Besides, I understood you threw yourself in to assist the woman out.'

Now Ambrose looked away, and Julius dropped the matter as they both farewelled the family and friends of the deceased, wishing them well. Once alone, Julius thanked the priest and gave the gravediggers the nod to fill the grave.

'Come then, we'll talk about it on the way back,' he said, walking away, and as they both arrived at the hearse wagon, he took the reins and climbed in, taking the seat next to Ambrose, who had entered swiftly as if keen to depart.

Julius gave him another curious look, which did not go unnoticed.

'There is nothing to talk about; I am just being cautious,' Ambrose assured him, his voice displaying an indifference that rang hollow.

'Grandpa told me about your nightmare.'

Ambrose threw his hands in the air. 'Why?'

'Maybe because he was concerned about you. As am I.'

Ambrose scoffed. 'There is nothing to be concerned about. It was a bad dream. Here I am in the light of day, business as usual.'

Julius nudged the horses forward, ensuring all mourners had departed before steering the hearse through the cemetery gates and continuing his discussion.

'I don't care about the business, Ambrose, or that you are here reporting for duty. I am concerned for you. What has you worried? We've been around graves and cemeteries for years, and you have never expressed concern before.'

'Nor am I now,' Ambrose reminded him.

'Did you fear somehow you might be left in that plot?'

'Of course not. Will was with me, as were the gravediggers.'

Bemused, Julius let the matter rest momentarily, knowing his brother would respond when he could articulate his thoughts. Sure enough, within a short period, Ambrose explained with a sigh.

'I was in the grave with a dead person, and the dirt was piling in around us. There was a joke about leaving me there—nothing more than a few words said in jest—but the sense of being there with dirt shovelled upon me felt foreboding. What if Will hadn't returned or had somehow been prevented from doing so? What if one of the gravediggers had turned on me?'

Julius nodded as he thought. Ambrose's concerns were irrational, but many fears were, except for those who suffered them.

'Not wishing to make it about business, but your fear is a little worrying given what we do for our living,' Julius said. 'You know you would die quite quickly if buried and not in the coffin? The weight of the soil and no oxygen... it would be over in no time.'

'Comforting, thank you, brother. But...' Ambrose gave a small shake of his head.

'Tell me.' Julius insisted.

'I don't fear that. I fear... it's ridiculous, forget it.' He looked away.

'It cannot be ridiculous if it has you standing back from the grave and having nightmares.'

'One nightmare.'

'Tell me.'

Ambrose took a deep breath. 'What if I am never found, and I spend my eternal life in a grave without my family?' He held up his hand. 'See, it is ridiculous. And do not say we will all meet on the other side; I will be buried alone.'

Julius frowned as he considered a suitable response. He thought about his brother's fear and realised how the death of their parents had affected them all so differently. He was fourteen when they passed away, and it had changed his life. As an adult, he was soberer in nature, craving security, both emotional and financial, and overprotective of those he loved. Ambrose was eleven and Phoebe nine years old at the time, but now he saw the insecurity and fear of abandonment behind his brother's over-confident façade. He wondered how their history might manifest in his little sister.

Julius nudged his brother, having found a simple answer. 'There is a simple solution.'

'There is?' Ambrose said, giving him a sceptical look as Julius steered the horses and hearse into the backyard of *The Economic Undertaker*.

'Of course. Send your spirit to talk with Phoebe, or if you can't do that, ask Uncle Reggie to tell us where you are. He has appeared on behalf of two spirits with messages for Phoebe. Tell her where you are, and we will retrieve you to our care.'

Ambrose stared at his brother and then huffed with laughter. 'Why did I not think of that?' he asked, smiling as if a load had fallen off his shoulders.

'Because it is well known I am the smart one,' Julius said in jest, and Ambrose laughed.

'On this occasion, I will bow to that.' He slapped Julius on the back and jumped from the hearse, a lighter man.

Julius smiled and shook his head, handing the reins to Charlie with thanks. Two fires were put out, and both siblings were happy again. He exhaled with relief and followed Ambrose into the office.

After two hours of revisiting their notes and files, Detective Harland Stone sat back in his chair. 'I have a theory, Gilbert, but before I voice it, I think we need to have a tea break while I clear my head.'

'I, too, have several interesting facts to share, Sir. I will fetch us tea and biscuits then.'

Harland thanked him and removed himself to the bathroom, pleased to leave the confines of the office and breathe some fresh air. He chatted with a few people along the way, assured several that they had a strong lead even if he did not feel confident, and returned to his office to find the tea and biscuits waiting. He had come to not dismiss Gilbert's facts out of hand. While sometimes they seemed irrelevant, they have, in several cases, been quite pertinent.

Lord knows what he will come up with today, Harland thought.

Gilbert returned moments later, patting his face with the cold water on his hands.

'I am ready, Sir.'

'Would you like to share your facts first?' Harland asked as both men returned to their desks with tea and biscuits.

Gilbert thought for a moment. 'No, Sir, they may be irrelevant, so I shall wait to see if they support your theory, if I may?'

Harland nodded. 'Over the past hour, I have considered everyone who might be involved, including other children who may have discovered the deception. There is one person I would like to investigate... it is a long shot. George Stockton.'

Gilbert frowned. 'George Stockton? Mrs Winifred Stockton's husband?' He began ruffling through his files.

'Yes, the wet nurse's husband, the doll maker, whom you called on this very morning.'

Gilbert paused. 'And, coincidentally perhaps, the husband of the last surviving *Stork*. Why George Stockton now, Sir?'

'The constable on duty said something that stuck with me. He spoke with Stockton last night when he went to warn them and believed him to be sober. But his wife had told me he'd been out drinking with the boys and got in late, startling her.'

'That is interesting,' Gilbert said.

'My thoughts exactly. Stockton might be completely innocent, but I am curious. He made dolls and tin soldiers; his work inspired Frances and Frank Crandle to start a doll hospital, and he knew the ladies. Did he know what they were doing?'

'If he did, why would he take so long to revenge their actions? Unless he just found out recently,' Gilbert said, drinking his tea and reaching for a second biscuit. 'Interesting theory, Sir, but what would be his motive?'

'Yes, my theory has some holes. Why would George Stockton feel the need to revenge their actions? Surely not because his toys were used as ruses? Unless he has an emotional involvement. But the fact that his wife is the last person standing is curious. Perhaps he frightened her deliberately last night when he came in late.'

'If he met Liddle and Dellow at the pub, perhaps they worked it out together – the two babies were delivered by his wife with the help of the *Storks*. He might be disgusted; I wonder if he is a religious man,' Gilbert mused, then shook his head. 'But he would have to be very disgusted to murder three women unless, as you said, he is somehow emotionally involved. Like a parent, godparent or is a little ill in the mind.'

'Yes. It is worth talking to him today. I am at a loss if he is not the guilty party. Tell me your facts, Gilbert.'

'I have several to share, Sir, but one is particularly relevant to your theory.'

'Go ahead; I'd welcome it if it supports our case,' Harland said keenly, finishing his tea and grimacing at the weak brew.

'It's about the dolls, Sir. I wondered how the original dolls and tin soldiers were being acquired. After all, not many people keep a doll for twenty or thirty years. I haven't any of my childhood toys.'

'Nor do I,' Harland agreed. 'Go on.'

'Well, maybe George Stockton is making new dolls and tin soldiers that he leaves behind at the crime scene. An interesting fact, Sir, is that the eyes were painted on dolls in the 1860s and 1870s when Mr Stockton first made the dolls. Now, in the 1890s, the technique is to use glass eyes. I noticed that the doll we retrieved from Nurse Faithful's brother had glass eyes, so a doll maker has made it recently.'

Harland smiled. 'Gilbert, that is excellent.'

'Thank you, Sir,' Gilbert grinned, delighted.

'Let us begin with the doll hospital. I want to know if Mr Crandle was acquainted with Mr Stockton.'

'Ah, good thought, Sir, although I believe his grief over Mrs Crandle's death is genuine.'

'As do I, but I want to know if he had much to do with Stockton's toy and doll-making interests. Then, to the pub that Stockton was supposedly at last night to see if he was there and if so, what time he left. We will finish with the man himself,' Harland said, heading for the hat rack.

The two men, energised, departed with a new skip in their step.

Chapter 32

Julius looked left and then right and, deciding it was safe, pulled Violet towards him for a quick kiss. She happily reciprocated, then laughed, pulling away.

'We are engaged. I don't think anyone would be too outraged by our actions,' she said.

'Nevertheless, we shall do this right. I have just redeemed myself with my sister and brother, so I don't wish to have you angry with me.'

Violet looked at him, surprised. 'Do tell. What did you do that put both offside, I can't imagine?'

'I defended Phoebe's honour without consulting her, and I was absent at a funeral where Ambrose had to pull a young lady from the freshly dug hole when she cast herself upon her mother's coffin. He got his suit dirty.'

'Good heavens, you are diabolic,' Violet laughed. 'I am sure I cannot marry you now.'

He grinned and pulled her closer. 'At least you know what you are getting into.'

'Yes, I am definitely having second thoughts.' She gave him a quick kiss and smiled. 'You did your best with Phoebe even if you might have gone about it the wrong way; as for Ambrose, well, goodness me, it shows how close you both are.'

'Does it?' Julius asked, surprised.

'Of course. Your brother meets with duress and immediately assumes you will save the day. Perhaps the experience was good for him, in a roundabout way.'

'Perhaps,' Julius considered her words. 'But I am pleased with your assumption – that he would look at me to fix the problem. I always want to be that for Ambrose and Phoebe, and you and Tom.'

'And I shall be that for you. We are soppy this morning.'

'You are right, Miss Forrester,' Julius teased, going all formal. 'Please get back to work, or I will have to dock your salary.'

'Yes, Sir,' she said and kissed him quickly again before they left the meeting room and joined the two ladies in the front of the store, who were suddenly very engrossed in their work.

Julius addressed Mary. 'Miss Pollard.'

Her head shot up, and she looked terrified. 'Yes, Sir.'

'I wanted to thank you. I believe you have designed a beautiful wedding dress for my fiancée, and even though I haven't seen the design, nor am I allowed to,' he said with a glance at Violet, 'my future wife is delighted with it.'

Mary blushed profusely, and Nellie Shaw nodded wisely.

'Thank you, Sir, it was my pleasure. Truly.'

'You will be the most beautiful bride,' Nellie said and sighed at the romance of it all.

'You will be,' Julius agreed, and he departed with a bow to each lady, charming them all.

Detective Harland Stone was surprised to find the *Doll and Teddy Hospital* open for business and Mr Frank Crandle, proprietor, behind the desk, talking to reporter Lilly Lewis.

'Miss Lewis!' Gilbert exclaimed.

'Mr Crandle, Miss Lewis,' Harland acknowledged them both, his expression relaying his surprise at seeing them as he closed the store door behind him.

'Hello, detectives. It's always a pleasure to see you,' Lilly said with sincerity and a smile.

'I am sure it is,' Harland teased her, 'and timely for your story, no doubt.'

'No doubt,' she agreed. 'I am here speaking with Mr Crandle about his lovely wife and their business.'

Frank Crandle looked uncomfortable. 'I know it is unseemly to be open for business so soon after Frances' death, but I can't be idle. She is everywhere, and I have to keep my hands and mind busy, or I don't know what to do without her – we have always been Frances and Frank, now...' His voice hitched.

'Very understandable, Mr Crandle,' Harland sympathised.

'It was Robert Louis Stevenson who said, "Keep busy at something: a busy person never has time to be unhappy", even though, of course, you will be pained,' Gilbert added hurriedly and looked relieved when Frank Crandle agreed.

'Right you are, detective. I'll get a girl in to help soon, to serve at the counter while I continue my repairs.' He addressed Lilly, 'With your permission, Miss, I shall just tend to the detectives.'

'Oh, please do,' Lilly said, keen to know their line of enquiry.

'Thank you,' Harland said, hurrying along. 'We would like to speak with you about George Stockton.'

'George?' Mr Crandle asked, surprised. 'Is he all right? Is Winifred?'

'Fear not, they are both well, Sir,' Gilbert answered. 'How would you describe your relationship with George Stockton?'

Frank Crandle did not have to consider and answered, 'We are acquaintances, nothing more. I have a good decade or more on him in age, and I have met him only a handful of times because our wives were part of the little group they fondly called the *Storks*, but that is the extent of our connection.'

'Did he purchase any dolls or toy soldiers from you of recent?' Harland asked.

Frank looked surprised. 'No, but his work changed our lives. He suggested we start this business because he was inundated with requests to repair toys once people knew how talented he was; that didn't interest him, but I liked the idea, and I've always been good with my hands. Then Frances got a small inheritance, and we were able to open the shop.'

Harland's eyes narrowed, and Gilbert immediately recorded that piece of news, neither believing her windfall was an inheritance but more likely a payoff from the insurance money.

'I see,' Harland continued. 'Did he make dolls or soldiers for you to sell?'

'No, we only sell the donated dolls and teddies we repair, but oddly, George did ask me to keep any of his original toys for him should they ever be brought in. You know about the tin soldiers and dolls he made for the *Storks*? The toys would have to be nearly thirty years old,' Frank Crandle said.

'We do know of the *Storks'* gifts,' Gilbert said. 'When did he ask you to look out for them?'

'Only very recently. I just happened to have one of the soldiers in the shop, and Frances recognised it. She was going to tell George so he could collect it.'

Again, Harland and Gilbert exchanged quick looks, and Lilly asked bluntly, 'Was that the soldier found on the stairs the night of Mrs Crandle's death?'

Harland gave her a frown and a look that reminded her he would be asking the questions.

'I could not say,' Mr Crandle said, confused. 'I got in late, and the next morning, having found Frances dead... I can't tell you anything that happened.'

'Mr Crandle, you have been most helpful. Thank you,' Harland said.

'If you will excuse me, Mr Crandle, I shall depart with the detectives,' Lilly said and, offering the storekeeper her thanks, she slipped out as Harland held the door open for her.

'What are you thinking, detectives?' she asked, 'that George Stockton has killed all the *Storks* except his wife!'

'We do not want to draw that conclusion just yet, Miss Lewis, but it is a line of enquiry we are pursuing,' Harland said in a most restrained manner.

Lilly grinned. 'How exciting! May I come with you?'

'You don't know where we are going,' Harland reminded her.

'But it will be something to do with George Stockton.'

Gilbert smiled, and Harland rolled his eyes. 'Very well, we will check his alibi last night. Come along then.'

Harland hailed a hansom, and in moments, the three were on their way.

Chapter 33

On hearing footsteps coming down the stairs, Phoebe looked up from her worktable to find her grandfather descending. She laughed at seeing him hiding behind a large green plant in a beautiful cream-coloured pot.

'A delivery for you, my dear, from the floral shop, and not a flower in sight!' Randolph said, entering her workroom with the large plant in his arms.

'Oh, it is magnificent, Grandpa, and will lift the room beautifully. It is perfect; I do hate it when the flowers die, and now this will live on.'

'If it prospers like you in quiet, gently lit spaces.'

Phoebe smiled. 'True. The pot is very tasteful, too.'

'Yes, I suspect the sender knew the colourings of your room. Where would you like her?'

'Her?' Phoebe laughed. 'Then I shall name her Florence the fern, and if you could put her on the table under the window, please, Grandpa, that would be perfect.' Phoebe hurried to move the vase from the table.

On settling it, Randolph plucked the card from the pot and handed it to her. 'That does look lovely there,' he said, stepping back.

Phoebe opened it and smiled. 'It is from Detective Stone, thanking me for the tip-off that the *Storks* were in danger. Oh, and a message begging my patience.'

'The poor fellow, I suspect he is smitten,' Randolph said. He winked at Phoebe, and she playfully hit him with the card.

'I shall leave you and Florence to it then,' he said, departing with Phoebe's thanks.

She gave Florence some water, her heart pattering faster than usual. Harland knew her well enough to gift her something unique and different that would last, and the message was most endearing. Phoebe studied his handwriting – firm and very legible. She read the card again, hearing his voice, low and steady, saying the words he had committed to writing.

'Miss Astin, my sincere thanks for your help once again. I hope you will save me the promised dances at Miss Yalden's dinner party this Saturday

And she read it again, and a few more times throughout the morning, each time with a smile upon her face and a heart full of hope.

The publican—a middle-aged man with ruddy features—was preparing for a lunchtime crowd and greeted the detectives and Miss Lewis as his first customers. He was not quite as welcoming when Harland introduced themselves.

'Sure, I know George Stockton. He and his mates have been coming here for years,' he said. 'Not a bad bloke. What's he done?'

'Nothing, hopefully,' Harland said. 'Was he drinking here last night, and if so, did you see what time he left?'

'Well, funny you should mention that, Detective,' the publican said, 'because I don't always notice the comings-and-goings when I'm busy, but in this instance, I did.'

'Why is that, Sir?' Gilbert asked, hurrying him along before the expected arrival of the lunch customers.

'Well, George was in here with his usual mates, but he came over to buy a round and bought one short. I asked him if he meant four drinks, and he said no, he had business to attend to, so he bought them the round for his shout and left after delivering it to their table. He didn't return.'

'What time was that, Sir?' Harland asked.

'Let me think.' The publican blew out his cheeks as if challenged. 'After eleven, that's for sure.'

Harland continued, 'Were these drinking friends two younger men by the name of James Dellow and Nathanial Liddle?' Harland asked.

'No, some of his workmates around his own age, but he knows those lads and speaks with them often. They're friends of his son, who's just old enough to drink here.'

'Son?' Gilbert asked and pulled his notebook from his pocket. 'I thought Mr and Mrs Stockton only had daughters.' He flicked back through his notes.

The publican shrugged. 'Couldn't tell you.'

'Do you know where George Stockton works?' Harland asked.

'That I do. He's got a second-hand store on Stanley Street. Always been handy at doing up things and has made quite a success of it through the shop.'

'Excellent, thank you for your time,' Harland said, and the men departed, Lilly hurrying behind them.

'Where to now, detectives?' she asked.

'To see Mr Stockton himself,' Harland said. 'Miss Lewis, perhaps you should—'

'I would love to come, please, Detective. I assure you of my discretion,' Lilly pleaded.

'Right then, why not,' Harland said with a sigh.

As Gilbert and Lilly spoke of other matters, the thought that Miss Astin should have received his plant by now buoyed Harland, and he hoped she might think more fondly of him as a consequence.

The hansom took the three across town, and pulling up at the front of *Stockton's Second-Hand Goods and Chattels*, Harland spotted two of the constables on day shift.

'Gilbert, will you ask them to remain nearby in case we need them?'

'At once, Sir,' Gilbert said, signalling the men.

On entering the small store crammed with everything from chairs to jewellery to toys, Harland and Lilly made their way to the back of the store, and Gilbert hurriedly joined them. They could hear hammering, and after a ring of the bell on the counter, George Stockton appeared. His face gave him away.

'Ah, I've wondered when you might find your way here.'

'Did you, Mr Stockton, why is that?' Harland asked.

'What is it, Pa?' A tall man, barely of legal age, came from the back room; he looked the spitting image of his father. Gilbert had confirmed from his notes that George Stockton only had daughters with his wife.

'This is your son, then?' Harland asked.

George Stockton's shoulders slumped, and he looked at the young man behind him and smiled. 'Yes, it is, and I am mighty proud of him.' His son beamed.

'You were separated from him at birth?' Gilbert asked, realising the connection.

George Stockton's eyes narrowed. 'By the *Storks*. Those despicable women,' he spat the words out.

'Perhaps we had better go to the station and start at the beginning, Mr Stockton,' Harland suggested. 'Should we be collecting the two brothers?'

'What two brothers?' George Stockton asked, covering for them and obviously bluffing.

'The two young men you have been seen talking with regularly – James Dellow and Nathanial Liddle, and please don't tell us they are not brothers. We know the story, Mr Stockton,' Harland said, closing down the second-hand store owner's denials before he could begin them.

'They did nothing,' George answered in a weary tone. 'But yes, they are victims, that's for sure.'

Harland nodded, and he breathed easier for the first time that week.

It was early afternoon when the men gathered at the station, and Harland and Gilbert began their interviews. Lilly Lewis had been sent away, as expected, but was told to prepare her story and, as agreed, Harland or Gilbert would provide the facts should an arrest be made. Content with the agreement, she departed.

'We've done nothin' illegal,' Nathanial Liddle said in his uncultured voice as he sat sprawled across a chair while the brother he only recently met sat beside him in a most composed fashion.

'Nat is right,' James said, his speech highlighting his education and savvy understanding of the law. 'You are wasting your time, detectives.'

'We know that, gentlemen,' Harland said, surprising them and his partner, Gilbert. Harland's strategy was to ensure the brothers believed they were not suspects in the murder and thus to elicit as much information as possible to charge George Stockton with the crime.

'Oh, right then,' James said, 'so why are we here?'

'We've arrested George Stockton concerning the death of the ladies of the *Stork* friendship group. You know them?' Harland did not wait for an answer, adding, 'We understand he was under duress. A terrible affair.'

Nathanial nodded in agreement. 'Mum was inconsolable when we told her what we believed had happened. She would have loved James and Jane. She would have found a way to keep us all together.'

'Maybe so, maybe not,' Gilbert said. 'We understand that your mother had much to contend with at the time.'

'She did that,' Nathanial agreed. 'Dad was dead, her family in Ireland, and his family didn't want to know about us.'

'Tell us why you dumped your sister at the miniature display, James?' Harland asked abruptly, and for a moment, he thought James would deny it, but the young man drew in a deep breath and began.

'Everyone thinks if you have money, you've got nothing to complain about, but Jane and I had an awful childhood. I told you about our father's cruel nature. I hold him responsible for the deaths of my mother and sister. If we'd stayed with Mrs Liddle, our real mum, we might have struggled, but Jane and I would have had brothers and sisters and a parent's love.'

'Your biological father—Nathanial's dad—died after your conception but before you were born. So regardless of whether you were a Dellow or a Liddle, you would have had the love of a good mother,' Harland reminded him.

'That's true,' James conceded, 'but Mum was oppressed. From the moment my so-called father walked in the door, she walked on eggshells. I thought she would follow Jane to the asylum, but I reckon she hung on for my sake. He as good as killed her.' James shook his head in disgust, his dark hair, needing a cut, flopped into his eyes before he swept it back in a practised move.

'Why did your father want to have children then?' Gilbert asked.

'Because he was a God-fearing man and wanted to be seen to have the perfect family, someone to carry on his name,' James scoffed.

'It must comfort you to know you are not your father's real son?' Harland asked.

'If you are trying to trap me into saying I killed those women because of that, well, I won't, Detective, because I never did,' James said smartly.

The boy was bright; there was no doubt about it, and Harland could not deny that the resemblance between the boys was striking. 'Continue then. Why did you dump your sister's body when she passed away?' Harland reminded him of the question.

'It's not a crime, is it?' James scoffed and, when the detectives did not answer, continued. 'The asylum didn't want me taking her out; she was too ill, but she begged me too, and I could never deny her anything. We were twins; we were one. But she died in my arms, and I was so angry.' He stopped talking, closed his eyes, and Nathanial touched his shoulder.

'You're not alone, brother.'

James opened his eyes, awash with tears, and with a nod of thanks to his brother, turned back to Harland. 'It pained me to abandon her there, but Jane and I spoke about it. I told her what Nat and I had figured out, that they weren't our real father and mother. I stopped Nurse Faithful in the street one day and asked her. I just came out with the question, and her look of shock gave her away until she gathered herself enough to deny it,' he said, his voice low and angry.

'She took off pretty quickly that day,' Nathanial scoffed.

'And avoided us every day after,' James agreed. 'So Jane and I wanted to draw attention to what had happened but didn't know how to do it, and she was worried about me, that I'd do something that would ruin my future. So, we came up with the idea of the doll connection. It started when I met George Stockton. He played darts with Nat and me a few times at the pub, and we got talking. He started working it out. No one could believe Nat and I weren't kin, and when Ma Liddle, that's what I call my real mum now that I've found her, well, she asked for mine and Jane's birthdate, and they were the same as the death date of her twins, she began to wonder. So did George Stockton.'

'Ma had got a windfall from the insurance,' Nathanial said. 'Call it what it was though, payment for James and Jane, or as Mum called them, Mordecai and Edie.'

James agreed and continued in his educated voice. 'George didn't want to believe it but couldn't stop digging; he had his reasons and asked his wife about us because she was a *Stork,* but she denied everything. So he started looking for this woman he used to love years ago. She was a widow, and they had a child, but he was still married and couldn't be with her. Do you know what happened to the kid?'

'In broad terms,' Gilbert responded.

'Right,' James said, studying both detectives. 'Well, she confirmed the date of the death of their baby; it was a boy, and then George became convinced his son never died. He asked around in the neighbourhood about babies delivered by the *Storks* that month and found a boy who was born that very day, and he tracked him down. He looks a hell of a lot like him.'

Nathanial shrugged. 'Might be his son, might not be, but he's convinced it is, and the lady he loved, Amelia's her name, she had the baby taken from and got a huge insurance payout too.'

Leaving the young men, the detectives entered the next interview room where George Stockton slumped in a chair, looking as if his world had ended. The detectives sat.

'I don't expect you to understand, but I've only ever loved one woman and only ever wanted a son. I could have had them both,' he said wistfully until his face twisted in anger. 'Those women playing God, they had no right.'

'You are correct about that, Mr Stockton,' Gilbert said.

'No court of law would disagree,' Harland agreed, 'but you played God too, Mr Stockton, when you took the lives of Charlotte Faithful, Louise Killick and Frances Crandle.'

'Ah, but I didn't, detectives. I did nothing but terrorise them. If their fear and guilt led to heart conditions and their untimely death, well, I was not to know that.'

Harland studied him.

'I swear on my beautiful son, whom I have only recently found, that I did not kill those women, but I did scare them to death,' he grinned as he said the words.

'How can you be sure they did it?' Gilbert asked.

'My wife, Winifred, kept records of all the babies; they probably all did. She told me she didn't, but I found her book listing them all. That's why I knew Nathanial and James were brothers. Charlotte Faithful delivered the twins, and Winifred assisted. The dates were in her book. There was a boy born to Amelia, the woman I loved, and if he had survived, I would have left Winifred, looked after that boy, and adopted her sons. Winifred and I should never have been together; I got her pregnant and did the right thing.'

'So, you would have abandoned your wife and daughters to be with the woman you loved even if you could not make her Mrs Amelia Stockton?' Harland asked.

'Yeah, I would have. Winnie and I were both miserable. She never liked me working in a second-hand store; it wasn't good enough for her. She was making an income, and I would have provided something for the girls; they'd have survived. But those *Storks* thought they were helping Amelia because she was a widow with two sons and a third on the way. My boy.'

Harland paused, considering George Stockton's confession. 'Mrs Frances Crandle was smothered. That is not natural causes.'

Both detectives knew that wasn't quite true. A pillow was left askew and may or may not have been used, but Harland bluffed to get a reaction; the man before them remained calm.

George Stockton held up his hands as if showing he had no tricks up his sleeve and nothing to hide. 'No, she covered her face with her pillow in terror as I marched around in my toy soldier suit.' He laughed at the memory. 'Then she began gasping and clutching at her chest. I didn't move the pillow or touch it.'

'You did nothing to help her, and you brought on her death,' Harland confirmed and looked surprised when George admitted it.

'Yes. She caused me excessive heart pain, too, detectives, but my heart is strong enough to bear it. If I collapsed from finding I had a son, and my heart gave out, would she be charged with murder?'

Harland saw Gilbert's expression as if he was weighing up the argument and spoke before he had the chance to do so.

'That is not for us to determine, Mr Stockton. Someone locked Mrs Killick's windows, and she could not escape the fire.'

'But I didn't set the fire, detective,' George Stockton said, looking smug. 'I gave her a little fright; if she dropped her lamp or could not push her way out of the window, that is not my doing. In this hot weather, sometimes the windows swell and seal. But I am curious,' he said, cocking his head to the side, 'what led you to me? The man who saw me at the toy shop that night?'

'What—'

'We had several pointers,' Harland said, cutting off Gilbert. They did not know there was a witness who saw George Stockton that night, but now they would do their best to find him. 'My partner pointed out that your original dolls had painted eyes, and the new dolls you left at the scene, dressed in the same manner, had eyes made from glass. Therefore, we knew they were being made anew.'

'Good Lord!' George exclaimed. 'My, that is fine detective work.'

'Thank you, Sir,' Gilbert said with a modest nod. Both detectives were unaccustomed to being praised by the criminals they were arresting.

'Right then, if you are finished with me, can I go?'

Harland's eyes widened with surprise. 'Of course you may not go, Mr Stockton. I am charging you with wilfully frightening to death Miss Charlotte Faithful, Mrs Frances Crandle and Mrs Louise Killick.'

'But you can't! That is outrageous!' He stood as if to run, and two police officers entered the room to restrain George Stockton.

'I am not unsympathetic to your case, Mr Stockton,' Harland said. 'But know that the ladies had the best intentions even if what they did was also against the laws of the court and possibly the law of God. It will be up to you to prove your innocence in the same court.'

As they watched Mr Stockton led away, Gilbert shook his head.

'It is the strangest of cases, Sir. Three dead women who all died in a manner somewhat violent and lonely, but without being touched.'

'Strange indeed,' Harland agreed, 'and over, thank goodness. I will be happy if I do not see a doll, teddy or toy for some time.'

Chapter 34

The Courier – late afternoon edition

DEATHLY DOLLS TERRORISE WOMEN
BABIES TAKEN FROM THEIR FAMILIES
HISTORIC INSURANCE DECEPTION

The Courier concludes its exclusive report by Lilly Lewis and Fergus Griffiths.

Treasured dolls and tin soldiers have been given as gifts to children since time immemorial, but for three women, the gift was deadly. *The Courier* recently reported that Roma Street detectives Harland Stone and Gilbert Payne considered the deaths of Nurse Charlotte Faithful, Mrs Frances Crandle and Mrs Louise Killick suspicious.

Found at the death scene of each woman was a doll with brunette hair, blue eyes and a yellow dress hand-stitched with cornflowers, or a tin soldier handsomely crafted. But they were not gifts; they were reminders of a time past and a deed done, and each deathly doll contributed to their deaths from fright.

It has been a most challenging case for the detectives, but readers can rest easy as the culprit has been caught. He is not without a sympathetic story, as are all the victims in this tragic tale unwoven by our intrepid detectives and private investigator, Mr Bennet Martin, whose path we crossed again during this investigation.

Today, the only living *Stork* is Mrs Winifred Stockton, but had the detectives not solved the case, her days may have been numbered at the hands of her husband: Mr George Stockton, 50, the owner of *Stockton's Second-Hand Goods and Chattels*.

George Stockton has been charged with the deaths of the three ladies. The other *Stork* member, Mrs Esther Banes, died of illness 23 years past.

Our story begins 25 years ago...

Phoebe finished reading the article and putting down the newspaper, looked at her grandfather to discuss.

'What a terribly sad story.'

'A moral dilemma and a right mess,' Randolph agreed, summing it up. 'Miss Lewis did a wonderful job yet again. She has an engaging way of weaving a tale.'

'She does indeed,' Phoebe agreed, proud of her friend.

'I agree with what that young man James Dellow said in the article: money is not everything, and the love of a family is worth more than gold.'

'As do I, Grandpa. In the years that you and Grandma struggled along with us, it was still a good life, was it not?' she asked.

He smiled. 'Despite the pain of missing your parents, which we all felt, the tight-knit family we had, all there for each other, made for the best of times.'

Phoebe felt herself getting misty-eyed. 'Yes, I could not agree more, Grandpa.'

'Now you must all go your own ways and hopefully start your own families. Your parents won't know the joy of being grandparents, but your grandma and I will do our best to stay young and useful.'

Phoebe laughed. 'I could not imagine you any other way.'

Chapter 35

THE LADIES OF THE *Vexed Vixens* had spent the morning with Emily at her townhome, helping to prepare for this evening's dinner dance. Emily had hired a caterer and two serving staff, insisting that as she never entertained, it would be done right on this occasion. Now, the ladies stood around the dinner table, finalising the placement of settings, discussing what they intended to wear, and checking the place cards.

'It is wonderful you can join us,' Phoebe said to Emily's cousin, Isabelle—a young woman of the same age, who was best described as an English rose in a harsh Australian climate—pretty and slender, with fair skin and hair, and deep brown eyes.

'Oh, the pleasure is mine, Phoebe,' she said as the ladies insisted on being on a first-name basis. 'Although I am sure my cousin has exaggerated my piano-playing abilities.'

'I have done no such thing; you are most talented!' Emily declared with a smile. She was quite the opposite in appearance with her olive skin and dark brown, glossy hair.

'Thank you, Cousin,' Isabelle said. 'I shall enjoy seeing you dance to my selection of polkas and reels,' she teased, making the ladies laugh at the thought of such spirited dances with the men in attendance.

'We'll do our best to keep up with you, and you must take your turn at dancing,' Emily assured her before adopting a mischievous look. 'Now, I hope we have the seating right. Are you sure you want to sit beside Detective Stone, Phoebe? And Kate, it was Mr *Ambrose* Astin you wanted next to you, was it not?'

Kate placed her hands on her hips. 'No, you might be right, Emily. Perhaps you should put me next to Detective Payne.'

Emily laughed. 'Oh, touché, Kate dear.'

'And yes, I am happy to sit next to the detective,' Phoebe said and admitted, 'although I am quite nervous about it.'

'Understandably,' Lilly said, patting Phoebe's hand. 'I am sitting next to Mr Martin, and while I am not nervous about that, I will do my best to challenge him. He's a most interesting man and quite surprising. I confess I thought he was an English fop, but he has many layers.'

'Perhaps you bring that out in him,' Violet suggested. 'But I am sure I am sitting next to the most handsome man present,' she said of her fiancé.

'You will get no argument from me,' Phoebe said with a laugh and quickly added, 'goodness, don't tell Ambrose I said that!'

Kate grinned with good humour. 'He would never believe it.'

'You are right; you know him well already,' Phoebe said with a smile.

'Now, Isabelle, you are sitting next to me, and on your left will be Dr Tavish McGregor,' Emily said. 'He is quite the extrovert and a very intelligent man, the coroner no less.'

'With a lovely Scottish accent,' Lilly added. 'Opposites attract after all.'

'Oh, I am happy just to be in good company and play the piano,' Isabelle blushed. 'I am not expecting to lose my heart.'

'Then rest assured, you will not be short of conversation with Dr McGregor,' Kate said. 'I have been with him on several crime scene locations, and you will struggle to get a word in.'

'Goodness me, how daunting to witness such a thing,' Isabelle exclaimed.

'It was the first time,' Kate mused, 'but thankfully, none of the scenes have been too harrowing. I have only filled in when a police photographer was not available. We know very little of Dr McGregor other than he is a clever, charming, and a most gregarious Scottish man.'

'I know a little more,' Phoebe said. 'Julius has told me a bit about his friend.'

'Ooh, do tell,' Lilly said with interest.

'Well, he is one of nine children.'

'Good heavens!' Violet exclaimed. 'How wonderful it must be to have many siblings. I often wish Tom and I had more.'

'As one of six, with five brothers, I promise you, dear Violet, it is not that exciting,' Lilly said drily, making everyone laugh.

'Even more interesting,' Phoebe continued when encouraged, 'is that Tavish's name means twin, and he has a twin brother back in Scotland! Dr McGregor came out here for work five years ago and has not returned. That is a little about him.'

'Goodness, and I thought one of him was larger than life,' Lilly said.

'I cannot wait to see them all in evening dress,' Kate gushed. 'I am so pleased you made the evening formal, Emily.'

'I wanted a chance to wear our gowns,' she said sheepishly. 'I am sure the boys are not as excited about dressing up as we are.'

'It will put them at best advantage,' Phoebe declared, and the ladies moved away from the table, gathered their belongings and prepared to leave.

'Best we begin our preparation as well,' Kate said with a roll of her eyes. 'My mother has organised a hair appointment for me. I told her it was dinner with friends, but as soon as she saw your invitation, she decided I had not told her the full story, and as eligible men were present, I must be preened.' She looked to Phoebe and grinned, 'but it will be worth it.'

'I hope my brother appreciates your efforts,' Phoebe teased, 'otherwise, I will make sure he does. I also hope Detectives Stone and Payne are not called into work this evening.'

'As do I,' Emily said and sighed. 'But that will be our lot should we fall in love with the men who keep our city safe.'

Several hours before he was due to depart for Miss Emily Yalden's dinner dance, Harland Stone began his grooming. He had checked his dinner suit earlier in the week and had it, along with his best dress shirt, pressed. He shaved and buffed his shoes to a shine with a vigour that would have made his schoolmaster proud.

Harland didn't feel nervous about seeing Miss Astin; far from it. He felt empowered. But if he had any fears, it was about losing her before he truly had the chance to win Miss Phoebe Astin's heart and hand. He had never really known great affection or love, which, as an only child, one would think he might have. But his wealthy father, keen to ensure his son attended his alma mater, shipped him off to board at a young age.

Harland recalled some facts Gilbert had shared about children in care or separated from their parents at an early age from the case they had just worked; he found himself in agreement with the sentiments. The isolated child could stand on his own two feet and be adept on social occasions. Thus, Harland was comfortable in most social groups. But children who boarded or were institutionalised learnt early not to express their emotions, to which Harland could attest. More so than most men, he did not speak of his feelings, nor was he comfortable doing so. As an adult, this proved challenging in an intimate relationship as several ladies he had once wooed had soon lost interest, playing second fiddle to his career with no verbal reassurance of affection.

Harland vowed not to make that mistake with Miss Astin, with limited success thus far. He knew that she too was different. She didn't crave company or socialisation and seemed assured of herself without the need to seek compliments. Would she feel deserted if work took a great deal of his time? Would she claim him to be unromantic like the other ladies had done? Time would tell, but somehow, he believed it would be different; they were kindred spirits, and for the first time, his desire for her was more important than all else in his life. He had never known that feeling and, truthfully, he did not like the vulnerable position it put him in.

Across town, Ambrose and Phoebe Astin were both in the final throes of dressing. It was fair to say that Ambrose fussed more than Phoebe and allowed his grandmother, Maria, to preen him. His hair was not right, his tie was crooked, and so on until he was pronounced perfect.

'That I always knew,' he announced with a wink and a grin at his grandmother, who laughed.

'Ah, it does my heart good to see my beautiful grandchildren dressed for a night out and looking so happy,' she sighed, pressing a hand to her heart as Randolph joined her.

'It is a shame Julius did not dress here as well so we could admire him in his dinner suit,' Randolph agreed, 'but with his wedding coming, we'll have a chance to dress formally again.'

They both turned to watch Phoebe coming down the stairs.

'Phoebe darling, you look absolutely beautiful,' Maria said. 'So like your mother, it takes my breath away.'

'Both great beauties,' Randolph said with a look of melancholy.

'You look lovely, Phoebe,' Ambrose agreed, of his sister in a pale pink dress with cream lace and pink roses stitched along the hem. It sat on the edge of her shoulders, showing her milky neckline. Phoebe wore her pale blonde hair down, secured loosely at the back with a matching cream lace ribbon. A touch of blush and pale pink on her lips made her appear quite ethereal.

'I do love this dress,' she said of the gown her grandparents had bought her for a birthday gift a year ago, 'but I rarely get a chance to wear it.'

'It is most becoming. We knew it would suit you beautifully,' Randolph said, preparing to drive them in the covered trap. 'Are you sure you do not want me to collect you at a designated hour?'

'No, but thank you, Grandpa. Who is to say how the night will pan out?' Phoebe said.

'You will see your sister home safely, Ambrose?' Maria asked, but it was more of an order.

'I shall. Or I will arrange a police escort for her,' he joked, and Phoebe made a face at him. 'Come then, the night beckons.'

Julius had organised a hansom cab to collect Violet at her residence, so they had the pleasure of arriving at the dinner together. Knowing she and Tom would reside with him in a matter of months filled him with a mixture of pleasure, relief and fear. He was no stranger to losing those dearest to him, and the thought that everything was going so well and could it last, plagued him. He often wished he had Ambrose's lightheartedness.

Having arrived with a bouquet to gift the hostess, Emily, and a corsage for Violet to wear, Julius gazed across at his fiancée as she pinned it on.

'I hope we will be seated next to each other tonight,' Violet said, knowing full well they were but teasing him.

Julius looked surprised and then dismayed. 'Oh no. It's not one of those dinner parties where we all change seats every ten minutes? I see Ambrose and Phoebe all day; I do not see you anywhere near enough.'

'Thank you, Julius,' she said, smiling at him sweetly. 'Perhaps we'll have to sit next to someone we don't know.'

'Then I'll be next to the lady playing the piano as I know everyone else quite well.'

'I'll be next to Dr McGregor, I imagine.'

'Perhaps we should detour and go out to dinner instead,' Julius joked, and Violet scolded him.

'We are sitting together; do not fear,' she said and laughed at the narrowed-eyed expression he gave her.

Arriving at Emily's, they alighted from the hansom, his hands around her waist as he lifted Violet down. With a brisk knock on the door, they quickly found themselves among the guests and the last to arrive. He felt instantly at home seeing his siblings' faces, along with Harland, Bennet and Tavish; it would be a good night.

Violet joined the ladies, delighting in her friendship group, and Julius accepted a glass of wine from one of the serving staff.

'You will need to stop calling me Sir for the night,' Harland was saying to Gilbert, as Julius approached them. Both men looked smart in their dinner suits.

'I don't think I can do that, Sir, sorry.'

'I understand,' Harland said.

'Well, you scrubbed up reasonably well, Harland,' Julius teased, and his friend grinned.

'Will I pass muster?'

'Just. Ah, here's Bennet.'

'What a fine night this is, and how fortunate are we to score an invitation?' Bennet asked, joining them and watching Miss Lilly Lewis the whole time.

'Most fortunate!' Dr Tavish McGregor agreed as he joined the men in time to hear Bennet's conversation. 'Who is that beautiful young lass with the look of an English rose and the manner of a princess?'

The men studied the ladies as they busied themselves with admiring each other's dresses and ensuring the dinner details were going according to plan.

'As that describes all the ladies, Doctor, could you be more specific?' Gilbert asked, arousing laughs amongst the men.

'You will go a long way, young Gilbert,' Tavish said, slapping him on the back. 'I speak of the young lady who just placed the music sheet on the piano. The fair maiden.'

'I believe that is Miss Yalden's cousin, Miss Isabelle Yalden,' Gilbert advised him.

'Isabelle, thy name is Beauty!' Dr McGregor said loud enough that the young lady wearing a white dress with a blue sash looked toward him and blushed profusely.

Julius nudged the coroner. 'Would you say subtlety is one of your best features?' he joked, and Tavish chuckled.

Lilly Lewis, on overhearing, laughed and moved to join the men, bringing Phoebe and Kate along with her. Emily and Isabelle went to the kitchen to check on the caterers while Violet studied the music sheets on the piano stand.

'You have outdone yourselves, ladies,' Bennet offered with a small bow.

'As have you, gentlemen,' Lilly responded. She wore a pale blue silk and lace dress featuring small puff sleeves and a fitted bodice. She scrutinised them, wrinkling her nose. 'I see haircuts were had, shoes shined—some better than others—shirts pressed and…' she hesitated long enough to sniff the air, 'fragrance adorned.'

Julius looked somewhat alarmed by her assessment; Harland and Gilbert appeared impressed by her reading of the room; Ambrose was looking at Kate and likely did not hear her, and Bennet Martin laughed.

'Nothing gets past you, Miss Lewis, and I hope my shoes are satisfactory. I had my clerk buff them for the occasion,' he said in jest. 'I can only assume that you did little preparation, being such a natural beauty.'

She laughed. 'Very good, Mr Martin.'

Julius excused himself to join Violet at her beckon and saw Harland approaching his sister from the corner of his eye. The look he gave both of them warned he was watching as a dutiful brother would.

Harland acknowledged Julius's look with a brief nod and moved to speak quietly with Phoebe.

'Miss Astin, you look beautiful this evening, but I can't recall a time when you did not.'

She smiled, self-conscious but delighted. 'Thank you, Detective.'

'Perhaps you might call me Harland?'

'And you must call me Phoebe, but expect Julius to frown a great deal about that,' she said in jest, and Harland chuckled.

'As expected. If I were your brother, I would be fiercer than Julius.'

'Then it is a good thing you do not have a sister,' Phoebe said in jest. 'Thank you for the beautiful plant. I am pleased to report that Florence is doing very well.'

'Florence?' he asked, surprised and laughed.

'I am not normally in the practice of naming plants, or any other items for that matter,' she assured him, 'but Grandpa asked what I would call her, and I thought, why not, as we will be sharing my room daily. Florence seemed a perfect name for a fern.'

'She will expect me to visit,' Harland teased.

'No doubt.'

'Ladies and gentlemen, I invite you to take your seats for dinner,' Emily announced, and as each guest moved to the dinner table, there was no doubt all present were pleased with the seating arrangements.

As Phoebe observed the dinner party unfolding around her and the night progressing too fast for her liking, it felt wonderful to be amongst friends and family. She rarely sought the company of others, but here she was blessed among those she loved, her exclusive group.

There was her first true friend, Kate, whom she had met at school and stayed close to in the years since. Then she had met Emily through Kate, who was tasked with photographing the *Miss Emily Yalden School of Deportment* debutantes; the three ladies had become firm friends. Dearest Lilly she met when the reporter was responsible for the births, marriages and deaths column of *The Courier* and had come calling regularly as death interested her much more than the other two topics, and now Violet, who will soon be more than a friend and Phoebe could not wait to call her sister.

In her position in the middle seat of the table with discussion underway on both sides of her and opposite, Phoebe was privy to many conversation threads. She heard the whisperings that she was not meant to hear – her brother, Ambrose, asking Kate—who looked most striking in a mint dress with white lace trim—if he may be considered her beau and her cheerful response.

'If you are free tomorrow, perhaps I could show you one of my favourite things,' Ambrose said.

'That sounds rather ominous, Ambrose,' Kate teased. 'Will I like it?'

'It is not me, if that is what you mean,' he joked. 'It is a place I love. Bring your camera if you like and capture it, like you have captured my heart.'

'Oh, Ambrose, what an invitation. What girl could refuse?'

'A sensible girl,' Ambrose teased, 'but come along anyway.'

To her left, Phoebe heard Detective Gilbert Payne and Emily enjoying many shared points of view and looking all the happier for it. Emily was wearing a most becoming bracelet, a gift from the young detective who insisted he could not give the hostess flowers like everyone else, his heart on his sleeve and his motive hopeful.

'But do you really think women should keep working once married?' Emily asked.

'If they wish to do so, then of course they should. But if their husband has the means to support them and the lady wishes to look after him, their home, and eventually the family, then surely any man would work their hardest to provide for her.'

A perfect answer, Detective Payne, Phoebe thought as she then caught Violet showing off her engagement ring—to Julius's amusement—to Bennet Martin.

'Goodness, that is stunning,' Bennet said. 'Business is going well then?' he asked Julius with a grin and a wink.

Violet had said for Julius's ears and Phoebe eavesdropping, 'I love talking about our future, but I confess I will be happy when we are married to talk of other things. I feel that the only conversation people know to have with me now is about my pending marriage.'

'I know what you mean,' Julius had answered. 'Let's agree that talking will not be our priority after the wedding.'

Phoebe almost burst out laughing but did her best not to appear to be listening. She loved how Violet brought out Julius's lighter side.

'No talking? Whatever shall we do?' Violet asked with playful innocence.

'Leave it with me,' Julius assured her with an engaging look, 'I'll think of something.'

Phoebe turned just in time to hear Lilly quietly questioning Dr Tavish McGregor.

'Now, Dr McGregor, I thought a man as gregarious as yourself would seek the same, and here you are, taken by the demure and pretty Miss Isabelle Yalden.'

'Ah, Miss Lewis, an astute observation as expected from a reporter of your calibre,' Tavish responded. 'When one works and lives with death every day, and my job is to find the means and manner in which crimes against a person have been perpetuated, to see a gentle lady of quiet beauty reminds me of the importance of what we do. To protect those who must be protected, to keep our world from their eyes, even...' he added with a twinkle in his eyes, 'if the young ladies think they are most capable of taking care of themselves.'

'Well said, Tavish,' Bennet piped in, entering the conversation late. 'I know this female reporter who is most challenging, but I am determined to treat her as if she were spun gold.'

Lilly laughed at his antics. Phoebe smiled at the group and moved from their lively banter to return to her own small party seated on her right, where Harland had finished conversing with Kate and Ambrose and returned his attention to her.

'May I call on you tomorrow, Phoebe? Perhaps we could enjoy a walk or a ride. Ideally, before my next case begins and I find myself calling on you in a professional capacity.'

'That would be delightful, thank you, Harland. I hear there is a very good miniature display in the Botanic Gardens,' she teased, and he laughed.

'Excellent. We shall be sure to avoid that.'

Then the music began, and Phoebe turned to see Isabelle seated at the piano. During the evening, Violet and Phoebe took a turn playing so that Isabelle could enjoy a spin on the dance floor, but for now, Harland rose, extended his hand and with a small bow said, 'Let us show them how it is done, Phoebe. And if that fails, you will have time to recover before heading home.'

Phoebe laughed. 'It might be me who does damage to your toes.'

'Then it will be my honour to endure that.'

Phoebe gave him a look reflecting her admiration for him, and with that, she placed her hand in his, and they made their way to the dance floor.

THE END

Author's notes:

I was home from school one day, sick (aged ten or so), and at lunchtime, I watched a classic Australian television drama called *Matlock Police*. I recall little about the episode except that it was about a woman who had lost her child somehow, but in the backyard of her house in the dark of night, a doll sat next to a music box playing the tune *Frere Jacques*. It was the scariest scene, and even now, decades later, I remember it. It inspired the deathly dolls.

While this novel is fiction, I try to be as accurate to the era and location—1890 in Australia—as possible. Here is a little explanation for those who enjoy knowing the facts behind the story.

There really was a Queensport Aquarium in Brisbane from 1889 to 1901 that had daytime steamer trips to the aquarium and evening moonlit excursions to dance and hear a band perform, all under bright electricity – a marvel of the time. The steamer departed from a city wharf to the venue on the Brisbane River at Hemmant. It also included a zoo with panthers and tigers. When the Brisbane River flooded in 1893, many animals escaped but were recaptured.[1] It closed in 1901, but Julius and Violet may well have enjoyed an evening there.

When speaking of brilliant criminals, I hoped that Ambrose could include Professor James Moriarty, the genius villain of the Sherlock Holmes novels. But he did not appear in the book series until 1893—three years after my book was set—and was introduced briefly in a short story titled *The Final Problem.*

I also wanted to feature a ballerina twirling in the music box with all its prettiness and innocence, but the little dancing ballerina that many of us grew up with in our music boxes came long after 1890. However, the music boxes of this era were beautiful wooden boxes with often many choices of musical pieces, from Gilbert and Sullivan through to rousing patriotic tunes. If you want to hear the *Home Sweet Home* tune played in the dark of night as it was in poor Nurse Charlotte Faithful's backyard, you can listen to it played on an antique music box[2] as listed below in the references.

Gilbert's interest in psychology and whether it is best to prepare before seeing a death scene was cited from the study of emotions in the text, *The Principles of Psychology* by William James (1890) – a pioneer in his lifetime. Those interested in our early psychologists and their impact on what we understand today can read more in *New Ideas in Psychology*, Vol. 46, August 2017.[3]

Women were dying for beauty's sake as the powders and tonics developed up to the 19th century often included arsenic and other poisons. The advertising made the products very appealing; women trusted they were safe and the products would assist them in being their best selves. A lady of consequence, the Countess of Coventry, Maria Gunning, was considered very beautiful, but even on her deathbed, she would not be without her foundation containing white lead – the product that contributed to her death. You can read more about it in a very interesting article in *The Conversation* (link below).[4]

While insuring a child's life might seem suspicious and unnecessary today, in the late 19th and early 20th centuries, the practice was more common than you might think. In fact, in the early 1900s, there were over 70,000 children's insurance policies in Australia.[5] This might have been the reason that the very first bill to be passed into law by the Federal Parliament was the Life Insurance Companies Bill, introduced in November 1904 by the Member for Darling Downs, Earnest Littleton Groom, to regulate insurance of the lives of children under ten years of age. Mr Groom explained in his speech that:

> "The general practice is for persons of the poorer classes to insure the lives of their children for amounts of £7, £8, and upwards so that if the children die at an early age, they will be able to provide for their burial. These assurances are prompted by motives which honourable members must applaud, since they spring from feelings of self-respect and honest pride. The average cost of a funeral is, I am informed, in Sydney about £4 10s, and in Melbourne, £5, and there are also incidental expenses for medicine, mourning, and so on."[6]

Where suspicion does fall, however, is when insurance is considerably more than would be needed for a funeral, medicine and mourning, and that is exactly what Mr Groom addresses in his speech, saying:

> "It has been felt, however, that if persons could assure the lives of children for unlimited amounts, assurances might be taken out for

improper purposes. The Bill provides a safeguard against that."[7]

Lilly cited some of the Reverend Dr Talmage's beliefs about the value of newspapers. Rev. Dr. Talmage was an American preacher who inspired many with his orator skills and wisdom. During his life, his sermons were published in over 3000 journals. He spent the latter years of his life on the lecture circuit and died in 1902.[8]

The mention of the unidentified bodies of men and women in the morgue—the men being the larger group—was factual and taken from a Melbourne newspaper report in 1897. It was a sad state of affairs indeed.[9]

Also by Helen Goltz:

THANK YOU FOR READING another volume of the Astin family adventures. I look forward to your company for the next book in the series! In the interim, perhaps one of these titles may interest you:

Miss Hayward & the Detective Series (historical mystery/romance):

Murder at the Carnival

The Artist's Missing Muse

Mystery at the Asylum

The Mortician's Clue (featuring Phoebe and staff from The Economic Undertaker)

Murder in Bridal Lane

The Clairvoyant's Glasses (paranormal/romance)

Volume 1 – A vision unexpected
Volume 2 – Time has a shadow
Volume 3 – Love knows no bounds
Volume 4 – Fate comes to call
Coming soon... The Raven's Son

The Jesse Clarke series (cosy mystery):
Death by Sugar
Death by Disguise
Death by Reunion

The Mitchell Parker series (crime thriller):
Mastermind
Graveyard of the Atlantic
The Fourth Reich

Writing as Jack Adams (mystery suspense):
Poster Girl
Delaney and Murphy childhood friends' series:
Asylum
Stalker
Cult
Hitched
Carnival
Coming soon... Forgotten.

The Lady Mortician's Visions (historical mystery/romance/paranormal twist)

The Missing Brides

The Fake Child

The Dastardly Debutante

The Deathly Dolls

The Potent Perfume

The Watery Grave

The Vanishing Groom

The Fallen Angel

Writing as Ally Adams:

The Saints team (contemporary romance):

Team Lucas

Team Tomas

Team Niklas

Team Alex

Spies in Love (contemporary romance):

My Boyfriend the Spy

I Spy My Guy

Stand-alone titles:

The House on Findlater Lane (mystery/romance paranormal)

The Forgotten House (historical romance)

Three Parts Truth (mystery suspense)

Morphers (middle grade fiction)

With journalist Chris Adams:

The Grave Tales series (non-fiction) x 9 titles:

Grave Tales: Brisbane Vol.1

Grave Tales: Great Ocean Road – Geelong to Port Fairy

Grave Tales: Sydney Vol.1

Grave Tales: Bruce Highway

Grave Tales: True Crime Vol.1

Grave Tales: Queensland's Great South West

Grave Tales: Melbourne Vol.1

Grave Tales: Queensland's Scenic Rim & Surrounds

Grave Tales: Tasmania.

About the Author:

HELEN IS A HYBRID-PUBLISHED, Amazon best-selling author. After studying English Literature, Media, and Communications at universities in Queensland, Australia, and obtaining a Counselling Diploma, Helen has worked as a journalist, producer and marketer in print, TV, radio and public relations. Born in Toowoomba, she has made her home in Brisbane, Australia, with her journalist husband, Chris, and Boxer dog, Baxter.

Connect with Helen:

Website: www.helengoltz.com

BookBub:www.bookbub.com/authors/helen-goltz

Facebook: www.facebook.com/HelenGoltz.Author

Instagram: https://www.instagram.com/helengoltz1/

1.   Queensport Aquarium. (2021, January 14). In *Wikipedia*. https://en.wikipedia.org/wiki/Queensport_Aquarium

2. Home Sweet Home playing on a vintage music box: https://www.youtube.com/watch?v=ICOzwf0F1fU

3. Lacasse, K. (2017). Going with your gut: How William James' theory of emotions brings insights to risk perception and decision making research. *New Ideas in Psychology, 46,* 1-7. https://doi.org/10.1016/j.newideapsych.2015.09.002

4. McNeill, Fiona, E., *Dying for makeup: Lead cosmetics poisoned 18th-century European socialites in search of whiter skin,* The Conversation, February 28, 2022. Retrieved 27 September, 2023 from URL: https://theconversation.com/dying-for-makeup-lead-cosmetics-poisoned-18th-century-european-socialites-in-search-of-whiter-skin-176237

5. Heriot, Dianne, The Life Insurance Companies Act 1905: the first private members' bill to pass the Parliament, *National Library of Australia,* 19 December 2017. Retrieved 5 November 2018 from URL: https://www.aph.gov.au/About_Parliament/Parliamentary_Departments/Parliamentary_Library/FlagPost/2017/December/The_Life_Assurance_Companies_Act_1905

6. Heriot, Dianne, The Life Insurance Companies Act 1905: the first private members' bill to pass the Parliament, *National Library of Australia,* 19 December 2017. Retrieved 5 November 2018 from URL: https://www.aph.gov.au/About_Parliament/Parliamentary_Departments/Parliamentary_Library/FlagPost/2017/December/The_Life_Assurance_Companies_Act_1905

7. Heriot, Dianne, The Life Insurance Companies Act 1905: the first private members' bill to pass the Parliament, *National Library of Australia,* 19 December 2017. Retrieved 5 November 2018 from URL: https://www.aph.gov.au/About_Parliament/Parliamentary_Departments/Parliamentary_Library/FlagPost/2017/December/The_Life_Assurance_Companies_Act_1905

8. Thomas De Witt Talmage. (2023, September 23). In *Wikipedia*. https://en.wikipedia.org/wiki/Thomas_De_Witt_Talmage

9. MORGUE MYSTERIES. (1897, December 17). *The Herald (Melbourne, Vic. : 1861 - 1954)*, p. 5. Retrieved October 22, 2023, from http://nla.gov.au/nla.news-article241621587